SORCERY
OF
WORDS

MOA ERIKSSON

CONTENTS

To Mom,
For always being there for me and for being the best mom anyone could ask for. I wouldn't be where I am today without your constant support. I love you.

Content Warning

Thank you for choosing to pick up this book! Before we get to the good stuff, I want to make you aware of a few possible triggers. This book contains on-page internalized acephobia, anxiety, panic attacks and mention of bullying. If any of these are triggering for you, please put your mental health first.

If you, or anyone you know, suffer from mental illness, don't suffer in silence. There is help to find. I have a few links and numbers to Swedish mental health resources below, as well as links to sites with global links.

Swedish links

1177.se: Find information about mental health as well as how and where to get help.

Umo.se: For youth under 25. Find information about mental health. If you are under the age of 25 (can depend on your region), you can also get help here.

Swedish numbers

1177: You can call this number at any time of the day for coun-selling and guidance about your health.

90101: Suicide hotline. You can call this number anonymously if you or someone you know has suicidal thoughts.

112: In case of an emergency risk of suicide, call this number.

Some regions also have on-call psychiatric emergency rooms. Numbers to these can be found at **1177.se**.

Global links

Find a Helpline: findahelpline.com

CheckPoint: checkpointorg.com/global

HelpGuide: helpguide.org/find-help

Chapter 1
Dream Dog

"Are we still on for tonight, Lia?" my best friend Clara asked as we left the classroom.

"It's Thursday! You know I'd never miss a Thursday night," I told her.

Clara smiled and practically skipped ahead of me, clearing a path through the throng of students hurrying to get home. "Did you bake anything?"

I rolled my eyes. "Do you really need to ask?"

I dealt with stress and anxiety in one way: baking. And Clara had a sweet tooth the size of Sweden, she didn't seem to ever get full, and she was always more than happy to sample anything I made.

"I just need to go home and walk Kiwi before I come over," I said. "Mom's working late tonight at the hospital, and Tilda has dance class."

"Sure," Clara said. "How's your sis doing, by the way? Ninth grade kicking her ass?"

I laughed lightly as we stopped in front of the lockers. "Yeppers. But she seems to be doing better than I did, at least." I unlocked my locker, carefully stowing my Math book into its assigned spot, and grabbed my coat.

"At least there's that." Clara shrugged on her coat with a grimace, no doubt remembering our ninth year. "So, meet at four?"

I nodded and wrapped a fluffy scarf around my neck. "Yeah, that'll give me plenty of time to walk Kiwi. See you!"

I grabbed my bag from my locker, waved good-bye to Clara and a few stragglers from our class and left.

It took about ten minutes for me to ride my bike from school to the flat I lived in with Mom and Tilda. Opening the door, I bent down to catch Kiwi, ruffling her soft fur as she jumped up and started frantically licking my face, acting as though I'd been gone for eight years rather than eight hours. I made a mental note to book her an appointment with the groomer soon; her black-and-white fur wasn't quite long enough to hide her eyes yet, but it was getting there.

Standing up to grab Kiwi's leash, I had to shield my eyes from the setting sun, which could be seen through the bay windows covering one entire side of the living room. The sun glinted off of the several photos covering the walls, pictures of me and Tilda and Kiwi, chronicling our entire lives.

I focused back on Kiwi, who still jumped around, swishing her tail.

"Lie down," I told her sternly. It took another try before she listened, but even then, her body vibrated with excitement, knowing what was coming. Most days, I didn't even bother to take off my shoes when I got home, knowing Kiwi would be waiting for her walk. Come rain or shine, this was our routine, and there was comfort in knowing that.

Once I'd put the leash on Kiwi, we walked into the cold autumn air. The sun hadn't quite set yet, but a few stars were already peeking out. Kiwi and I kept to well-lit streets and walked along the edge of the forest. Well, calling it a forest wasn't quite right, it was more of a grove in the middle of the city. It was part of what I loved about Visby; it was a nice compromise between city and countryside.

As we took our long walk, the cool autumn wind bit my cheeks, and I burrowed into my coat. I watched Kiwi walk along, completely unaffected by the cold in her thick fur. My mind drifted to the first time I'd met Kiwi.

'Kiwi is a shih tzu who has black and white fur. She is very fluffy. She has a short nose and very big blue eyes.' Nine-year-old me put her pen down in search of some colouring pens. A tickling sensation on my lower leg made me look up from the paper. My gaze landed on a small dog sitting at my feet. I exclaimed, loud enough for all my classmates to turn to look at me. I didn't even notice, I just dropped down to the floor and hugged the little ball of fluff. Kiwi – because it was Kiwi, as impossible as that sounded – wiggled and started licking my face. I couldn't keep myself from laughing.

At least until our teacher, Ylva, came to check what all the noise was about. She towered over me, and I shrank down and buried my face in Kiwi, seeking comfort in her soft fur. I could tell she was upset with me. Her face was all stiff and her eyebrows were lowered in that way adults did when they were really angry about something.

I hugged Kiwi tighter.

"What is that doing here?" Ylva asked, and I cuddled up to Kiwi, who just kept licking my face.

"Umm..." I started, but how could I explain that the dog had appeared from the page of my notebook? That sounded crazy even to my nine-year-old ears.

"Is that yours?"

What else could I say? "Yes," I replied in my smallest voice.

Her face softened then, and she crouched down next to me. "She's pretty," Ylva said then, and her voice didn't sound as upset now. "Come on, let's go outside. I'm sure she needs some fresh air."

I stood up with Kiwi in my arms and let Ylva lead us outside.

"You're not supposed to bring your pets to school," Ylva told me, and she looked really serious. "Some of your classmates are allergic to pets. Do you know what that means?"

I nodded. I was allergic to grass and oak.

"They could get really sick if you have your dog here at school."

"Okay," I said. I still didn't know how to explain that the dog hadn't been with me that morning.

"I think we better call your mom, okay?" Ylva said, but it was in that weird way adults sometimes spoke, when they made it sound like a question but really, they were telling you something. Like when Mom ask/told me to clean my room.

While Ylva called Mom, I cuddled with Kiwi. I couldn't believe my dream dog had appeared out of the blue like that. Almost like magic.

Mom got to the school quickly. Too quickly. I knew she'd never let me keep the dog. Tilda and I had asked for a dog for a long time, but she had always refused us, said we didn't have time. We did.

When Mom showed up, I put on my best pretty please-*look, and prepared to start begging. Mom talked to Ylva for a while, and then she told me we were going for lunch.*

I followed her to the car, still hugging Kiwi to me, even though she'd started wiggling a lot. What if I set her down and she ran away? I couldn't risk it, not when I'd finally gotten my dream dog.

In the car, Mom looked at me for a long time. I started wriggling like

Kiwi, and Mom finally spoke. "Lia, sweetie, there's something I need to tell you."

I opened my mouth to start pleading, but Mom kept talking before I could.

"You have a rare type of magic, sweetie, that allows you to create things with your words."

I looked at her with wide eyes. Magic? Wasn't that impossible?

I looked down at Kiwi. The proof that magic was actually possible.

"What does that mean?" I asked Mom.

"It means that when you write, you can make things appear."

I didn't say anything for a while. Magic? I could actually do magic? "That is so awesome!"

Mom laughed a little. "Yes, it can be awesome," she said with a smile on her face. "But you also have to be careful, and learn to create only what you mean to, so you don't have any more accidents." She looked at Kiwi.

I nodded. Maybe if I behaved and learned to control it, she'd let me keep Kiwi. "Okay. I'll learn to control it, I promise! Can we keep Kiwi?"

Mom blinked. "Kiwi?"

I nodded, my dark curls bouncing around my face. "Yes! Because she looks like the dog Kiwi that I was writing about!"

Mom laughed. "I guess we'll have to go get some stuff then, if we're going to take care of a dog."

I squealed, and Kiwi licked my face, excited. "Hey, Mom? Can you do magic, too?"

She looked at me and smiled. "Yes, I can. But I don't have to write things I want to create. I just have to say them."

I widened my eyes. "That's so cool!"

Mom laughed. "Yes, very cool."

I blinked back to reality and my eyes immediately moved to Kiwi who skipped along, tail held high. I walked between two copses of trees when my neck started prickling. When Kiwi stopped to do her business, I discreetly looked behind me, right as an icy wind hit me right in the face. I shivered and hunkered down in my scarf as the leaves rustled in the screaming wind.

Was it just me, or was that shadow moving?

Kiwi let out a low growl, and my eyes shot to her and found her looking in the same direction as the shadow, tail low between her hind legs.

My stomach tightened as my heart started racing, and I looked back towards the shadow, but found nothing but stillness. An almost eerie stillness. Even the branches seemed to have frozen in place, even though the wind still whistled through the trees.

Another shiver raced down my spine, not from the cold this time, but I forced myself to turn away from the shadow, to keep walking, telling myself it was nothing but my imagination. But the feeling of being watched didn't go away.

Clara and I met outside our favourite café, Fiket – I know, a café called "The Café", not exactly the most creative name. It was a small place by Visby City Wall, with two floors where you could sit. Clara and I always picked a corner with a pair of well-worn armchairs on the top floor.

Every Thursday, without fail, we'd sit there for hours and talk about anything and everything, or we'd sit and read, not needing anything other than the other's presence. Then we would go to her or my place, watch a movie and eat way too much of my latest baked creation.

"She's so unbearably shy, but she's also really funny and sarcastic once you get to know her," Clara gushed about her crush, Alva, as she tucked a short warm blond strand behind her ear. "And she's so cute. I mean, have you seen the way her bangs fall into her eyes? All I want is to reach over and brush it away."

I couldn't disagree with her. Alva was very cute, in a girl-next-door kind of way. She had dark hair that looked unbelievably soft, tawny skin, and these big, blue eyes. And though she was usually very serious, she had a genuine smile that made your lips lift automatically back at her.

I laughed at Clara's wide-eyed expression and dreamy sigh. Because of her warm, light skin, she didn't blush as fiercely as I did, but her cheeks were definitely tinged a little pink. "You really do have a thing for the shy ones, don't you?"

She wrinkled her nose in confusion. "What are you talking about?"

"Well, you know, I was also really shy, and then you came to our class and took me under your wing," I explained to Clara, reminiscing about the day we'd first met and how fast we'd become best friends, like it was the most natural thing in the world.

Everything seemed like the most natural thing in the world with Clara.

"I didn't take you under my wing." Clara frowned and narrowed her eyes. "We became friends. There's a difference."

I raised my eyebrows at her vehement reaction. "You *so* did. Don't you remember, you told that girl off for being mean to me? And then you just sort of grabbed me – like, metaphorically – and forced me out of my shell."

Clara widened her eyes. "Is that how you see it? Like I saved you somehow?"

I shrugged. "Well... yeah. Kind of."

Clara shook her head. "No. Nope. Nuh-uh. I told that girl off because that's the decent thing for *anyone* to do. And I didn't 'take you under my wing'. I became friends with you because you were really nice and funny, and we had a lot of fun together. Still do," she added, staring at me.

I stared back for a second, then shook my head. "Okay, I get it. You didn't take me under your wing."

"Good." She paused and looked at me. "What about you? No guy – or girl – that you're interested in?"

I shrugged and squirmed a little, twirling a dark brown curl around my pale finger. My skin felt too tight and I wanted to disappear.

I'd never had any real crushes. Or, well, I had, but I never thought about kissing them and all the stuff Clara talked about. I imagined holding hands and watching movies together, which made me feel about ten years old. Eighteen-year-olds always thought about kissing and all that romantic stuff, right? What was wrong with me that I had zero interest in doing that, even with my crushes?

Clara looked like she wanted to push but decided against it. "So, did we decide on a movie for tonight?"

I nodded. "*Me Before You*, right?" We always cried watching that movie; still we watched it over and over again.

Clara moved on to complaining about schoolwork. It was getting close to the end of the term, and we were swamped with it. I struggled to push down the little ball of dread that settled in my stomach. In an attempt to lighten the pressure over my chest, I dug my nails into my palms a little, hoping the slight pain would drown out the pain that grew inside of me.

"... like, it can't come as a surprise that Christmas is coming up, so why don't they plan ahead, you know, to make sure we don't have every test the last freaking week of school?" Clara paused and looked at me. "Lia? Are you okay?"

I opened my mouth to say fine, but we both knew that was a lie. Clara knew me well, and she could tell by looking at me that something was up.

"Anxiety?" she asked, keeping her voice low.

I shrugged. It meant everything to me that she was always there for me, but sometimes I didn't want to talk. Sometimes it helped telling her about the anxiety. Often, though, I didn't know why the constant knot in my stomach expanded, why pressure started suffocating me, why everything inside hurt so bad I could do nothing but curl in on myself and wail. Those times, it was easier to just try to breathe through the pain until it lessened and then let it be there without analysing it too much. Or it would eclipse everything else in my life.

Thankfully, Clara knew me well enough to know when I needed to talk and when I needed to be distracted, because she took a breath and launched into a story about something funny Alva had said while I made sure to keep my breaths slow and even to keep from spiraling.

When we left the café to go to Clara's place, I couldn't help but sneak glances over my shoulder, though, looking for the moving shadow I'd seen earlier. Jesus, I was getting paranoid if I was this worried about a freaking shadow, but that thought didn't stop me from looking behind us for the third time in as many minutes.

"I was thinking," Clara said, and now that we were standing, she stood easily a head taller than me, "maybe we need something a bit more light-hearted than *Me Before You*. What do you think about a comedy instead?"

I looked at her and found her looking at me with a small frown. My stomach clenched. I hated when I made her worry, which I knew she did a lot. She was great like that, but I didn't want to be a burden to her and forced a smile.

"A comedy sounds great." It took everything in me to not look behind me again, but I managed to keep my eyes turned forward.

"How about... Oh! How about Bridget Jones? That's always fun to watch." Clara's voice rose with excitement.

"Bridget Jones sounds great." My smile was more genuine this time.

The rest of the walk, I kept my focus on Clara and our conversation instead of my paranoia, but it took a lot of effort. When we finally got to her house, her mother stuck her head out from the kitchen to greet us.

"How are you, Lia?" she asked as we stepped into the kitchen.

I smiled genuinely. "I'm good." It was mostly true. "What's for dinner?"

"Meatballs with potatoes and gravy. Hope you're hungry."

My stomach took that opportune moment to growl, and Clara laughed.

"Well, dinner's ready in five minutes. Clara, your dad's in the study, why don't you go get him?"

We all sat down to eat, and Clara's mom asked, "So, what was the best part of your day, Lia?"

Familiar with this tradition, I answered, "Definitely having coffee at Fiket with Clara." I rarely replied with something different on Thursdays.

Clara was next. "Sorry, Lia, you know I love our coffee dates, but the best part of my day was that Alva and I talked for almost an hour after school today."

I couldn't help but smile. God, I hoped Alva was secretly gay or bi or something, and that things could work out between them.

"The best part of my day was that one of my students finally understood how equations work." Clara's mom smiled.

"And the best part of my day was that I got my favourite for lunch," Clara's dad said.

We ate the rest of the dinner mostly in silence. When Clara and I went upstairs to find a comedy to watch, my thoughts strayed back to the mysterious shadow.

The next day, the shadow still wasn't far from my mind. The knot in my stomach had gotten worse since the day before, making it difficult to take deep breaths. Thankfully, on Fridays we only had two classes in the morning and Clara and I grabbed lunch when we were finished with History.

When we headed back to our lockers to get our things, we were stopped by a guy in the hallway – Axel, if I remembered correctly. He and Clara knew each other, but I couldn't for the life of me remember how they'd met.

"Clara!"

I held back a sigh. Since Clara was a lot more outgoing than me, she knew a lot of people, so this wasn't an uncommon occurrence. But with how I felt at the moment, I wanted nothing more than to get home and hug Kiwi.

"I'll see you Monday," I told Clara, waving a little as I headed for the lockers.

She started to move towards me, but Axel pulled her into conversation, and she just waved back. I knew she'd call me later. She knew me too well and cared too much to leave it be.

I hurried home, and after a quick walk with Kiwi, I went upstairs to my room, followed by the black-and-white ball of fluff, and sank into bed. Kiwi immediately followed, laying down next to me, head resting on my lap.

I let my hands sink into her fur and felt the soft strands sift through my fingers. When the knot in my stomach didn't relax, I picked up my notebook. Kiwi, knowing what this meant, jumped down from the bed and wagged her tail, looking up at me with expectant eyes.

I laughed at her eagerness, then opened my notebook to the last used page and started writing.

After I'd created Kiwi, Mom had taught me how to control my abilities, and nowadays, it was rare that something happened out of my control – thank God. It would've been really awkward in ninth grade when we were writing about volcanoes if one had appeared in the middle of the classroom. And learning to control my magic had other benefits, too.

The first thing I had learned was that I had to write what I wanted to create. Other creators could use their magic by speaking the words, but those like me had to write.

The second thing I learned was that intent was key.

I focused my mind on what I needed, and imagined it bursting into existence as I wrote the words.

Before I knew it, the place that used to be the door to my wardrobe opened into a swirling blue mist. Kiwi started bouncing up and down. I lifted her up and stepped into the swirls.

Chapter 2
Escape Reality

I had created the meadow three years earlier. It started out as a way to get away when I needed privacy, but recently, it had become a place where I could go and escape reality. It became a place where I could relax, even when my anxiety got bad. And it really was escaping reality – as far as I could tell, it existed on a plane different from the real world.

Birches surrounded the little clearing, and tall grass and flowers of all shapes and colours filled the place. I was always careful of venturing into the surrounding forest. At some point, the forest ended abruptly, and I had no idea what would happen if I accidentally stumbled outside of the boundaries of my creation. Maybe I'd stumble straight into space, or end up back in my room? Something told me I'd be better off not testing that, so I stayed far away from the edge.

Some days, the sunlight streamed through the trees into my meadow. Other days, it was the moon, along with a million and one stars, to be precise. It depended on my mood. It was a grey and rainy day in the real world, and I craved sunshine, which is what met me when I stepped through the doorway.

I put Kiwi back on the ground, and she immediately started running around. Like me, she stayed away from the surrounding forest.

Maybe she could sense the danger of going too far. Or maybe she sensed my trepidation about it.

I lay down on the grass and closed my eyes, listening to the birds chirping, the gentle rustling of leaves, and Kiwi's quiet thudding steps in the grass. The knot in my stomach started loosening, and my breaths felt deeper than they had all day. The constant churning of my brain calmed, focused on the soothing sounds, the flowery scents in the air, the feel of the soft grass against my back. Muscles that seemed to always be tense, relaxed.

Something light landed on my stomach, and I opened my eyes. Kiwi stared down at me with big eyes, tail swishing. When she saw that I was looking at her, she jumped down and started bouncing up and down. I laughed and stood up. The bouncing got worse. I let my gaze wander the meadow and found what I was looking for.

The minute I grabbed the twig and showed it to Kiwi, she froze, eyes glued on it. Only her tail moved.

"You want this?"

She jumped up, trying to grab the twig, but I pulled it out of her reach. I didn't make her wait very long, though, before I threw it for her. She spun and set off after the twig. Then she raced laps, holding it proudly in her mouth.

A chill raced down my back. I spun around, in time to see a shadow moving into the trees.

Kiwi stopped by my side and started barking. Dark clouds gathered, blocking out the sun. I shivered in the sudden cold. A sharp wind swept through the meadow, rustling the leaves. My heart sped up. No one else should be able to enter. I could bring others, but it should be impossible for anyone to enter on their own. That was how I'd created it – so that no one could enter without my specific "key" – and creators couldn't change each other's creations. That was one of the basic rules of magic. We couldn't change already existing things, we could only create new things.

Panic made me freeze as a raindrop hit my forehead while the wind picked up further, turning into a storm. The beautiful birch trees that surrounded my creation felt dark and ominous as they swayed violently. A loud *snap* made me jump and spin around just as a thick branch fell through the heavy foliage. Another heavy raindrop hit the middle of my head, then another, and another. The cold drops seeped into me, settled in my bones, and I shuddered.

Then the sky opened up and rain pelted me. My hands shook as I grabbed my pen from my pocket, but I couldn't find my notebook and tears blurred my vision along with the rain. I sank into the grass and felt around, hoping to find something, any flat surface, that I could write on. I finally found a somewhat smooth rock, grabbed it, and started writing, wanting to get out of there as soon as possible. The pen slipped from my wet hand, and I grabbed after it blindly. Then finally I managed to write the line that would take me back home.

> *Blue swirls open into a doorway leading back to my bedroom.*

My handwriting was so shaky it was barely legible, and when the doorway didn't immediately spring into existence, my heart nearly stopped beating for a moment. When the air in front of me finally started swirling into a blue mist, I grabbed Kiwi, who still stared intently into the trees and growled, and stepped through the doorway.

Darkness enveloped me for a long moment that stretched out forever, and for the first time since I'd made the meadow, my chest tightened in fear. *What if I can't get out? What if whoever changed the meadow had also changed the doorway?*

Then, finally, I saw the plastic plant that stood in my bedroom window, and I stumbled into the room. My big toe got caught on the rug, and I landed hard on my hands and knees, the fall only slightly softened by the fake lambskin rug. The pulsing pain in my palms and knees barely registered past the chaotic storm raging inside of me.

Soaking wet and shaking, I curled into myself, hugging my stomach in a desperate attempt to ease the pain inside. What just happened? How did someone else get into my meadow? No one should be able to do that without my permission, creator or not.

You didn't actually see anything, though. The thought snaked unbidden through my mind. All I'd seen was a shadow, but what if I was seeing things? No one else could enter, not without the key, the specific words that opened the doorway to my meadow. But then... how had the weather changed? Was my safe space breaking?

Kiwi licked my face, and I laughed, but it turned into sobs. My breath came in short gasps, and tears streamed down my face, though I barely noticed it. My meadow, my one safe space, had been taken away. My heart beat so fast it hurt, and I knew I needed to calm down. But I felt violated – my one safe place had been turned against me.

I forced myself to look up at the painting I had above my desk. I followed the shape of it with my eyes, breathing in time with it. It was an exercise I'd learned when I first started having panic attacks, and it usually worked. My breathing slowed down, little by little, along with my heartrate. My chest still felt tight, but at least the panic attack had passed.

My head turned on its own, until my gaze landed on my closet door. The doorway had closed itself, but just the sight of my closet had my heartbeat picking up again. Dread and fear mixed with anxiety and settled inside me until I shook with the overwhelming emotions. What could be powerful enough to cause such a drastic change in my meadow?

And would I ever be able to get it back?

CHAPTER 3
SORCERY

Since it was Friday night and Mom had the evening off, the three of us – Mom, me and Tilda – had dinner together and a game night. Because of Mom's job, we couldn't have a regular set day as game night, but we tried to do it once a week.

It had been just us for as long as I could remember. I had no memory of our dad since he'd abandoned us right after Tilda was born.

"How was your week?" Mom asked me and Tilda. "Anything new at school?"

I shrugged. "It was fine. We've got a ton of examinations next week, but I don't think it'll be any trouble."

Tilda gave the biggest sigh. "It's crazy! Why do all the teachers have to schedule their tests for the same week? Don't they ever talk to each other?"

"Yeah, I remember what it was like in ninth grade, so much stuff that needed to be done before the gymnasium." I smiled at her. The Swedish equivalent of high school required a lot of preparations. "It gets better, though."

"Well, you've only got a few weeks left before break, so try to focus on that," Mom said. "And I'm sure you'll both do fine."

After dinner, Tilda volunteered to take Kiwi for a walk while Mom and I cleaned up. We started working, and for a while, only the clinking sound of dishes could be heard, until Mom asked, "How are things really?" She started loading the dishwasher. "I know the end of the term can be really stressful."

"My anxiety's been a bit worse," I said, "but it's not too bad. Really."

Mom looked up at me and her eyebrows drew together. "You know you can talk to me, right? Whatever's going on."

"I know, Mom," I said. "I promise I'll tell you if things get bad."

She looked at me for a long moment. I met her eyes briefly before focusing back on my task of putting the leftovers in the fridge. Any longer and I'd break down and tell her everything. "I know you think I worry too much, but I don't want things to get as bad as they were before. And I need you to know you're not alone. You have people who care, people you can turn to for help."

"I know that, Mom." It was true. But the last thing I wanted was for her to worry even more.

Before she could press me further, the door opened, and Tilda's voice floated through the flat. "We're home!"

I gave Mom a small smile, then yelled back, "Are you ready to lose at Monopoly?"

Mom had to work all weekend, and I spent Saturday catching up with the latest release from my favourite author. My thoughts were still spinning after what had happened in my meadow, and it was a relief to be able to focus on Poppy and Casteel's latest obstacles. They sure had bigger issues than me, at least. Tilda was doing something with her friends, and I stayed curled up in my comfy armchair, Kiwi resting on my feet, for most of the day. Getting lost in my books was one of the few things that could calm my anxiety, and I never said no to a full day of reading.

On Sunday, Tilda and I had a *Marvel* marathon. It was one of few things we had in common, so we took every chance we got to watch the movies together, see the new ones in the cinema, or binge-watch the latest show.

I took Kiwi for a quick walk while Tilda prepared breakfast, and then we curled up on the sofa, me with a fluffy blanket and a cup of tea, her with a hot chocolate with whipped cream and marshmallows. We watched the first movie mostly in silence, focused on our breakfast, while the wind howled outside. About halfway through the second movie, Tilda got up and walked to the kitchen. I heard her rummaging through cupboards for a while, then a deep sigh and a whisper, and then she came back into the living room holding a bar of chocolate.

I narrowed my eyes. "Did you just create that chocolate?" Unlike me, she didn't have to write anything to create – she just had to say it, and with the proper words and intention, it would appear in her hand.

She shrugged and sat down on the couch, but she couldn't keep a smile off her face.

I sighed. "You know we can't use it all willy-nilly like that," I admonished.

She raised an eyebrow. "Willy-nilly? What are you, five? And besides, it's just small stuff. It's no big deal." She held the chocolate out to me and grinned. "You know you want it."

I gave her another disapproving look, but the chocolate with its yummy pieces of fudge was impossible to resist. "Seriously, Tilda, you need to be careful what you create. You know the consequences."

She sighed and popped a piece of chocolate in her mouth. "Yeah, yeah. I know. I'll be more careful."

After classes on Monday, I had some studying to do for our Psychology test the next day, so I decided to go to the school library for a while. I always got more done when I studied at the library – or really anywhere other than at home. Even if the house was empty, it was too tempting to cuddle up with Kiwi and read a book, or hang out with Tilda, or do literally anything other than what I was supposed to be doing. I didn't mind, though. When we'd had our first Psychology class the year before, the subject had quickly become my favourite, and I'd realised I wanted to help kids like me.

I was focused on my reading and didn't notice someone approaching me until they set down their MacBook on the table next to me and asked, "Is this seat taken?"

I looked up and smiled at Noah. "No, go ahead."

He sat down, gesturing at my book. "Psychology?"

Noah and I had met our first year at the gymnasium, through Clara. Clara met him through some mutual friend of theirs, and in her mission to pull me out of my shell, she'd introduced us. It had taken a while for us to become friends, since I'm totally awkward and have no idea what to say to strangers, but Noah had persisted, kept starting conversations with me in the corridors, something I was eternally grateful for. He was a really nice, boy-next-door kind of guy (which I preferred by far over the clichéd bad boy) and he was easy to talk to, something that was rare for me.

I blinked back to reality. "Yep. We have this big test tomorrow, and I feel like I don't know any of it."

Noah laughed. "This coming from the girl with the practically perfect memory?"

"It's not perfect, I've just found a good study technique that works for me."

"Fair enough," he allowed. "And here I was going to ask if you wanted to grab some coffee, but I'm guessing I can't pull you away from your books?"

I bit my cheek and rolled my neck to release some of the tension that had gathered over the last couple of hours. I had been studying for a while, and I felt fairly confident about the test – though my confidence would disappear by morning, but then, I felt like that before any test, no matter how much I studied before.

"I should probably take a break, anyway," I said.

Noah smiled. "Perfect."

Our school had two cafeterias. The one we went to was in a small room, with a cosy atmosphere, dim lights and a constant smell of fresh coffee. The people who worked there always took a moment to chat with you about school. There were candles on every table and a comfy couch in one corner. That's where we sat down after we ordered – him a cup of coffee and carrot cake, me a cup of tea and a toffee cookie. I immediately took a big gulp of citrusy tea, and scalding hot water burned my tongue. I swore as I choked on the burning liquid.

"Are you okay?" Noah asked, eyebrows drawn together.

I nodded, though it took me a second before I could reply. "Hot."

He grinned. "I've heard that about boiling water."

I narrowed my eyes at him. "Ha. Ha. Very funny." I bit into my cookie, and the toffee melted on my tongue. The first bite crunched, then gave way to soft, chewy toffee.

"I found out something interesting." Noah lowered his voice. "There's a coven of sorcerers living on Gotland."

My eyes widened. Other than Noah, I'd never met anyone else with magic, except my mother and sister. "Really? Where?"

"They live scattered all over the place, but they meet in the forest in Stenkyrka, really close to the Virgin."

I snorted. "Of course they would meet at a cliff where a tragic love story ended and a young virgin fell to her death. Where else would a coven of sorcerers gather for their secret, clandestine meetings?"

Noah laughed. "Right? Could they be any more cliché?"

"How did you even find out about that?" I blew on my tea and took a careful sip. "That seems like something they'd want to keep quiet."

"My mom told me," he said. "Apparently, some lady approached her and told her about it. Offered to let us join."

"Oh? So, are you? Going to join?" I picked up my cup in an attempt to keep my hands busy.

Noah shook his head. "No, Mom told her we were fine without a coven. We mostly try to stay under the radar, and joining a coven feels kind of counterproductive to that, doesn't it?"

I snorted. "Yeah. What do they even do out there? Virgin sacrifices?"

Noah grinned. "Just practise their magic, I think. I don't know, Mom didn't ask too much about it. She said it was a community for creators and sorcerers where they wouldn't have to hide their magic. Apparently, she really emphasised the importance of keeping magic a secret. Like we couldn't figure that out on our own. I think we've all read enough history to know what a bad idea *that* is."

I snorted. "Yeah, we'd have to be exceptionally stupid to let everyone know about our magic. Did you meet her?"

Noah shook his head and took a bite of his cake.

"So, how are the twins doing?" I asked. "Has their magic appeared yet?"

Noah sighed. "Yes, it has. The flat is a hurricane most days – when it's not flooding, that is."

"Sounds like when Tilda was discovering her magic." I laughed at the memory. "Once, she was telling me and Mom about dolphins – she had a project at school about them – and then, all of a sudden, we had a dolphin in our living room." Needless to say, we hadn't been able to keep *that* creation. We'd had to shove the poor thing into the trunk of the car, which was an adventure of itself, then let it into the Baltic, hoping it might survive the cold ocean.

Noah laughed.

"Do they have one affinity, or do they control all the elements?" I didn't know too much about sorcery. Hell, I didn't know enough about creative magic, either. Everything I knew, my mom had told me. It wasn't like we had any instruction manuals to help.

"Well, sorcerers in general can control all elements, though the girls seem to be using mostly one element each. Water and air. Our apartment looks like a warzone these days. Though it could be worse. At least they aren't burning the place down."

I laughed. As we moved on to talk about school, I looked at him closely, trying to feel something. I didn't want to admit it, but mine and Clara's conversation, and my realisation that I'd never been attracted to anyone, had me rattled. Noah was good-looking. He was tall and dark-haired, with golden-brown skin, dark brown eyes and a warm smile. He had this classically handsome face; sharp cheekbones, full lips, long lashes. I could recognise he was good-looking, but it didn't stir anything in me, like Clara talked about. I found some people good-looking, but it never amounted to anything more than an appreciation of beauty. Like looking at a pretty painting. No butterflies, no sweaty palms, no nothing.

I sighed. Why couldn't I have a normal crush like every other seventeen-year-old girl? I hung out with this totally gorgeous guy all the time, and I felt nothing beyond friendship.

Noah paused, looking at me. "Are you okay?"

I shook myself out of my depressing thoughts. "Yeah, just... stressed, I guess."

"Are you still thinking about the Psychology test? Because you'll do fine – you always do."

I nodded, because it was easier to claim it was because of school – it often was – than to explain that I wished I was attracted to him. Sure, we were close friends, but that would be weird.

"You know what I think?" He smiled. "I think you should try riding."

That was random. "Uh, what?"

"I really think riding could be good for you," he explained. "I mean, when you ride, you have to be completely focused on what you're doing. You have to be in the moment. I think you could use that. Plus, horses are actually great for anxiety. There's scientific proof."

Really? That didn't sound right to me, but then, I was open to trying anything that could reduce my anxiety. "Okay?" I said hesitantly.

Noah smiled. "You don't even have to ride; you can just pet the horses for a while."

I was still not sure about it – I'd never been around horses before – but if Noah thought it could help, what harm could it do? Just the thought of sitting on a horse made my palms feel damp, but if I only had to stand next to it and pet it? My mind supplied images of crushed toes, but I shoved them away. If it could make me feel better, it was worth a try, wasn't it?

After that, Noah set about distracting me from my stress. "Did you know that the dot over lowercase i and j has a name?"

I raised my eyebrows at the randomness of the question. "No, I didn't know that."

Noah grinned. "It's called a tittle. Means a tiny part of something."

I laughed. "That's... random. Why do you even know that?"

He shrugged. "Why shouldn't I know that?"

I shook my head in amazement and sipped my tea, letting him pull me into easy conversation.

My heart thundered in my ears as I stared at the open notebook on the desk in front of me. I'd had to dig out an older notebook, since I'd left my current one in the meadow after I'd panicked so badly, and the pages were filled with my neat handwriting. I had thought about going back constantly since Friday, even though the thought was enough to send me into a panic attack. Still, I wanted to hope it had been a fluke, because I needed the comfort of my safe space.

Hands shaking, I started writing in the margin, my handwriting squiggly from my shaking hand. The doorway opened up, and I stepped through, my eyes sweeping over the place in case it turned wrong again. Kiwi was downstairs with Tilda – no way would I risk bringing her when I didn't know what was waiting for me.

The meadow was normal. The sun warmed my cheeks, and I could hear the trees rustle in the breeze. I let my gaze scan the surrounding forest, but I saw nothing out of the ordinary. No shadows. No clouds. No rain.

I let myself breathe out, tension seeping out of my shoulders. A sound of branches snapping behind me, and my shoulders tensed up again. I spun around and came face to face with a stranger, half his face covered with a white mask.

CHAPTER 4
WHITE MASK

I backed away, my heart hammering in my chest, and the sky darkened. *Oh no, please, not again.* My foot got caught on something and I fell, landing hard on my butt. The man took a step forward, and I backed away, shaking my head. "Please..." My voice dropped into a whisper that could barely be heard over the wind that tore at my hair and bit at my cheeks.

I looked up at the stranger now towering over me.

He stilled. "I'm sorry I scared you." His voice was deep, low. "I just wanted to talk to you."

"Who are you?" I asked, proud when my voice only shook a little.

The side of his mouth that I could see rose into a smile. "I'm Erik."

I dug my shaking hands into the grass, trying to ground myself, but my heart still beat hard and my breathing was shallow. My thoughts raced, almost too fast to follow. *Had he been here last time too? Was he the shadow I'd seen? Had he been following me when I'd walked Kiwi? Why was he here?* How *was he here? What did he want with me?*

A fat raindrop fell on my head, and I jumped. I desperately grasped onto one thought. "You're the one who was here last time, aren't you? You started the storm?"

Erik shook his head. "I was here last time, but I didn't start the storm. You did."

I gaped at him, disbelief momentarily overshadowing my panic. "No, I didn't! I don't control the weather like that, not without writing it—would you stop doing that!" The rain fell properly now, cold raindrops making me shiver. "Stop making it rain!"

"I'm not doing anything." The calmness of his voice t made me want to scream. "You are. It's the only explanation."

I blinked once, twice, breathing hard. My fingers dug into the ground. "How did you get in here?"

"I'm a creator *and* a sorcerer, like you, though I create things by speaking them." *Like Tilda.* It didn't slip my mind that he didn't really answer my question. "And I really couldn't do this – okay, I could create a storm, but changing something in a world that you've created would be difficult. I swear I didn't start that storm, and I'm not creating this one."

He's lying. The thought brought some clarity to my panicked thoughts. *I need to get out of here.* I looked around, trying to find my notebook, but I must have dropped it in my shock, because it lay in the grass between me and Erik. I looked from it to Erik and back again. Did I dare move closer to him to grab it?

Erik must have noticed my gaze, because he bent down to pick up the notebook and pen. He moved closer to me, and I flinched. My muscles clenched so hard it hurt, but he just put them down next to me and moved away. I let go of my almost convulsive grip on the grass to grab my notebook and pen, barely even noticing the dirt stuck under my fingernails.

"I know this must seem really strange," Erik said gently. His hair stuck to his forehead, and a raindrop slid down his face. "It's just...

well, I've never met anyone else like me before, and I thought…" He looked away. "I thought maybe you could understand."

I looked up at him, uncertain. I didn't really understand what it was like to be completely alone like that. I had my family, and Noah and Clara, who all knew about my ability. But I could imagine what it must be like to not know anyone else with magic, and I felt bad for him.

I sighed. "Alright. Just… don't come here uninvited again, okay? It's a bit eerie, not knowing if someone will be here when I come." I didn't let go of my notebook and stayed tense and ready for anything, but I was willing to give him a chance.

The rain stopped and the sky cleared. The wind slowed into a light breeze, and I felt the heat from the sun on my face, warming me. I wiped the rain from my face, my wet clothes sticking to me.

What the hell is going on with my meadow? Could it be possible that Erik wasn't doing it? If so, did that mean I was doing it? That I was a sorceress? *That's impossible. I would've noticed before.* After all, Noah's sisters were ten, and already their magic had awakened. The same age creators were when their magic first appeared.

Erik sat down opposite me, a healthy distance away. Now that I wasn't panicking, I took the time to look him over. With his black clothes, and dark, almost black hair, he could've easily blended with the shadows, if it weren't for the shocking white of his mask. He must've been around my age, but it was hard to tell because of the mask. "Thank you."

"I thought it was impossible to be both a creator and a sorcerer." It was part statement, part question.

Erik shrugged. "It's not like there's a handbook or something. The only way to know if it's possible is if you met someone who is both." He gave an ironic smile. "And, being both myself, I think it's pretty evident that it can happen."

He had a point. Still, I couldn't believe that I could be a sorceress. It couldn't be possible. Could it?

I decided to change the subject. If I was going to let this guy into my safe space, I wanted to get to know him. It seemed only fair, since he was in a place that was incredibly private to me. "How did you find me?"

He smiled wryly. "It was a complete accident. I created a doorway to take me to a meadow, and accidentally ended up here."

I frowned. "So any creator could accidentally stumble upon this place?" The thought settled in my stomach like lead. What if someone else had been here when I wasn't?

What if someone else had been here when I was?

Erik nodded. "In theory, yes, they could. But you can protect it from other people. I can show you."

I hesitated, twisting my fingers through the grass. Could I trust him? But the thought of other creators getting into my safe space made my eyes sting and my stomach feel like it was full of needles. *This is my only safe space – I have to protect it from strangers.* "Okay. How do I do it?"

"There is this protective spell that you can use – that you can write, just like when you create anything else." Erik leaned forward. "It will only protect a specific place, though. You can't use it to protect yourself. And it only works if you're in the place you want to protect. You can't do it from somewhere else. But once it's there, it stays, until you remove it."

I nodded. I just needed to protect the meadow, anyway. "What is it?"

"With this incantation of protection, spirits of evil intent shall encounter redirection."

I wrote the incantation down and looked up to see a faint shimmer close over the clearing like a dome. My eyes widened. "Wow. So, no one will be able to enter now?"

Erik shook his head. "That's not quite how it works. No one who wants to harm you or your meadow will be able to enter. People with pure intentions, like the spell says, will still be able to enter. But this way, you know you will be safe here."

I bit my lip, chewing it over. Did I believe him? *Should* I believe him?

But then, *I* had created that protection spell, not him. Words didn't lie, not when it came to magic, and besides, I had filled that spell with so much intention I could practically feel it in the air. It wasn't perfect, but it would keep *spirits of evil intention* away. Whatever that meant.

I sighed. "Okay. So how are you a sorcerer and a creator?"

Erik's mouth twitched. "Well, my guess is one of my parents was a sorcerer and the other a creator."

I raised my eyebrows. "You guess?"

"Yes."

I looked down at my bouncing knee. The shortness in his voice made it clear that he didn't want to talk about it, but my untameable curiosity was my biggest fault, or so my mom liked to say. *He's inside your one safe space – the least he can do is answer some of your questions.*

I looked back at Erik but couldn't quite meet his gaze. "Want to elaborate?"

His mouth turned down at the corner. "My mother was a sorcerer, I believe. I don't have many memories of her, but I am pretty sure she used the elements. My father left before I was born, so I have no way of knowing if he was a creator, but it would make sense. As far as I know, magic is inherited, but who knows?"

It did seem like magic was indeed inherited, considering the only people I knew who had magic – which admittedly wasn't that many – also had parents with magic. But like he'd said, it's not like we had a handbook or something to help us figure stuff out.

"Did your mother... pass away?" My voice dropped low.

Erik smiled, but it wasn't a happy smile. "No. She left when I was six or so."

I inhaled sharply. "Then who raised you?"

"No one." Erik looked away then, staring intently at the trees surrounding us. "I was found by a circus director, who took me in, but he didn't raise me. He let me join his circus, paraded me around as his freak for years."

I stared at him in horror. How could something like that be allowed to happen in Sweden, in the twenty-first century?

"I'm so sorry," I whispered, my heart clenching in sympathy.

Erik's eyes swung back to me and flashed, and I shrank back. "I don't need your pity." His hard voice made me flinch.

"It's not pity." I forced my voice to come out stronger than a whisper. "It's empathy. There's a difference."

He looked at me, eyes narrowed, then finally nodded. "Alright. I'm sorry."

"Are you still with the circus?" The question slipped out before I'd even decided to ask.

His whole demeanour changed between one heartbeat and the next. He stiffened, and his eyes grew hard as diamonds. I could practically feel frigid air radiating off of him.

The warm sunlight disappeared, and I looked up to find dark clouds covering the sun once again. My eyes shot to Erik.

"No," he said shortly.

I looked away, staring unseeingly at a bright pink flower next to him as rain once again pelted me. His strong reaction scared me and reminded me that I really didn't know him at all. For all I knew, he was lying to gain my trust. And the dark clouds had shown up right when he grew cold. It had to be him doing it. "I should go," I said finally.

His face softened. "Please don't."

"I have to. It's getting late."

"How can you tell? The sun is still shining."

"The position of the sun changes, though," I explained. "Depending on the time in the real world." It had taken some adjustments, a lot of trial and error, but after months of missing dinner, I'd finally managed to get the sun and moon to show me the time. It wasn't exact, but good enough that I could tell when afternoon turned into evening.

"That's creative." He looked away, then back at me again, his eyes imploring me. "Can I please see you again?"

I hesitated, but then remembered the protection spell. If he meant me harm, he wouldn't be able to come back. "Fine. I'll meet you tomorrow, here, same time."

He nodded, and his entire body relaxed. "Thank you."

I didn't say anything, just picked up my notebook and wrote myself home.

CHAPTER 5
RAZOR SHARP TEETH

"That was horrible," Clara complained as we sat down in the school cafeteria to eat. At noon, the place was packed with students, and I had to lean in to hear her over the noise. "I have never done so badly at a test before, I swear."

I laughed. Clara always said that after our tests. "I'm sure you did fine," I told her. "You're so good at Psychology."

Clara picked at her food, wrinkling her nose. I couldn't blame her. The scent of curry overwhelmed everything else, and the curry concoction in question looked anything but appetizing. "Still, that was a lot more difficult than I expected. I don't think I got the second question right."

I started to reply but was interrupted. "Is this seat taken?"

I looked up and found Alva standing there, shifting from foot to foot. "Nope," I told her with a smile. "Go ahead."

She smiled and sat down next to Clara, who transformed at the sight of her crush. No longer picking at the questionable chicken curry, she smiled, her whole face brightening.

They were such opposites to each other – Clara outgoing and the life of the party, Alva shy and anxious, dark golden-brown hair and tawny skin to Clara's warm blond and pale skin.

"So, how did you guys do on the test?" Alva asked and looked down at her food, tucking her dark hair behind her ear.

I looked at Clara, expecting her to be quick to reply, but she stared at her food like it held the answers to world peace. Clara, who was the most outgoing person ever, couldn't even find the words to tell her crush how the Psychology test went. I wanted to laugh. "I think it went okay," I told Alva, since my best friend had clearly gone mute. "But it's hard to tell." I didn't usually consider myself superstitious, but when it came to exams, I didn't want to jinx it and avoided ever saying it went well. I couldn't explain it, but it was the only superstition I allowed myself.

"I know, right?" Alva agreed. "How did it go for you, Clara?" She looked at Clara, who blushed. Blushed! I'd never seen Clara blush before. What alien had replaced my best friend?

"Okay, I guess," Clara mumbled.

That's it. I couldn't look at this. It was too painful. So I did the only thing I could think of – I kicked Clara under the table (maybe I read too much). But I succeeded in getting her attention. She squawked and finally looked up from her food and raised her eyebrows at me. I mimicked her expression, then subtly (probably not) looked at Alva. Clara sent me a dark look, but at least I'd gotten her out of whatever that mood had been.

Back to herself again, Clara started talking to Alva. "It went horrible," she exclaimed. "And was it just me, or did she ask questions about things we haven't even talked about yet?"

Alva smiled slightly. "The questions were a bit different from the practise ones, but I didn't think there was anything totally new."

Clara launched into an animated reply with a lot of gesturing. Relieved that she was back to normal again, I went back to eating.

I tried to focus on the conversation and even participate a little, but my thoughts kept drifting to my meadow.

The more I thought about it, the more Erik freaked me out. I felt awful for him, for everything he had been through and for how mistreated he'd been. If he was telling the truth, that is.

Something about him felt off, and really, what were the chances he had stumbled upon my meadow by accident? It felt like too much of a coincidence.

And the whole thing about me being a sorceress? I had a hard time believing that, too. I definitely would've noticed it sooner. I'd never had any accidents connected to the elements. Only when I'd written things and they had appeared next to me, like Kiwi.

Not to mention, I had a feeling Erik was holding something back. There was something he wasn't telling me, the question was what. And could I trust him anyway?

"Lia?" Clara's question forced me out of my thoughts. She stood up, holding her tray and looking at me. Alva had already gone ahead to drop off her tray. "Is everything okay?"

I shook my head to clear my thoughts. "I'll tell you later," I told her and tried to smile reassuringly, but it probably looked more like a grimace.

Clara looked at Alva, then back at me, frowning. Finally, she nodded and followed Alva.

The rest of the day was hectic, so Clara didn't get a chance to push, which I knew she would do the second we had a moment to ourselves. I knew I needed to tell someone about Erik, but for some reason, I didn't want to.

Still, I'd read enough books to know that not telling anyone would lead to trouble, so I would.

After school, I expected Clara to corner me, and she tried to, but Alva interrupted us, asking to talk to Clara. She opened her mouth, taking a small step towards me, and I knew she was going to tell her no, so I practically shoved her towards the brunette. I didn't want my issues to stand in the way of Clara's crush.

I quickly grabbed my bag from my locker and closed it with a small click. Calling my good-byes over my shoulder, I gave them their privacy as I headed home.

When I got there, I decided to take a long walk to clear my head a little. The pressure on my chest had been increasing all day, along with the cramp in my stomach, so I hoped it would help. Kiwi wasn't home, which meant Tilda had already taken her on a walk, but that didn't matter. I left my bike outside our flat, then started going in the direction of the forest.

Walking usually calmed me down, but this time, it wasn't working. The pressure over my chest was still there, making it hard to breathe. I pressed my fingernails into my palms, hoping the bite of my nails would distract me from the inner turmoil, but I was so focused on the anxiety in the pit of my stomach that I barely felt it.

I was so caught up in my head that I barely heard the crying at first. When I did, I stopped and listened. It sounded like a small child crying in the forest.

I turned towards the sound. "Hey! Is anyone there?"

The crying stopped for a second, before a child screamed. "Help! Help me!"

My heart started racing, snapping me out of my panicked thoughts. "Where are you?"

"Help!" The voice got more and more desperate.

I looked up and down the road, hoping there would be someone else around who could help, but no luck.

My stomach cramped as I grabbed my phone from my pocket and turned on the flashlight. Pushing branches and thorns out of my face, I walked into the forest. The sound of the child crying and screaming for help intensified. My heart beat so fast it was painful and I shook all over, but if a child had lost their way or was in danger, I couldn't leave them there.

"Ow!" A thorny branch dug into my hand as I pushed it out of the way and continued further into the forest.

The streetlights were starting to fade from view, leaving me mostly in darkness, when I finally saw the child. They were tiny, probably no more than two or three years old. It looked like they'd gotten stuck somehow. When I got closer, I could see the child's translucent, almost blue-ish skin. Dark hair fell in an oily tangle down their back, and only a thin, torn tunic protected them from the cold autumn air. They had circles under their eyes, so dark they looked like bruises, and the eyes were almost black.

I couldn't tell if the child was a boy or a girl, because of their state. Dressed the way they were, they would probably freeze to death if they didn't get inside soon.

"Hi," I said gently. "I'm Lia. I can help you. What's your name?"

"I don't have a name," the child cried.

I frowned as a chill raced down my spine. My whole body screamed at me to run. Something was seriously wrong here. I continued walking towards the child, but more hesitantly and slowly now. I felt silly for being scared of a child, but every instinct in my body screamed at me to run. My every muscle tensed, ready to run.

"Okay," I murmured. "Do you know where your parents are?"

"I'm alone!" the child cried shrilly. I jumped and almost dropped my phone.

"Okay," I repeated. "Can you come here? I'll help you get out of here."

The child nodded and started walking towards me. Apparently, they hadn't been stuck. Maybe they'd been lost and scared.

As the child got closer, I started shivering and my hands started shaking. I couldn't stop myself from backing away a step. Then they reached the light of my flashlight, and I gasped for breath. The child smiled, showing off razor sharp teeth.

I turned on my heel and ran.

Behind me, I heard the trees rustle as the wind picked up, and the child – creature? – screamed. Still, I didn't dare look back, didn't stop until I reached the streetlamps again. The creature had gone quiet by then. I chanced a look into the forest, shining my flashlight to search for the scary child. What I would do if it did chase me, I didn't know. I shook so badly I could barely hold my phone, and my face stung from a combination of cuts and scrapes and the cold, biting air.

The trees had bent from the strong wind that somehow hadn't touched me at all. It looked like it had parted around me like the Red Sea for Moses. I was too freaked out and terrified to even begin to understand that.

The child was gone.

Safely hidden away in my room, I called Clara and Noah, asking them to come over as soon as possible. What had happened with that child was not normal, and the wind that somehow didn't touch me wasn't normal, either.

Ten minutes later, the doorbell rang. Footsteps sounded up the stairs, I heard a knock on my bedroom door, and Clara stuck her head in.

Once we were all seated in my room, Clara looked at me, her brow knotted with concern. "What's going on, Lia?"

I took a deep breath and told them everything, about the storm in my meadow, about meeting Erik, and the scary child that disappeared. Clara and Noah listened, not saying a word while I talked, though their looks were of equal horror. By the time I was finished, I wanted to cry – again.

"Oh my God," Clara murmured. Silence descended on the room. The TV blared downstairs, and I stared at my shaking hands, trying to process everything.

"I don't think it's a good idea to see this Erik guy again," Clara stated, finally. "I mean, we don't know if he's connected to that... child, but he sounds creepy, and the fact that he can get into your meadow really freaks me out. How is that even possible?"

Noah nodded. "I don't know. There's really very little we know about it. I can ask my moms, but I don't know if they'll know anything since they're both sorceresses. You could ask your mom, though, see if she knows."

I bit my lip, frustrated that there were so many questions and no answers. "Yeah, I'll ask," I said.

Clara sighed. "Do you know of any creatures from Scandinavian folklore that could fit this thing?"

Noah shook his head. "Not exactly my area of expertise. I didn't even know those creatures were real – *if* that's what it was."

Clara sighed. "Let's look it up, see what we can find. A human child wouldn't disappear like that, that's for sure." I opened my laptop, and the soft whirr of the computer filled the room as the three of us waited. None of us spoke as I typed in the search engine, *Scandinavian folklore creatures child.* I clicked the first link that popped up and read out loud, "A myling is the spirit of an unnamed child which has been killed and buried in secret by its mother." I shuddered before forcing myself to read on. "It can usually be found haunting the place it was buried, screaming and crying, begging for someone to help them. The only way to put the myling to rest is to give it a name and bury it in holy soil."

I stared at the screen in horror. "Oh my God. That's... horrible."

Clara made a choked sound. "We have to find it then, and put it to rest."

I moved my horrified stare to her. "You want to go digging for a child's corpse?" My voice rose at the end, giving it a slightly – or very – panicked sound. "Are you actually crazy? We should call the police."

Noah looked green. "And tell them what? 'Hey, I saw this creepy creature from mythology in the forest, and now I think there's a child buried there. Could you please go dig for it?'"

I gaped at him. "You agree with her? It's... it's... insanity!"

Noah grimaced. "Maybe, but... what's the option here? Just leave the poor child there? We can't do that. What if someone is missing their child? They deserve closure."

Acid rose in my throat. I opened my mouth to argue, but what could I say? It's not like we could ask an adult – they would never believe us. And Noah was right. What if a parent – a dad, since apparently the mom was the killer here – was missing their child? Not to mention the child deserved better than to be unnamed and left in an unmarked grave. It – they – deserved some peace.

I stared down at the screen again, at the picture on the screen depicting a child no older than five, six, their skin a greenish-grey tint, their clothes ripped, hair tangled. The eyes, like black holes of nothing, seemed to stare right at me.

Can I really go grave-digging? Do I have a choice?

Chapter 6
A Child Buried

Clara and Noah had to leave before we could reach a decision on the grave-digging business. Once they'd left, I sank down into the softness of my armchair and breathed in deeply, catching the scent of the orchids placed on the little table next to the chair – the latest of a long line of plants. Unlike my mom, I had the opposite of green fingers. Any plant that entered my room would, sooner rather than later, perish. And still I kept trying.

My laptop whirred softly, and I listened to the clicking of the keys as I entered my password, letting it ground me in the here and now. It didn't always work, not when things were at their worst, but to my surprise, it kept the anxiety at bay this time.

A knock on the door interrupted my focus, and Tilda peeked inside. "Can I come in?"

I nodded, and she stepped inside, closing the door behind her. "What was that all about?" she asked and sat down on my bed, opposite me. I twirled in my chair to face her. "Did something happen?"

I chewed on my lip, unsure of how much I wanted to tell her. As my little sister, I didn't want to include her, but I also thought it would be a good idea for her to be aware of the possible danger so she could be careful.

"Yeah," I finally said. "I met this strange guy when I went to my meadow yesterday, who claims to be both creator and sorcerer, and then today, there was a really freaky child in the forest that I don't think was human. I went to help them, but ran when I saw them, and they chased me through the forest. So we should probably be careful."

Tilda frowned. "That's so creepy! Are you okay?"

I met her wide eyes. "I'm fine."

She narrowed her eyes. "Sure. Of course. Why wouldn't you be, after being chased by a creepy child in the forest and having your safe space invaded by a stranger? No big deal."

I felt some of the tension leave my shoulders. Tilda's calmness made me feel a little less freaked, and the familiar sarcasm soothed my nerves a little.

I shrugged. "It was scary, but I wasn't hurt or anything. I'll be fine."

Tilda let out an exaggerated sigh. "You're hopeless. Fine. I'll let it go." She looked away and stared out the window, quiet for a long moment. "If the creepy child thing wasn't human then what the heck was it?"

"According to my trusty friend Google, it's a myling – a child killed and buried by its mother."

Tilda's face tightened. "That is... disturbing in so many ways." She shuddered. "Just promise you'll be careful, okay? I don't like this at all."

Neither did I. "I promise."

She nodded and stood. "Good. Now I have to go finish my Maths homework or my teacher might actually kill me."

I rolled my eyes at her exaggeration. "Sure he will."

She put her hands on her hips and pouted. "He really might. He hates me!"

I snort-laughed. "Well, then you'd better go do your homework."

She stuck her tongue out at me and left, closing the door softly behind her.

I turned back to my laptop to open up the essay I worked on, hoping to get something done while distracting myself at the same time, but when my eyes drifted to the little clock in the corner, I jumped up. I'd completely forgotten about meeting Erik. I'd told Clara and Noah that I wouldn't meet with him, but something in me protested the thought.

Before I could talk myself out of it, I grabbed my notebook and wrote.

As the doorway opened up, I stepped through, clutching my notebook, and the darkness transported me.

When I stepped out, sunshine greeted me, warming my face. I immediately relaxed a little, my muscles releasing some of the tension. Stillness and quiet ruled the meadow, which was a nice change from the windy fall weather. Instead of the whining sound of the wind, only a soft rustling of leaves could be heard.

I looked around and spotted Erik sitting at the edge of the treeline, frowning. When he saw me, his face lit up in a wide smile.

"I thought you weren't coming," he admitted.

I smiled back. "I lost track of time. It's been an eventful day." I settled opposite him in the grass and told him about the creepy child.

His brows knitted. "That sounds like a myling."

I stared at him. "How did you know that?"

He looked away and shrugged. "I never really had any friends or anything, except this little girl who talked to me sometimes at the circus, so I didn't have a lot to do growing up. Since I had magic, it felt right to learn more about the folklore and mythology around here. I never expected it would actually be useful, though."

My heart clenched for him, but I kept my feelings to myself, remembering how he'd snapped the last time I expressed sympathy for him. "If there's a child buried here, we need to help them somehow. They deserve some peace." My voice sounded a lot more certain than I felt. I felt more like hiding out under my bed. "How can there be a child buried in the middle of the city?"

Erik's eyes glazed over. "Would it be such a surprise, considering the history of Gotland? But there might not be."

I chewed the inside of my cheek. There was, in fact, a mass grave in the middle of Visby, a remnant from the war with Denmark in the Middle Ages. Well, slaughter was a more accurate word, since the people of Gotland were farmers and didn't know squat about fighting. "Fair enough. What else could it be?"

"Well," Erik mused, "someone could have created it."

I froze as the realisation hit me. Why didn't I think of that? "But... why would someone want to create something out of mythology? What could be the purpose?"

Something gleamed in his eyes, but it disappeared before I could put my finger on it. "That's the question."

My breath caught as my palms turned clammy. "We need to go look for a grave, then. If it was created, then we won't find one, and if it weren't..." I trailed off, my stomach turning to acid at the thought of digging up a corpse.

A look of panic flashed across his face. "Why would you look for a grave? If there's a mythological creature there, you should avoid it."

He rushed through the words.

"But they deserve peace. And their parents deserve to know what happened to their child. Plus, knowing if the myling was created or if it's an actual spirit of a dead child could help us."

He shook his head. "It's a bad idea," he said firmly, that look of panic still on his face.

I decided to drop the subject, not wanting it to turn into a fight. The thought of going grave-digging made my stomach turn, but Erik's total rejection of the idea raised some questions. Why was he so against the idea of us looking for this child? What was he scared we would find?

The next day, the hallways at school were quieter than usual. While students stood off in groups like they usually did, their conversations were hushed and there were no laughs. In fact, most people were looking off in the distance, distracted.

Clara waited for me at the lockers, her face settled into a deep frown, eyes shiny. My stomach clenched. Whatever had happened, it couldn't be good.

I frowned. "What's going on? Did something happen?"

Clara looked away for a second. "One of the students in our year is missing," she said, keeping her voice down. "Axel – you know, the guy I talked to on Friday?"

My breath whooshed out of me. "What do you mean, missing?"

"No one has seen him since yesterday morning. He wasn't at school.

His parents haven't seen him, and neither have his friends. They reported him missing last night, and the police are here talking to his classmates."

The always-there pressure on my chest increased, and my stomach knotted. "Oh my God," I murmured, unsure what to say.

A kid missing? Surely he must've been staying with a friend or... something. Something else was just... it didn't happen on Gotland. Disappearances, kidnappings, murders... that was rare. Historically, sure, but I could only remember one recent murder, which had happened that summer. It had been huge news because it was such a shock, a murder happening right in the middle of Visby.

The entire day felt off. We still had regular classes, but no one could focus, we all kept talking about the missing student, and none of the teachers told us to be quiet or to focus on our studies. The hallways were less loud than usual, everyone talking in hushed voices. We even saw the police in the hallways on the way to lunch.

The quiet, tense mood in the hallways settled on my chest like a rock, and I found myself struggling to keep tears from falling.

When our last class of the day finally finished, Clara came home with me. No one else was there yet, so we took a walk with Kiwi. Neither of us said much, too caught up in our own heads. When we got back, we went right upstairs, Kiwi hot on our heels. We both settled on my bed, and Kiwi curled up at my feet.

As soon as we closed the door behind us, Clara started talking. "I know you don't like the idea, but we really can't just leave that child buried in the forest. We can't tell anyone about it, so really, I don't see any other option than to go look for it ourselves."

I sighed, but I'd made up my mind after Erik's reaction the day before. "I know. I don't like it, but you're right. If there's a child buried there, we have to do something."

Clara frowned. "What do you mean, *if* there's a child buried there? We agreed it had to have been a myling, so there has to be a body."

"It was definitely a myling," I said, shuddering as I remembered the child. "But, what if it was created?"

I didn't quite want to believe it was a real myling, because if they existed, God knew what other creatures from folklore and mythology might exist. Although, if someone had created the myling, there was a chance they would make other creatures, so maybe it didn't make much of a difference.

I walked past that place every day with Kiwi. If there was an actual child buried there, wouldn't I have noticed it sooner? And it would've reached the news if the disappearance was new.

Clara stared at me, her mouth open as she worked through that bit of information. "I didn't think about that. Can you really create mythological beings?"

I chewed my lip. "I mean, I created Kiwi before I even knew what magic was, so why not these creatures as well?" I shivered. "I don't even know what's scarier; if there is a child buried there, or if there is someone creating creatures from folklore on Gotland."

Clara looked at me with wide eyes. "What if there *is* someone creating them? What the hell could they want with Gotland?"

"I don't think I'll ever be able to sleep again," I muttered, shivering at the thought that this might be just the beginning. If one creature from mythology could come to life, what's to say all of them wouldn't? *Oh my God...*

"Well, going digging will help us find out which it is; a real myling or a creation."

My stomach clenched. "I know. We need to call Noah, then, and make a plan. I'd rather have it over and done with as soon as possible."

We quickly decided that Noah would meet us outside of my place at midnight. That was late enough that our families should be asleep, and we didn't want to wait too long, since we had no idea how long it might take us to dig up a grave. We all needed to be at school the next day, after all.

Acid churned in my stomach by the time we hung up. "I need to not think about this for a while, or I might go hide in my meadow and never return."

"Let's talk about something else," Clara decided, her face a greyish-green. "Axel has to have left or something, right? Like, he must've run away from home. Right?"

I bit my lip hard and pressed my fingernails into my palms, but it did nothing to distract me from the pressure growing inside. *That was her idea of a better subject?* "I don't know. I mean, kids running away? That sounds more like a movie to me. Do people actually do that?"

Clara shook her head. "But what's the alternative? He was... taken?" Her voice dropped to a whisper.

I had nothing to say to that. The ticking of my wall clock filled the room.

"Is it just me or is the timing really funny?" Clara continued. "I mean, first you meet this strange guy who has magic like yours, then last night and the myling, and now a guy from our school is missing? Could it really be a coincidence?"

The thought had snaked its way into my head a few times throughout the day, but I had pushed it down every time. If I really thought about it, I might not leave my room out of fear.

"I don't know," I said, finally. "But how could it be connected? I mean, Erik and the myling are both connected to the magical world, but Axel can't be. I'd know if someone else at our school had magic."

But would I? Would I recognise someone like me if I saw them? I realised how much I didn't know about my magic and the people like me.

"Let's change the subject to something a little less depressing," I said. "As far as distractions go, that was a pretty crappy one."

Clara grimaced. "Sorry. Yes. Fun topic to discuss." She hummed to herself, then her face split into a smile. "Noah mentioned you agreed to go riding."

I didn't say anything and let the ticking of the clock fill the room once again. "He said it was really good for anxiety to be around horses, and if it could help…" I didn't need to finish the sentence. Not with Clara.

She squealed like a baby seal. "Well, I think it's a great idea! So, you and Noah have been spending a lot of time together…" She wriggled her eyebrows and grinned. "Are you interested in him?"

I shook my head frantically. "No!" I grimaced at the vehemence in my voice. "I mean, no. We're friends, that's all."

Clara laughed. "You know it's okay if you like him, right? It would be really cool if you two started dating!"

"I'm not interested in him like that." The words were firm. "We're just friends."

Clara's eyes widened. That might've come out a little harder than intended. "That's fine, too," she backtracked. "Obviously, girls and boys can be friends without either of them being interested in anything more." She paused and looked at me for a long time. "Is every-thing alright? You know you can talk to me, right? About anything."

I nodded. "I'm fine."

I wasn't.

The truth was, I was pretty sure there was something really wrong with me. Clara talked all the time about her crushes and how hot some girls were. But I'd never felt like that about anyone. I'd never looked at anyone and wanted *more*. I mean, I dreamed of falling in love and being that close to someone – I was a true romantic – but when I looked at people, I didn't feel butterflies in my stomach. I couldn't even imagine kissing someone.

I was weird. I mean, I was eighteen, I had never been kissed – and not because no one had been interested, because there had been a guy a year before. But when he'd tried to kiss me at a party Clara had dragged me to, I had run away. The thought of kissing him had made me feel icky. That wasn't normal. My only hope at this point was that I was a late bloomer. That had to be it.

Really, I wished I was interested in Noah. He was always willing to listen, to help, and could usually make me feel better. He would be a great boyfriend. Why couldn't I feel something for him? Why didn't I get butterflies or nervous when I looked at him?

I shook my head, trying to clear it. Another subject change was well-needed. *Maybe I should make a list of bad subjects.* "So, what did you and Alva talk about yesterday after school?" That should properly distract her.

Clara frowned a little, but thankfully dropped the subject. "Oh, I totally forgot about that! She asked if she could do the Communica-tions project with us. I said she could. She can, right?"

I laughed at her wide puppy dog eyes. "Of course. As long as you'll be able to focus with her around, I'm fine with it."

Clara didn't even bother to deny it. "Hmm, well, probably not, but this is such a great opportunity to spend time with her! I can't pass up on it!"

I laughed again. "Are you going to go all quiet and stare at your lap again? Because I can't watch that again. It's too painful."

Clara punched me playfully in the shoulder. "Shut up. We had a moment yesterday after school, I'll have you know. Maybe she's a closeted lesbian?" she mused, and her eyes lit up.

"Maybe," I agreed. "Anything's possible."

"Yeah," Clara murmured. "Hey, let's find some cutesy romcom to watch while we wait, okay? I might go crazy from the anticipation."

That's exactly what we did. But the funny moments didn't distract me for long from what we had to do. No amount of awkward moments could get my head off the fact that we'd be returning to the place I'd seen the myling, this time in the middle of the night.

Chapter 7
Grave-Digging

My glove-clad hands gripped the shovel hard while Clara and I waited for Noah. The time had slowly ticked past midnight, and I couldn't stop bouncing on my toes. Where was he? Why was he late? Had something happened to him?

Clara reached out to put a hand on my shoulder. "Breathe, Lia."

I realised I'd been holding my breath and took a quick, short breath.

"Good. Now a deeper one. It's only been four minutes. He'll be here."

That didn't stop worst-case scenarios from spinning around my head. What if he'd encountered the myling on his way and had been hurt? What if he'd been attacked by another creature? What if he'd been kidnapped? What if he lay hurt and dying somewhere between my apartment and his, and no one was there to help him?

I grasped at my chest, my heart beating painfully hard. My vision blurred.

"Lia!" Clara's voice was sharp. "Breathe. Take a breath." I gasped for breath. "Not one of those gasps. You know how it works. I'll count for you. Breathe in—one, two, three, four. Hold it—one, two. Breathe out—one, two three, four. Hold—"

"Hey, sorry I'm late," Noah said as he slowed his bike down next to us. He looked between me and Clara, eyebrows furrowed. "Is everything okay?"

"Perfect," I squealed. My heartbeat slowed down, leaving me feelings shaky and a little dizzy.

Clara shook her head. "This might be the worst idea I've ever had, and I've had a lot of them. Let's do this." The hand already resting on my arm gripped my jacket as we started walking. The weight helped ground me in the moment. I forced myself to focus on that feeling, on the icy wind blowing in my face, the way my fingers stiffened despite the gloves.

It only took a few minutes to walk to the place where I'd seen the myling. I led the way into the forest, stumbling over roots. Clara followed with a flashlight, showing the way, and Noah was last. After what felt like an eternity, I came to a stop, staring at the spot where I'd seen the creepy child. It was in front of a particularly gnarled tree. Thorny, dead bush covered the space in front of it. Lovely.

Clara followed my look and grimaced. "Are you sure it's not somewhere else? Maybe it was that tree next to it?" The tree next to it was a birch, the ground in front of it covered in some dead leaves and nothing else.

"Nope, this is the one."

Clara groaned. "Of course, it's this one." She looked at me, then Noah. "Well, I guess there's nothing to do except start digging, then."

"Where's your problem-solving spirit?" Noah stepped forward with his shovel and started hacking at the thorny branches. I copied his movements. Soon we were all hacking away, sweat dripping down my neck from the exertion. At least the physical activity distracted me from my worry, though my heartbeat was still erratic, my breathing uneven, my hands shaky.

The branches thinned out, leaving the space in front of the tree mostly empty, the thorny bush almost completely hacked off. Noah looked up at me, the corners of his eyes crinkled with concern. "Are you sure about this?"

I wanted to hug him for asking, but now wasn't the time. If I stopped to think about it, I wouldn't go through with it. I gave a decisive nod, hauling in a thin breath, and drove the shovel through the underbrush and permafrost.

Or, I tried to. The shovel just bounced off the frozen ground.

"Well," Clara said, "that's anticlimactic."

Laughter bubbled up my throat, but I shoved it down. If I started laughing now, I might not stop, and this wasn't the best moment for it.

Noah stepped up next to me and took off his gloves, handing them off to me. My stomach clenched as he crouched down, lowering his hands to the ground.

I shivered, the sweat having long since chilled against my skin.

Clara and I shared a look. "What the heck is he doing?" Clara asked.

I opened my mouth to reply, but a loud wailing interrupted the quiet calmness of the night. I reached out, my hand grasping Clara's tightly. The air between Noah and the tree shimmered in the night, solidifying into the small shape of a child. The pale, blue-ish skin seemed almost luminous in the dark of the night.

Noah stumbled back, landing on his bottom with a dull thud. The child in front of him screamed. "Help me!"

My heart started drumming hard. "How can we help?" My voice squeaked out.

The child just wailed louder. I was closer to it now than I'd been before, and my body shook. Every cell screamed at me to run. I could see dead leaves and dry branches tangled in its oily hair. A thin, torn tunic barely covered them, and I shivered in empathy, my heart beating fast.

"We want to help you." Clara stepped forward. I stumbled after her, still gripping her hand. "Please tell us what we can do."

"I have no name," the child wailed.

"You need a name?" Clara asked. Later, when I wasn't growing lightheaded from lack of oxygen, I'd be impressed by her calmness.

The desperate crying trailed off. All-black eyes peered up at Clara. The child nodded, taking a step around Noah and towards Clara.

"Charlie. Your name can be Charlie. Do you like that name?"

The myling blinked. "My name... is Charlie?" Their voice was calmer now, though it was still shrill.

Clara nodded. "Yes. Your name is Charlie."

The child sniffed and started to fade. I stared as the outline of it grew fainter and fainter until it was completely gone, my racing heart the only evidence it was ever there.

I stared at Clara. "What was that?"

She shrugged. "Let's just get this done and get out. I don't want to chance that thing coming back, do you?"

I shook my head, and a full-body shiver gripped me. "There's still the issue of the frozen solid ground, though."

Noah gave a weak smile. "How lucky we have magic on our side, then." He lowered his hands to the ground in front of him. Steam rose from his hands, the ground shook, and split open in front of him.

Clara gaped. "Why in the world did we bring shovels if you could just do that?"

A short laugh. "Back-up. I don't like to rely too heavily on magic, if I can avoid it."

We peered into the hole in the ground. "No bones here," Clara stated. "Can you also put it back together?"

Noah lowered his hands once more. With a rumble, the dirt in front of him settled back into the hole. We repeated this routine around the whole tree, just to be safe, but found no bones.

Had we looked thoroughly enough? Did this mean the creature was definitely created?

CHAPTER 8
BEAUTIFUL CREATURES

Thursday came and passed without any other incidents. Axel stayed gone, and everyone at school stayed more subdued than usual, but people were starting to go back to their own lives and their own worries. I was shocked at how fast they seemed to stop caring, but at the same time, I did my best to not think about it, or my anxiety would overpower everything.

Thankfully, I had promised Noah that I would go with him to the stables that day, so I didn't have time to think too much about it. Instead, I spent the day stressing over the fact that I was going to the stables after school. It wasn't that I was scared of horses, but I had a lot of respect for them. They might be beautiful creatures, but they were also large and strong and you could get seriously hurt dealing with horses if you didn't know what you were doing. Which I didn't. I'd never even seen a horse up close before.

After school, I went home and put my unruly, dark hair into a braid and changed into a pair of yoga pants and a sweater, hoping it was good enough.

When I met up with Noah at his place, he took one look at me and laughed.

"You know the purpose of you coming with me is to give you less anxiety, not more, right?"

I grimaced at him. "Well, I'm not used to being around horses, so of course I'm a little nervous."

He stopped laughing. "But I am," he told me seriously, "and I'm not going to let anything happen to you. Besides, you'll only be around Skandika, and she's the sweetest. She's not going to do anything. She's great with beginners."

That made me feel a little better, and I could breathe a little easier. Still, the knot in my stomach didn't completely disappear.

It took maybe fifteen minutes for us to bike to the stables. As usual, exercise worked well against anxiety. By the time we parked our bikes outside, the knot in my stomach was barely there. It also helped that Noah was great at distracting me.

"Did you know that people around the world speak over six thousand different languages?"

I let out a surprised laugh as I parked and locked my bike. "That's... random."

Noah grinned. "I've got more where that came from. Do you know what trypophobia is?"

I shook my head, laughing. "No, what is trypophobia?"

"An aversion to irregular patterns or clusters of small holes. What about mellifluous? That's such a cool word, isn't it? Mellifluous."

"You are so weird."

"And I embrace that weirdness." He opened the door into the stall and held it open for me. "Well? What is mellifluous?"

"I have no idea." I stepped into the peaceful interior, the scent of hay filling my nostrils.

"It's a smooth and musical sound that's pleasing to hear."

I shook my head again. "Where do you get this stuff? Do you spend your free time googling random facts?"

"Maybe. Maybe I'm just a fountain of random knowledge." He grinned and turned to me. "Wait here, okay? I'm going to get Skandika from the pasture."

I nodded. He grabbed the headcollar and left me alone in the quiet. I waited, breathing in the scent of hay and horse, until he came back with a brown, slender horse.

Skandika had a black mane, dark brown hair and large, brown eyes. Noah stopped her a few metres away from me.

"Say hi to Skandika." He smiled.

I took a careful step forward, holding my hand out, palm up, to let her sniff me. She did, without hesitation, and nudged my hand.

"She wants you to pet her," Noah explained.

I carefully put my hand on her neck, and when she didn't bite me or step on me, I dared to go a little closer. Her skin warmed my hands, much warmer than I expected, her hair soft and smooth to the touch.

"She's beautiful." Awe filled my voice.

He smiled. "I know. And see, you're already less stressed."

He was totally right. The knot in my stomach was almost completely gone – it never really went away – and I felt calm in a way that was rare for me.

I laughed. "You're right. I do feel less anxious."

His smile grew. "I don't want to be that kind of person, but I told you so."

I hit his arm. "Shut up."

He laughed. "So, do you want to ride a little, or do you want to settle for petting her?"

My stomach clenched at the thought, but not in the tight, hard way that warned of anxiety. It was more of a fluttery, nervous but excited way.

"She won't throw me off, will she?" I couldn't quite stop my brain from producing the image of me flying through the air. She may not have been big by horse standards, but falling off would still hurt like hell.

"No." Noah gave me a reassuring smile. "I'll even lead her."

I chewed my lip. "Okay. I'll ride."

While Noah got Skandika ready, I mostly cuddled with her. I sifted my fingers through her mane and let my hand drift over her smooth coat while Noah brushed her and put on her saddle and bridle. Between that, and Noah's continued random facts, I felt my muscles relax and my whirling thoughts quiet down. I could be in the moment and enjoy it. She was so friendly and calm that it was impossible to stay on edge around her.

When we were finished, Noah led Skandika outside to a paddock. The sun shone, and should've been warming, but the cold air still bit at my cheeks. I breathed in the fresh scent of pine and looked around.

The stables and paddock were surrounded by trees on one side, and the pastures on the other, full of horses of all different colours and sizes.

Noah put a little stool next to the beautiful brown horse, helped me get into the saddle and gave me the reins. "Just tell me whenever you're ready, and I'll start leading her. And don't worry; she used to be a riding school horse, so she'll be nice."

I moved around a little to get comfortable in the saddle. "Okay. I'm ready." I blew out a breath.

Noah led Skandika into a slow walk. After a few steps, he looked back at me. "Doing okay?"

I nodded, unable to keep the smile off my face. It had been a long time since I'd smiled this much. "It's... really good," I said.

Noah smiled wide. "That's good. I'm glad you like it."

He led Skandika a couple of laps around the paddock, and we made small talk, but I was admittedly distracted by the slight bumpiness and the lovely view from horseback. My mind quieted down, and muscles in my back and neck relaxed even more. When we started on the third lap, Noah looked back at me again and asked if I wanted to trot a few steps.

My heart skipped. "Uh, okay?" It came out more as a question than an answer.

Noah chuckled. "Just a few steps, and I'll even hold your leg if you want. Okay?"

My stomach fluttered with nerves, but I nodded. *Please don't throw me off, Skandika.*

Noah fell into step next to me and put his hand lightly on my leg. "Hold onto the saddle if you want. Ready?"

I nodded again, grabbing the saddle, and Noah started jogging while telling Skandika to trot. After a moment, she did, and it got a lot bumpier. A little caught off guard, I lost my balance and held on tight to the saddle. Skandika took only a couple of steps before slowing down again, and I couldn't help but laugh a little while I righted myself.

Noah looked up at me. "Fun?"

I nodded, feeling more relaxed than I'd been in what felt like years. It was such a freeing feeling to be riding. All the new and exciting sensations crowded my mind, leaving no room for panicky thoughts and stressing over school.

"Want to take a few more steps?"

I nodded again, and Noah started jogging again, nudging Skandika into a slow trot. This time, I was prepared for the bumpiness, and managed to keep my balance for a few more steps.

By the time I got off, I felt more at peace than I had in a long time. I even laughed a little as I slid off the saddle. "Wow," I said, a little breathlessly.

Noah grinned. "That good, huh?"

I smiled. "I can't remember the last time I felt this calm."

His smile widened. "Well, you're welcome to come here with me anytime you want."

"I might just take you up on that offer."

When I got home, both Mom and Tilda were already there, and the scent of my favourite food hit me right away, a mix of cheesy goodness and bacon.

"Hi!" I yelled. "I'm home!"

Mom stuck her head out of the kitchen. "Hi, honey," she said.

"How did the riding go?"

"It went well." I hung my coat on the rack. "We're having car-bonara?"

"Yep. Would you take Kiwi for a quick walk before dinner? Tilda forgot when she got home."

"Of course," I told Mom, then yelled, "Kiwi! Time for a walk!"

I'd barely finished the sentence when Kiwi came running, tail wag-ging, nails clicking against the floor. I ran my fingers through her thick fur before I put on her leash.

I didn't take our regular walk through the forest, since I was still shaken by my encounter with the myling; instead, I walked past the playground, and around it.

"Lia!" a voice yelled from somewhere in the darkness. I looked around, frowning. Who would be at a playground this late? Most people had the sense to stay inside, where they were safe from the wind and rain that was classic fall weather on Gotland – although, to be fair, that was the weather every season on Gotland.

Kiwi started barking and pulling on her leash. I started to tell her to knock it off, when the voice spoke again, this time right behind me. "Thank God I found you!"

I spun around and came face-to-face with Erik. The light from the streetlights glinted off his mask, and his eyes looked almost black in the darkness. It looked like he stepped right out of the shadows.

My heart skipped a beat. It felt almost surreal to see him on the streets in my neighbourhood. "Uh, what?"

"I heard a teenager went missing and I got worried." He looked away, embarrassed, and scratched his neck. "I might have overreacted, but after what you told me about the myling..."

I gave him what I hoped was a reassuring smile. "I'm fine. It was some guy from another class. It's a scary coincidence, though." My stomach knotted.

Erik grimaced. "It is. You need to be careful."

"I am," I assured him, though I felt as worried as him. What the hell was going on here?

And what was Erik's role in it?

"Would you meet me in your meadow tomorrow?"

I blinked back to reality. "Why? What are you thinking?"

He shrugged. "Well, it might be a good idea for you to learn to defend yourself, just in case. And learning to use your sorcery would help you defend yourself. I thought I could teach you."

I kept my face carefully blank, not sure if I actually believed I could be a sorceress as well. Still, what did I have to lose? Worst case, it didn't work and turned out I was nothing more than a creator. I didn't believe Erik would try to hurt me. Apart from the feeling I had that I could trust him, he'd also had plenty of chances to hurt me, and he hadn't. Maybe that was naïve and stupid of me, but I wanted to give him a chance.

"Okay," I said finally. "Same time?"

He nodded and seemed to melt back into the shadow.

I sighed. What was my life becoming?

After dinner, I wrote in my notebook, creating new plants for my room, since my old ones were dying. Since I was horrible at keeping plants alive, my powers came in very handy. I stuck to creating smaller things, though, because of the cost of the magic. After I'd created my meadow, I noticed a large part of the copse of trees I walked by was missing. Not like it had been chopped down – it was simply gone, not a trace of it left.

My stomach still clenched with guilt every time I walked by it.

Needless to say, I was careful with what I created after that, not wanting to risk destroying something important. It wasn't an active choice I could make – magic chose something of equal value and close to the source of the magic to destroy and use to create the things I wrote. After the meadow, I stuck to creating only little things, like plants for my room, since I always had similar plants in my room that could be destroyed without causing damage to the world. God knew the world didn't need more things destroying the environment.

A soft knock on my door pulled me out of my focus. "Come in!"

Mom opened the door and stepped inside. "Hey," she said softly. "Everything okay?"

I hesitated. I didn't like lying to her, but I also didn't like making her worry. "I'm just a bit stressed." I settled on a half-truth. "There's been a lot at school lately."

Mom sat down on my bed, next to me, with a heavy sigh. "Do we need to get a new appointment with Helen?" Helen was my old therapist who'd helped me work through a great deal of my anxiety. Unfortunately, they didn't do long-term treatments, and when I started getting better, we had finished the treatment.

"It's not that bad," I told Mom. "We just have a lot right now, before the end of term." I gave her a reassuring smile. "I'll take a long walk tomorrow; that should help calm me down a bit."

She hesitated. "You sure we don't need to up the dose on your medication for a while?"

Upping the dose would mean things were worse than I wanted to acknowledge. "No, it's okay."

Mom hesitated for another moment, then hugged me tight, and we stayed like that for a few minutes. "You'll let me know if things get worse again, won't you?"

I nodded. "I promise."

Even after she let go of me, she stayed in my room for a while, and we talked about everything and nothing. I'd always been able to tell her everything; she was always supportive and had helped me a lot. She'd been the one to set up my first appointment with Helen; she'd been there during the bad days when I couldn't get out of bed; she'd picked me up from school countless times after I'd had panic attacks. A girl couldn't wish for a better mom. But the feelings of guilt kept me from telling her everything and making her more worried.

After a while, we went downstairs, and Mom, Tilda and I watched a few episodes of a Swedish crime tv-show we followed. It was based on a series of crime novels taking place on Sandhamn, about two childhood friends, a cop and an attorney. The books weren't as good as the ones that took place on Gotland, but I might be biased.

That night, when I went to sleep, I dreamed. But when I woke up in the middle of the night, tangled in my sweaty sheets, I couldn't remember the dream. The harder I tried to focus on the details, the fuzzier they became, until I couldn't remember anything at all. All I could remember was waking up in the middle of the night, in the middle of a panic attack. My heart racing, my breaths coming in short bursts, my hands shaking.

CHAPTER 9
A Million and One Stars

Blue swirls open up into a doorway leading to my meadow, lit by a million and one stars and a bright full-moon.

It was Friday, and time to meet Erik again. Meeting him the day before had made him feel more real than ever, but it did nothing to scare me off.

I stepped through the doorway and let the darkness close on me, then stepped out. For a moment, I looked up at the sky, glittering with stars like jewels, and the big, bright moon. The night sky always felt more magical here. The warm air washed over my skin.

"Beautiful." Erik stepped out of the shadows of the surrounding forest, and God, he looked beautiful too, in a dark, shadowy way. The mask shone in stark white against the dark backdrop.

He was truly fascinating to watch.

Was this attraction? This appreciation of beauty?

I paused and looked inside, trying to force some kind of a reaction to him, but nope, nada. I admired his beauty, was fascinated by the stark contrasts, but there wasn't so much as a tiny little flutter in my stomach.

"Now where did you go?" Erik's voice brought me back to Earth – well, was the meadow technically Earth? I didn't think so.

"Nowhere," I said and looked away. I couldn't tell anyone about my affliction. What would they think of someone who couldn't feel attraction? There had to be something seriously wrong with me.

He frowned a little but didn't say anything. "Are you ready?"

I nodded, though I still didn't believe him. "What exactly are you planning?"

"Well, magic in general, and especially sorcery, is triggered by emotion before you learn to control it. What kind of emotion is different for each sorcerer, though. Some by happiness or excitement, others by fear or anger. So the first step for us is to find what triggers your magic."

I raised an eyebrow, thinking this would be a long afternoon. "So you want us to go through every emotion and see if one causes me to lose control?"

Erik snorted. "Not quite. It's already happened once, hasn't it? All we have to do is figure out what you were feeling when you caused the storm."

I closed my eyes briefly. He wanted me to relive that horrible moment? Thanks but no thanks.

Erik must have sensed my discomfort – or maybe my face was that easy to read – because he hurried to say, "Humour me? Just for a minute, and if it doesn't work, we'll try something else."

I sighed but nodded. "Right. What do you want me to do?"

"Can you tell me what you were feeling that afternoon?"

I plopped down on the ground. If I was going to remember that feeling, at the very least I wanted to be comfortably sitting rather than standing. I set my hands down on the ground, feeling the soft blades of grass, and let myself remember the afternoon my meadow had been breached. "I felt... scared," I started, then shook my head. "No, that's not quite right. There was some fear, I think, but I felt... violated, like someone had broken into my most inner and private thoughts." My heart started beating faster, and a familiar pressure clamped down on my chest.

The ground beneath me shook and I jumped and looked at Erik, who had sat down opposite me without me noticing. "Did you do that?"

He shook his head and looked at me intently. "Definitely not. I'm not even sure I could do that here. The magic feels foreign, different from my own, and it wouldn't be easy to change it. Yet it draws me to it like a freaking moth to a flame."

My brows knitted. "You can feel the magic?"

"Yes. This whole place is nothing but magic. It calls to me and soothes my magic. You can't feel it?"

I shook my head.

He leaned forward and grabbed my hands, cupping them palm up. Then, still holding my hands with his, he murmured something too quiet for me to hear. A tickling sensation trickled across my skin, and as I watched, a fragile forget-me-not grew out of my hands. The air crackled with magic as I stared at the beautiful little flower in my hands. "Oh my God," I whispered as the aftershocks of magic zinged over my skin. "That's what magic feels like?"

Erik smiled, a small, secret smile. "That's what being here feels like for me."

I drew in a sharp breath and pulled away. *Don't let him get any wrong ideas now.*

A look of hurt flashed over his face, but it was gone in an instant. "So, what caused the outburst?" His words came out clipped, business-like. "What were you feeling?"

I didn't hesitate. That crushing pressure meant only one thing. "Anxiety." Of course it would be freaking anxiety. Why would anything ever be easy for me?

Erik nodded. "Right. Did you feel the magic when it burst out? Like a tingle in your fingertips or a knot unravelling in your stomach?"

I bit back the sarcastic reply that knots never unravelled in my stomach. They only ever did the opposite. "Nope," I said, scooting back a little when the closeness made me uncomfortable. "I didn't feel anything." Except for anxiety, I didn't add.

Erik pursed his lips. "Hmm. Then we'll just have to find it some other way."

"Find what?" I couldn't keep the slight annoyance out of my voice.

"The source of your magic." At my blank look, he smiled, amused. "Your sorcery rests somewhere in your body," he explained and leaned forward. "Before you can learn to control it, you have to find where it rests. For me, it's in my hands, and when I release it, my fingertips tingle. For others, it may rest in their heart, their stomach, their head. Only after you've found your magic can you start working on releasing it in controlled bursts instead of letting it be controlled by your emotions."

"Right, okay." I scooted back, uncomfortable with the proximity and worried that he'd get the wrong idea. "Well, I need to get back, so we'll have to continue some other time." I didn't know why I was being short with him, but I knew I needed to be alone, now. *I need space.*

Erik stood up quickly and held out a hand. Not wanting to be rude, I took it and let him pull me to my feet. For a second, our bodies were almost pressed together, and discomfort skirted over my skin. I pulled away and grabbed my notebook, needing distance from him, stat. I quickly created my doorway, and stopped only when Erik spoke my name.

"Same time tomorrow?" His voice rose in hopefulness, and I almost said yes, but I needed some time to think.

"I'll be busy this weekend." I softened my voice. "Monday?"

"Fine." He sounded annoyed, but I didn't let that soften my resolve. I waved goodbye and stepped through the blue swirls.

Alone in my room, I sank into bed and put my face in my hands. *What the hell is wrong with me?* Here was a nice guy who seemed interested in me and all I wanted was to run as far and as fast as my legs could carry me.

Why am I like this?

Chapter 10
If My Life Were a Book

That weekend, I took my bike and went to the library. It was Saturday, and I still couldn't stop thinking about seeing Erik outside of my meadow. It had made him feel much more real and knowing that he could find me in the real world, and not only in my clearing, made my insides feel shaky. Hoping to distract myself, I went to the library.

Some days, I was so grateful to live in a place as beautiful as Visby. There were the small, thick groves of trees and bushes that surrounded the neighbourhood, intersected with asphalt walkways, so it didn't really feel like living in the city. But ten minutes on the bike, and you arrived at the city centre, with shops and restaurants and cafés.

Then there was inside the city walls, cobblestone streets and beautiful old houses overgrown with ivy. I loved how mismatched the houses were; some made of brick, others wood; some big, some small. Brown, yellow, blue, red, even pink houses made the streets into a rainbow. The towers of the Sankta Maria church could be seen from anywhere within the city walls.

I could spend hours walking around, admiring the city I grew up in.

I rode my bike down the endless slopes and came to Almedalen. The water of the pond glittered in the sunlight, and the noises of the playground washed over me, a mix of happily screaming children and quacking ducks. Most of the children were at the playground, but some of them were feeding the ducks – something Tilda and I had loved doing when we were kids.

When I stepped inside the library, the scent of coffee and freshly baked goods hit me, but I walked through the combined foyer and café up the stairs to the fiction level of the library.

I browsed the shelves for a while, looking for something new to read, and breathed in the scent of books, letting the hushed atmosphere wash over me.

I found a contemporary that I'd been meaning to read for ages, about a girl with anxiety, who drew an online graphic novel. When I'd first read about it last year, I had been too caught up in my own anxiety to be able to read about it, but I thought I might be able to now. I also found a book by one of my favourite authors, about this less-than-heroic main character who somehow gained superpowers through a near-death experience, and a new-to-me contemporary written entirely through texts which sounded cute.

I decided to stay and read for a while, so I took off my shoes and went up the stairs to the couches usually occupied by kids doing anything but reading. The couches overlooked the library's café and the park outside, which made it my favourite reading-spot. I decided to start with the fantasy book, because, in my humble opinion, the author must've made a deal with some demon to get her extraordinary writing skills, and her books were sure to capture me from page one and keep me distracted for the day.

After a while, I moved down to the foyer and café, got a cup of tea and a piece of raspberry pie – the same as I always got, for the last five years, and then I sat by the window overlooking the park, and once again immersed myself in the world of ExtraOrdinaries.

I don't know how long I sat there, reading and drinking tea – my favourite Kränku tea, from the local tea and coffee shop on Gotland. When I looked up, pulled out of the book by someone sitting down across from me, the sun had started to set, which meant around three in the afternoon.

It was a woman, probably in her thirties, if I had to guess. Her short, black hair shone, and her green eyes glittered. Dressed in a white dress shirt and a black, straight skirt, she smiled, a small, secretive smile, like we were sharing some kind of secret.

She gave off a kind of maternal vibe, a sweetness that made you want to trust her, made you want to confide in her.

"Hello, Lia." She met my eyes. "It's so nice to finally meet you."

I narrowed my eyes. "Who are you?"

"I'm Melinda, and I just want to talk to you." Her voice softened a degree. "I'm a writer, like you."

Writer was not the technical term for people like me – we were all grouped together as creators – but I got her meaning nonetheless.

After some consideration, I sat down. There were several people in the foyer, so there wasn't much she could do to me without people reacting. Our powers were in creating things, not changing already existing things, and that included other living beings. We couldn't make people ignore us, for example, or see something that wasn't there. I couldn't make myself into, say, a t-rex, but I could create a t-rex out of nothing. Though why anyone would want to do that, I didn't know.

Melinda smiled a little wider. "Thank you. I'm the leader of a local group of creators and sorcerers. We are a community to those of us who feel out of place among non-magic people. And when I find out about creators or sorcerers living in secret, I take it upon myself to see them and talk to them about joining our group – completely up to them, of course. As long as they follow the regulations, that is," she added, almost like an afterthought.

This must be the leader of the group Noah told me about.

"Okay." I dragged the word out.

"Maybe I can tell you more about what we do, and you can go from there? You don't have to make any decisions today, of course. You can take some time to think about it, talk to your family about it."

I said nothing, and picked at my nails. This woman had just approached me out of the blue, and I had no reason to trust anything she said. On the other hand, something about her made me feel calm and safe, and her smile was soft and almost maternal.

I let out a long breath. "Okay."

"We meet in Stenkyrka about twice a month – do you know where the Virgin is located?" Her voice dropped into a soft whisper.

The Virgin was a rauk – they were basically big, old rocks in different shapes that were pretty common on Gotland, made of limestone – which stood on a cliff in Stenkyrka. The Virgin, funnily enough, didn't look like a virgin, or even a person. It hadn't been named by its appearance, unlike many of the other rauks (one of which actually did look like a person), but rather after the story of the virgin who had supposedly fallen to her death at the cliff. Nevertheless, it had an interesting shape, with the rounded edges that came from the water corroding the limestone over time.

I nodded.

"Well, we meet there, and we talk and practice our powers – you know, it's very important to be able to control our powers, to make sure we don't accidentally use magic in front of non-magic people. It's of utmost importance that we don't reveal our existence to the non-magic world. We practice together and help each other learn and grow. It's a safe place to use our powers, in a community of people like us."

I stared out at Almedalen, at the kids running around the playground, the parents keeping a close look at them, the ducks waddling around the grass next to the pond. I hadn't felt like I needed a community before – I had my family, and Noah, and Clara, to an extent – but maybe they could help me learn more about my magic? There was so much I didn't know, and other than Erik, no one seemed to have any answers. Maybe a community of people like me wasn't such a bad idea?

I turned back to Melinda and found her looking at me expectantly. "I'll have to talk to my family about it." My instinct told me to trust Melinda, but I wasn't sure if my instinct could be trusted.

Melinda gave me a soft smile, and I couldn't keep the corners of my mouth from lifting in response. "Of course. Why don't I give you my number, and you can call me if you want to visit sometime? Or just if you want someone to talk to? And remember, just because you come to one meeting doesn't mean you're committing to anything. You can just come and visit and see how you feel about it." She grabbed a small notebook from her pocket, ripped out a page, and scribbled her number on it.

After promising to think about her offer, I left the library to head back home.

Brisk, cool air met me when I walked outside, and, to my surprise, it wasn't too windy. Gotland, being a small island, was usually windy; some days it was bad enough that I couldn't even take my bike to school because I'd be blown away. It was the one drawback of living on an island – well, that and the fact that sometimes, it felt isolated.

Still, most days, I loved living on Gotland. It was beautiful, and you were never too far from nature. And, while Visby was a city, it didn't feel like a big city, which I liked. I wasn't much for big cities. We'd visited Stockholm a few times, and while it was fun for a couple of days at a time, I usually felt a little overwhelmed by the end of the visit.

I decided to go to Noah's place to talk to him about my visit from Melinda. It didn't feel like a coincidence that she and Erik had appeared in my life at the same time.

I walked the bike up the horrible ascent back home. The only bad thing about Visby was that between the city centre and the harbour, there was a thirty-metre height difference. I hated the full work-out required to walk back up.

Darkness had fully descended by the time I parked my bike outside the apartment where Noah lived with his moms and two younger sisters. Once I parked, I texted Mom to let her know where I was, and then I knocked on the door.

After a minute, the door opened, and Ella, one of the twins, looked up at me. "Lia!" she exclaimed and sprang forward, wrapping her arms around me.

I laughed and hugged her back. Ella was an outgoing kid, loud and energetic. Her twin, Olivia, was more quiet and thoughtful, and didn't trust people as easily. It had taken me several months to get her to relax around me, while Ella had decided we were best friends forever the first day we met.

Once Ella let go of me, she yelled into the house, "Noah, Lia is here!"

Noah stuck his head into the hallway, smiling. One thing the three siblings had in common was that they all smiled a lot. And since their moms were the most optimistic people I'd ever met, it made sense.

Other than that, Noah looked nothing like his sisters. Ella and Olivia were identical, and both had long, light brown hair and bright blue eyes. Noah, though, had darker hair and dark brown eyes. Ella and Olivia closely resembled their mom Nina, while Noah looked a lot like their other mom, Jenny.

When Nina and Jenny wanted kids, they had decided against adopting, and gone with a donor instead. Jenny had Noah, and several years later, they went with the same donor, and Nina had Ella and Olivia.

"Welcome to the chaos." Noah waved me inside. "To what do we owe the pleasure?"

I stepped inside and slipped on the wet floor. I looked down at the puddle that covered the entire hallway. "What the———?" I looked up at Noah with my eyebrows raised.

Meanwhile, Ella skipped into the house and yelled for her sister to come.

"Oh, that." Noah chuckled. "I told you the twins are starting to develop their powers, right? Ella threw a fit earlier, and accidentally made it rain. Thankfully, it was contained to the hallway."

"Oh," I said, blinking. "So, their powers are affected by their emotions?"

Noah nodded. "Before they learn to control it, yes. Which is a lot of fun for the rest of the family."

I laughed. "I can see that. Is this a bad time? I can come back some other time."

Noah shook his head. "No, no, it's fine. Our moms are at a work dinner, so I'm babysitting the twins, but as long as you don't mind them... We were actually just about to start watching *Frozen 2*. Again. It feels like that movie is on every time I get home." He grimaced. "I know *Into the Unknown* by heart."

I snorted. "It could be a lot worse, you know. And besides, what did you watch when you were ten?"

"Not *Frozen*, that's for sure. Oh, we have some pancakes left over if you're hungry."

"That would be great, thanks."

I took off my coat, shoes and socks – thankfully the water hadn't soaked into my shoes, so my socks were still dry, and I wanted to keep it that way – and followed Noah into the living room, my feet splashing in the water, asking on the way, "Do they get tired using their magic?"

"A little," Noah explained. "They'd have to use a lot of magic to get really tired, but these outbursts can definitely be a little tiring for them."

We entered the living room, where Ella and Olivia were waiting. I dried my feet with the towel he handed me, and put my socks back on, then I plopped down on the couch. Ella and Olivia sat on either side of me while Noah put the movie on. Then he disappeared, probably to dry off the hallway.

The movie had just started when he came back and handed me a plate of pancakes. He sat down next to Ella, and met my eyes above her head and smiled. I smiled back as Anna and Olaf started singing in the background.

By the end of the movie, both twins had fallen asleep, Olivia leaning against my shoulder, and Ella with her head in Noah's lap.

"I have to put these two to bed," Noah told me. "If you can wait, we can talk once they're in bed."

I nodded. Noah gently shook Ella, trying to wake her up, and I did the same with Olivia. We guided them both back to their room and got them into bed. After half an hour, they were both sound asleep in their own beds, and Noah and I were back on the couch.

"I met the leader of the coven today," I said.

Noah blinked. "What?"

I told him about Melinda's appearance at the library, and what she'd said.

Noah thought it over for a minute. "Huh," he said finally. "I haven't seen her, but I'll be on the lookout. She asked you to join the coven?"

I shrugged. "That, and to make sure I don't use my powers in front of non-magic people. She put a lot of emphasis on that."

Noah frowned. "That does seem a bit strange. But then, I don't really know what's normal and not. Besides you, and my family of course, I've never met any other creator or sorcerer."

Neither had I.

Except Erik.

"I think we should just wait and see what happens. If she approach-
es one of us again, we'll take it from there. Okay?"

I nodded. She hadn't said or done anything to make me think she
wasn't exactly what she claimed to be. Maybe I was overreacting. Still,
why had she approached me now? I'd lived in Visby my whole life –
surely she could've found me sooner than this? Why wait until now?

I sighed and chewed on my lip. When Noah put his hand on my
arm, I looked up. We were really close. If my life had been a book, one
of us would've leaned in, probably both of us, and we would've kissed.

But my life wasn't a book. The thought of kissing Noah didn't make
me feel icky, like I had at that party, but I didn't feel butterflies, like the
girls in the books I read. I should've felt excited, but I wasn't. What the
hell was wrong with me that the thought of kissing an attractive guy
– a *nice*, attractive guy – didn't make me feel anything at all?

"What just happened?" Noah frowned. "You left the planet."

I blinked. That was not what I'd expected him to say.

"You know you can talk to me, right? About anything. And don't
tell me nothing's wrong, because I can tell. You look like someone
kicked your puppy."

Could I tell Noah about my, um, whatever it was?

He was better than Clara, at least. As much as I loved her, she was
and always had been very vocal about how hot she found some girls,
and how much she'd like to kiss her crushes. Compared to her, my lack
of interest in doing anything with anyone, beyond possibly holding
hands or hugging, was apparent. But Noah never talked about that.
Maybe that was because I was a girl and he thought it would be weird
to talk to me about hot girls, but either way, it felt easier to tell him.
Who knew? Maybe he could help me figure it out.

I sighed again. "I think there's something wrong with me," I blurted out before my mind had even decided to tell him.

Noah frowned. "Why would you say that? There's nothing wrong with you."

"No, there is." My voice shook. Was I really going to do this? "I don't like guys."

Apparently I was.

Noah's frown disappeared. "You like girls? There's nothing wrong with that."

I shook my head, hard. "No, I don't like girls, either." How do I explain this? "Clara is always talking about how much she wants to kiss her crushes, and stuff, and I don't. I might've had some crushes, at least I think I have, but the thought of kissing somebody makes me uncomfortable. Like, really uncomfortable. And not just nervous uncomfortable." I paused and took a deep breath to calm my racing heart. But as nervous as I was over how he'd react, it was a relief to have said it.

Noah rubbed his chin in silence, and I started freaking out. Oh my God, what if he thought there was something wrong with me? I mean, I did, but it would suck if he agreed.

"Have you ever heard of asexuality?" he finally asked.

I frowned. "No," I said slowly. "Why? What is it?"

"Asexuality means that you don't experience sexual attraction." Noah met my eyes. "Someone in my rainbow group is asexual, and they don't feel sexual attraction, though they do feel romantic attraction – meaning, they want to hug and hold hands and do other romantic stuff, but they don't like kissing. Or," he cleared his throat and blushed, "other stuff. Though asexuals can like kissing, I think.

They just don't feel sexual attraction."

I blinked. That was a lot of info all at once. "You're in a rainbow group?"

"Yeah. I'm bisexual," Noah explained.

"Oh." I let that sink in. "Thanks for telling me." I paused. "And you think I'm... asexual?"

"I don't know," Noah said. "But I think you should look it up online."

Asexual. Could I be that? After what Noah had told me, it sounded possible. And I liked that a lot better than there being something wrong with me.

Noah nudged me, and I looked up. "There's nothing wrong with you. Maybe you're asexual. Maybe you're not. There are a lot of labels that aren't well-known, and maybe you'll find one that fits you. But you don't have to use a label. Labels are for you, and if it makes you feel better to use asexual or any other label, go for it. If not, you don't have to. But whichever label you use or don't, there is nothing wrong with you."

My eyes stung, and I had to blink away tears. After wondering for years what was wrong with me, why I wasn't as interested in kissing as everyone else seemed to be, it was a relief to know there might be a word for what I was. And hearing someone else tell me there was nothing wrong with me felt really, really good.

CHAPTER 11
ASEXUALITY

When I got home, I hurried up to my room, barely stopping to say hi to Mom and Tilda, and opened my laptop. Once I had Google up, though, I hesitated, eyes glued to the little search bar. Afraid of what I might find out. Did I really want to know if I was actually asexual? Like it wasn't enough to be a socially awkward, anxious mess. Did I really need to add another misunderstood and stigmatised label to it?

But... what if it could explain some of the things I felt and experienced – or, more accurately, didn't experience? What if I could find other people who felt the same things?

Ultimately, my need for knowledge won out. Whether it made me feel better or not didn't matter, I just needed to *know*. I didn't want to be this... this wondering, insecure mess. I wanted – no, I *needed* – answers.

I typed the words *am I asexual* into the search bar and clicked the first link that popped up. A quiz. *Perfect.* I started the quiz and stared intently at the first question. *How do you feel about physical intimacy?*

My mind immediately brought up images of my first – and only – kiss, and my knee started bouncing. *Not great, Internet, not great.*

I chose the option for hugs and cuddles but nothing more – but really, how should I know, since my only attempt at physical intimacy was a totally ruined kiss?

The second question appeared. *When was the last time you had a crush on someone?*

I stared at the question for so long, my vision got blurry. My stomach clenched and my breath got short. Even though the answer was an obvious one, I couldn't quite make my finger press the option for, never had a crush. I kept staring at the screen, not quite seeing it, and I knew, without having finished the quiz, I just *knew* what the result would to be.

My hand shook as I finally chose an option and the next question popped up. The rest of the questions were about whether I found people attractive – yes, but it didn't make me feel anything – and how I felt discussing intimacy with my friends – awkward and out of place – and what I imagined a future relationship to be like – romantic? And it wasn't a surprise when the results told me I might be asexual. I read through the short text.

"You can identify as asexual and experience different levels of sexual and romantic attraction..."

"Well, that's totally unhelpful," I mumbled and heaved a sigh. "And what the freak even *is* attraction? How am I supposed to know what it is – and whether or not I feel it – if I've never experienced it?"

I Googled asexuality and found the same unhelpful definition: *Asexuality means not experiencing sexual attraction.* But how the heck was I supposed to know what sexual attraction was – and if that's what I didn't experience – if I had never felt it? I didn't know. It didn't make any sense.

And yet, reading about asexuality and, most important, other asexual people's experiences, made me feel... right, somehow. Like something clicked.

It was after one in the morning when I finally decided I wasn't going to figure out my sexual identity in one evening, and went to bed. Although, shutting my brain off wasn't that easy. It never was. I tossed and turned for an hour, my thoughts spinning around. *What about love? Can I still fall in love? Will I live my whole life alone – and, worse, lonely? No one to share life with?*

Tears filled my eyes. Loneliness wasn't something I was unfamiliar with. That ache inside, of being on the outside looking through the window, that ache and *longing*, it hurt. And the thought that that might be my life, it terrified me. I didn't want to be alone. I wanted to fall in love. I *dreamed* of falling in love. What if... what if I couldn't fall in love?

When the tears refused to stop, I grabbed my remote off the bedside table and turned on the television, quickly finding my comfort show. I closed my eyes and focused on the familiar sounds of the sitcom, and finally, my mind stopped spinning, and sleep claimed me.

I spent most of Sunday reading in bed. Since Mom had to work, and Tilda was going to the movies with her friends, it was just me and Kiwi, and she certainly didn't mind spending the day in bed. She settled on top of my feet, and we stayed that way until she hopped down and started skipping around my room. A sure sign she needed out, so I got out of bed and we went downstairs.

Since I had the whole day off, I decided to take a long walk with Kiwi. I bundled up, because late November on Gotland is freaking cold, and we went outside.

Frigid air met me when I went outside. Trying to breathe only resulted in a coughing fit, the air puffing into small clouds when I breathed out. I shoved my face into my scarf and set off at a brisk pace to get warm. We started around the little forest, and I got lost in my thoughts. I'd spent the entire morning trying not to think about what Noah and I had talked about the previous night, and my research, but finally, the thoughts caught up to me.

Could I really be asexual? Part of me tingled in excitement at finding an online forum with people who seemed to be like me.

But part of me freaked out. I loved romance. I practically lived and breathed romance books. Romcoms were my absolute favourite type of movie. And I dreamed of falling in love, getting married, starting a family. What would happen to those dreams if I was asexual? Sure, Noah had said that there was a difference between sexual and romantic attraction, but how do you separate romance from sex? Was that even possible?

What would it even mean to be asexual? Would I never have a family, like I dreamed of? Would I spend my life alone?

Still, I couldn't deny the small sense of relief knowing I wasn't alone in my feelings. Knowing there were other people like me out there.

Gah! Why does it have to be so complicated?

I heard someone call out my name and blinked back to reality.

"Lia! Hey!"

I looked around and found Erik standing at the side of the road. Behind him, kids were playing and shouting in the playground, while their parents were watching carefully.

I blinked, surprised to see him in broad daylight, among other people. When I'd seen him before, it had either been in my meadow or at night.

"Hi, Erik," I said hesitantly. Could I trust him? Sure, he hadn't done anything to hurt me, but he was a stranger. Was I being stupid, letting him into my life?

He looked almost shy, standing there with his hands in his pockets. "Look, I just wanted to say sorry if I freaked you out the other day. I didn't mean to."

People were staring. Not so much at me, but the white mask covering half of Erik's face wasn't exactly discreet. The parents were making sure to keep their kids away from where we stood. Not that I could blame them. After all, hadn't I reacted the same way?

Kiwi tugged on her leash, reminding me I still had a dog to walk. "Oh, uh, why don't you walk with us? Kiwi gets impatient if I stay still for too long."

He smiled, a small smile tinged with sadness, and I had to wonder exactly how lonely he was.

I knew what it was like to be lonely. I wasn't alone, no, I had a lot of people around me who cared about me. But when my anxiety got bad, I was overwhelmed by the feeling that no one could understand what I was going through. It had taken months of therapy before I realised that I wasn't alone in my struggles. I had people who maybe didn't quite understand what I was going through, but who were willing to try.

Maybe Erik needed to know he wasn't alone, too. And if I could help him with that, without putting myself in a dangerous situation,

I would. No one should have to be lonely.

I burrowed into my scarf as we started walking. The sun shone, not a cloud in sight, and even the wind had taken a break, but those days were always the coldest.

"You're in the gymnasium, right?" Erik asked.

I nodded. "Yeah. In my second year."

"Do you like it? What program are you in? Do you have a lot of friends?"

Whoa. I laughed lightly. "Um, I guess, Social Studies, and no, I really don't."

He frowned, like this bothered him. "Why don't you have many friends?"

I shrugged and looked away, uncomfortable. "I'm not outgoing enough. People find me difficult to get to know, I think. I don't know. I'm just... introverted, I guess."

Erik didn't say anything for a long time. I looked at him, wondering why he so quiet. He had a sad look on his face. "I'm sorry." He met my gaze.

I forced a smile. "It's okay. I have a few close friends and my family. I don't need any more."

This time, he was the one to look away, but not before I saw the deep longing on his face. "You grew up here?"

I nodded automatically, then realised he couldn't see that. "Yeah. I've lived in Visby with my mom and little sister all my life."

This made him look at me, a small frown on his face. "Not your dad?"

I shook my head. "He left when we were kids. Haven't heard from him since." That was something I'd rather not think about, so I decided to ask him about his childhood. Too late, I realised he probably wanted to talk about that even less than I wanted to talk about my dad. I grimaced. "I'm sorry. I understand if you don't want to talk about it."

He slowed to a stop and didn't say anything. Children laughed and screamed excitedly in the background. I was sure he wouldn't answer. But then... "My father left when I was five. My mother... she blamed me for it. Said if I hadn't been born, he would've stayed with her. Maybe he would've. I don't remember much of him, so maybe he hated me that much." He took a deep breath. "About a year later, there was a... an accident, and she couldn't deal. She left me in an alley, broke my leg to keep me from following her."

My mouth dropped open as shock and horror washed over me. How could a mother ever do that to her child? Not only abandon her child but actually hurt them?

Probably the same way a mother could murder her own child and bury them in secret.

My heart squeezed as I realised how horrifying his childhood had been.

"That's where Anton found me, hours later. I'd given up calling out for help by then. He found me in the corner of the alley, soaked through by the rain, shaking from cold and pain." The cold words made him sound almost detached. Like he'd long since stopped caring.

I shivered, more from his story than the weather. Coldness seeped all the way to my bones while I listened to him talking about his horrible parents.

"Anton made sure I got medical attention, then he took me to his circus. You know what happened there." He looked away, jaw ticking.

"It wasn't until years later, when I was well into my teens, when one of the trapeze girls helped me leave, made sure I got to Gotland. But people can be cruel, which is a lesson I should've learned at the circus, but I hoped… I hoped people would be able to ignore my scars. They couldn't. And since I had never gone to school, no one in their right mind would hire me for anything. So I slept outside, anywhere I could find some shelter from the weather. Until I found the abandoned tunnels underneath Visby."

Tears threatened to spill over. How could the world be so cruel? How could no one have stepped in and helped him? It was horrifying that something like that could happen. How could people be so heartless? A lot of people must have seen him paraded in that circus, and no one had stepped in to do something!

I reached out to touch his arm. It felt useless – after everything he'd been through, all I could do was try to comfort him? I didn't know what to do. Nothing I could do would make what he'd been through any less horrifying. "I'm sorry." My voice cracked, and I had to blink away my tears. "I'm so sorry."

His eyes flashed to mine, and I could see the shock in them. He didn't expect sympathy.

My heart broke for him.

Before I'd even decided to do it, I heard myself asking, "Would you take off your mask?"

His eyes widened, and he went quiet. I focused on him, and the sounds of children playing faded into the background. "That's not a good idea. I told you, people get uncomfortable when I take off the mask."

I chewed my lip. "Well, who cares about them?"

He looked to the side, turning the side of his face covered by the mask slightly away from me. "It's not pretty."

I stepped closer to him. "I don't care."

He stared at me, wide-eyed, and then, slowly, Erik reached up, his fingers brushing against the mask, but he stopped there, his entire body frozen. I held my breath, scared that a too-loud breath might stop him, and waited, looking into his eyes with a steadiness I didn't feel. After what felt like an eternity, he wrapped his fingers around the mask, but before he could remove it, we were interrupted by a loud hissing sound.

Chapter 12
Lindworm

I looked around, and gasped when I saw a huge snake only a few metres away from where we stood. It rose easily as big as me, with deep red scales and a darker mane – like a lion's mane. Its body was thick – thicker than most well-built men, let alone *me,* and its body twice my height.

Kiwi started whining and pulled hard in the opposite direction, and I let her pull me away.

Without taking my eyes off the snake, I breathed to Erik, "What is *that?*"

He drew in a sharp breath, eyes wide. "I think that's a lindworm," he whispered.

"A *what?*"

"A lindworm." Erik's voice lowered. "It's a creature from Norse mythology, a kind of snake and dragon hybrid. There are actually two versions of the lindworm; one good and one very, very evil."

As the lindworm slithered closer, it didn't take a genius to figure out which kind we were facing.

"Well, since you know so much about it, how do we get out of this alive?" I struggled to hold on to Kiwi's leash as she pulled and pulled away from the lindworm.

"The legends don't really say."

Of course they didn't.

"Well, then I vote for run." My heart hammered against my chest.

"Sounds good." Erik grabbed my shaking hand and tore off. The dragon-snake thing hissed behind us. Then I heard a whoosh and it rolled right in front of us. It had its tail in its mouth and *rolled* in front of us like a freaking wheel.

We skidded to a stop, and Kiwi let out a high-pitched whine as she threw herself backwards.

"Oh, I forgot they could do that." Erik frowned.

I backed away from the snake. "You *forgot* it turns into a freaking wheel? How the hell do you *forget* something like that?" I asked, incredulous. "What do we *do?*"

"Let me try something." Erik's voice lowered to a whisper. "*Die.*" He whispered the spell so intently it sent shivers down my back.

The lindworm hissed.

"Worth a try." Erik tore a stick off a nearby tree.

The lindworm attacked. It lunged at us, hissing and snapping teeth longer than my arm.

We stumbled back, and the teeth snapped so close to my face I could smell its putrid breath. A white, milky liquid dripped from its mouth. *What did the thing eat? Rotten corpses?*

Erik knocked me out of the way. "Don't let it spit on you." The calmness in his voice made me want to beat him upside the head. "Its spit will blind you." He swung the stick like a bat, like the lindworm was nothing but an innocent ball flying at his face. The lindworm flew backwards but it didn't deter it. It shook it off and hissed, toxic spittle flying everywhere, and attacked again.

I backtracked, stumbled, just as the snake bounced harmlessly off an invisible barrier. I would've fallen on my butt if Erik hadn't grabbed hold of my hand.

I wished intently for it to burst into flames, but I knew creating didn't work like that. I couldn't affect something that already existed. Which explained why Erik's whispered spell hadn't done much except annoy the snake.

Gravel crunched underneath my feet. My heart beat so hard it hurt. I gasped for breath, and the snake burst into flame. It let out a high-pitched scream, and I stumbled back several more steps as the flames grew brighter. With a final hiss, the lindworm disappeared in a cloud of black smoke.

"Oh my God," I breathed, and practically fell into the bench conveniently placed right next to me. "What just happened?" I raised my hand to push my hair out of my face, and realised it shook bad enough that I could hardly hold on to Kiwi's leash.

Erik sank onto the bench next to me, his eyes wide and full of fear. "You okay?"

I shook my head forcefully. "Not even close." I looked at the now empty playground. I hadn't even noticed people had run out of there, but they must have, when they saw the snake.

"Oh my God," I said. "All those people at the playground, they must've seen it, too. They aren't supposed to know magic exists!"

"They were probably too far away to see what it was," Erik said. "And I doubt any of them would assume it was a creature from ancient Scandinavian folklore."

Good point. "How *did* a creature from ancient Scandinavian folklore appear in the middle of a playground in Visby?"

Erik frowned and stared into the distance. "I have no idea."

My thoughts spun. "It must've been created."

Erik turned sharply back to me. "Why would you think that?"

I shrugged and looked away. "Well, I think the myling was created, so it's not such a stretch that the lindworm was, too."

"Why do you think the myling was created? I know I said it was possible, but it could also be the spirit of a real, dead child."

I shuddered at the thought, remembering the desperate wailing of the child. "Well, I..." I clicked my mouth shut. He had been firmly against the idea of going grave-digging, and I still didn't know why. How would he react if he found out we'd done it? "I don't know. I guess it just feels less unbelievable than thinking these creatures actually exist."

Erik stared at me, and my heart stuttered. What if he could tell I was lying?

He sighed and looked away. "I guess that makes sense." A pause. "By the way, that was clever, setting the snake on fire. Quick thinking."

I drew in a sharp breath. "You didn't do that?"

He shook his head. "No. The thought didn't cross my mind. I guess it should have. But it wasn't me."

I frowned. "Why didn't you?"

"Why didn't I what?" He kept his gaze trained on the horizon, refusing to meet my eyes.

"Why didn't you think of it?" He knew that creating wouldn't make a difference on something that already existed. Why wouldn't his first thought be to use the elemental magic?

He shrugged. "Panic, I guess." He looked over at me, and his eyes strayed to my shaking hands. "Are you sure you're okay?"

No, I wasn't okay. I had no idea what my life had become, but I needed it to stop. I had enough to worry about.

I shrugged. "I should probably go home, make sure Kiwi is okay."

Erik nodded. "Will you meet me in your meadow tomorrow?"

The first thing I did was call Clara and Noah and tell them about my encounter with the lindworm. I left out the part about meeting Erik, though. I didn't understand why I didn't want anyone to know about Erik. I just didn't. Less than half an hour later, they were both there. Clara made some tea for us, since I still shook uncontrollably. I hoped some hot tea might help.

We all sat on the couch. Thankfully, neither Mom or Tilda had come home yet, or I would've had some explaining to do.

The second I sat down on the couch, Kiwi jumped up and lay down on my lap. She still shook badly, as did I, but at least I'd gotten her to stop whining, which she'd done when we got home.

For a while, I let the mug warm my hands. I stared down into the cup as silence settled over the room. My aching muscles finally relaxed bit by bit, and the shaking subsided. I took a few sips before I told Clara and Noah what had happened with the lindworm and how it had burst into flame when I wished for it. That last part made Noah frown, and I paused my storytelling to ask what he was thinking.

"Well, that's a strange coincidence," Noah said. "And, well, before sorcerers learn to control their powers, it usually happens in one of two ways; they get really emotional, or they wish for something, usually not as specific as that, but maybe they wish for someone they're angry with to get hurt, and they'll be thrown down the stairs, things like that. And you being scared at that moment, plus thinking about the lindworm bursting into flame? That's way too coincidental."

I'd been thinking the same thing, but hearing it from someone who clearly knew more about sorcerers than I did freaked me out. "So, you're saying I'm probably a sorcerer, then. That I'm a hybrid."

Noah nodded. "It's the only thing that makes sense."

"How is that even possible?" Frustration coloured my voice.

"I don't know," Noah said, shrugging. "But as far as we know, there's no reason why a sorcerer and a creator couldn't be together and have kids, and why shouldn't those kids be hybrids?"

For the first time since I started considering the possibility of me being not only a creator, but also a sorcerer, I started actually thinking about how it could've happened. And what Noah said made perfect sense. There was no reason why a sorcerer and a creator shouldn't have a hybrid kid. And since my mom was a creator, that meant my father had to have been a sorcerer. Well, probably. I was pretty sure Mom wasn't both. She would've told us that, right?

If my father was a sorcerer, which seemed likely, did my mom know what he was? They had been together for a few years, but he'd left us when Tilda was one, and I was three. Mom rarely spoke about him. She always answered our questions, but it was obvious it hurt her to talk about him, so Tilda and I had stopped asking about him. Besides, he was gone and not coming back. What point was there in asking questions about a man we would never meet?

We were quiet for a long time, clearly having come to similar conclusions about my father, but none of us were ready to voice our suspicions. I didn't talk about my father. I didn't know much about him, except that his name was Johan, he was kind and caring, and he had loved me and Tilda for the short period of time he'd been with us. That explained why Mom had been so hurt and surprised when he'd left. From what she told us, they seemed to have been very much in love.

It all had me wondering how someone who supposedly loved all of us so much could up and disappear on us. Well, the few times I let myself think about him, I wondered. But most of the time, I preferred not to. He couldn't have cared that much about me and Tilda if he'd been able to drop out of our lives like that. It sucked that he had left, and some days I did wish I had a dad to turn to, but most days, it wasn't something I thought about. I had an amazing mom and a little sister who I was really close to, and we did fine on our own, without a dad.

"I know the most logical thing would be to ask my mom," I said finally, "but I can't. It hurts her too much to talk about my father, and besides, does it really matter how it happened?"

"No, it doesn't." Clara shook her head. "It doesn't change anything."

Noah nodded, agreeing. "It doesn't make a difference," he said. "I am curious about why you're only now starting to manifest these powers, since most sorcerers start manifesting their powers around ten. And you started manifesting your creative powers earlier. Why now?"

An interesting question. I had about as much control of this new magic as a ten-year-old throwing temper tantrums. That made me feel mature.

"Of course, what we need to be focusing on is getting your new magic under control," Noah said, as if he'd read my mind.

I snort-laughed, remembering how my creative magic had first started manifesting. "Right, it would be a little awkward if I accidentally set fire to the school."

Clara chuckled. "I wouldn't mind," she said. "If you could do it this week, before our Maths test, that would be great."

I laughed, and it felt really nice to laugh after the events of the last couple of hours – hell, make that the last couple of weeks. "I'm thinking no," I said in between bouts of laughter, "but I'll keep your request in mind."

Clara pouted, pretending to be angry, and it only made me laugh harder. When Kiwi raised her head to look at me judgingly for waking her up, I sobered up.

"Have you seen this Erik guy again after last time?" Noah asked, bringing me back to reality.

My stomach clenched, but I shook my head. I felt horrible lying to my friends, especially since they were only trying to help, possibly even putting themselves at risk, but I couldn't tell them about Erik. "No, nothing. I've been staying away from my meadow, so maybe he's been there, but I haven't seen him."

Noah nodded. "Alright, well, keep staying away from him. I don't like this at all."

I promised, while my stomach churned.

I'm such a bad friend.

But I still couldn't bring myself to tell them.

We made small talk for a little while longer, until Noah had to go home for dinner. Clara texted her parents to ask if she could stay the night, which was okay. Tilda and Mom came home a while later. Clara and I made dinner for the four of us, and we helped Mom clean up afterwards. The clock read past seven when we were finally done and could go up to my room, Kiwi hurrying to follow us up.

"So," Clara said as I closed the door behind me, "movie?"

"Yes," I said with a sigh, collapsing onto my bed. "I need something funny."

"You and me both," Clara said, and her voice still tightened with worry. "I'm not liking this situation at all, Lia."

Neither do I, Clara.

CHAPTER 13
GODS

On Monday, Noah texted me and asked if I wanted to come with him to the stables. I had tons of studying to do, but since I'd promised Mom to try and study less, I said yes. Internalised pressure played a big part in my anxiety; the pressure to always get perfect grades in everything. It meant I tended to study a lot more than what was healthy. Even a mental health professional telling me I was burning myself out had barely made a difference. Only when my anxiety got so bad I could barely go to school did I realise I wouldn't be able to get good grades if I was unable to attend school. That had finally gotten through to me.

That's how I found myself on a horse once again. This time, we took a walk through the forest, and Noah led Skandika while I mostly enjoyed the ride and the silence of the forest. As we were in the grips of a typical Northern European November, there were very few birds and insects around. No chirping could be heard, which meant only the sound of Skandika's hooves and Noah's and my breaths broke the silence. Our occasional quiet conversation felt loud in the peaceful forest. As we chatted, relief made me feel light when he didn't bring up our conversation from Saturday. I had spent many more hours googling asexuality, and every time I felt the same confusing mixture of feelings as I had that first night. I was not ready to talk to another person about it, even though I spent most of my waking moments thinking about it.

Reading about other asexual people's experiences made me feel... validated. I read all these stories about asexuals and I recognized myself in so many of them. But. I loved romance. I *wanted* romance. Didn't I? How could I love romance and still be ace? As much as I'd read about sexual and romantic attraction and how they were different and separate, it felt impossible. How could you separate the two?

What right did I have to call myself asexual, really?

How could I even know if I was asexual or not? How could I know that I didn't experience sexual attraction when I'd never felt it – when I had no idea how it would even feel?

Thankfully, Noah didn't bring up the topic of my possible asexuality. And even though neither of us talked about it, it didn't feel like we were avoiding the subject, exactly. We had plenty of other things to talk about.

Like my newfound sorcerer magic, for example.

"I've been thinking." Noah led Skandika into the stables.

"Oh no."

He punched me playfully on the arm. "Shut up."

I raised my hands in surrender. "Alright, alright. What have you been thinking?"

"Well, I've been thinking it might be a good idea for you to learn to use your sorcery."

My stomach clenched at the reminder of my lies. "Yeah?"

He nodded. "Yeah. First, because it's great if you don't accidentally make it rain inside the classroom if a teacher gives you a pop quiz or something."

I laughed. "Fair enough. What's second?"

Noah pursed his lips. "Well, it would be extra insurance if you could use your sorcery to protect yourself from whatever mythical creatures appear."

I nodded. "You're right."

He looked at me in mock outrage. "Why do you sound so shocked?"

I laughed. "Well..."

He grimaced at me. "Rude! I have lots of good ideas!"

We laughed as we put Skandika into her stall. "You think I need to learn to use my magic. Did you plan on teaching me or were you hoping I'd magically wake up one day and be an expert sorceress?"

He snorted. "Do you think you could do that? Because that would make things so much easier."

"Ha! I wish. No, I think you're going to have to teach me." Here's to hoping he won't figure out I've already been learning how to use my magic.

"Yeah, I figured as much. What are you doing tomorrow after school?"

"Other than worrying myself to death over mythological creatures? Not much."

We decided to practise in my meadow the next day after school. Noah felt better about me being there if I wasn't alone.

I'd have to ask Erik to stay away the next day, or I'd have some explaining to do.

As we grabbed our bikes and headed home, the constant pressure inside was almost completely gone, and I felt lighter – like I might float away on a cloud of relief.

When I stepped into my meadow, the stars were twinkling again, and Erik already waited for me. He stood still as a statue in the middle of the clearing, his back to me, and I wondered what he was thinking about.

The moment I stepped out of the doorway, he turned towards me, eyes full of shadows. The white mask, as usual, stood in stark contrast against his dark hair. I pushed away the disappointment at having been interrupted the day before.

Something had happened.

I furrowed my brow. "What's wrong?"

He shook his head as if to dispel the shadows, but it didn't lighten his mood. "Nothing important," he promised, but I didn't believe him for a second. "Ready to practise?"

I wanted to press him, but something in his eyes made me hesitate. I nodded. "Let's do this."

A shadow of a smile crossed his face, far too brief. "I like your determination. Yes, let's do this." He waved to the grassy ground, and I sat down. After a moment, Erik did the same, sitting down across from me like the last time.

My stomach clenched at the memory of how the last time had ended, and the way he had looked at me. *Please, don't let him get the wrong idea.*

"The next step is to try and find where your magic rests," Erik began. "But before we start practising, I think it might be a good idea for you to learn about where your magic comes from."

I frowned. "But we don't really know where the magic comes from."

"I've found some texts over the years that hint at it. And I have some theories."

"Alright, so where does the magic come from?"

Erik smiled. "The gods."

I raised an eyebrow. "The gods? Really?"

"Yes, really," Erik said. "According to legend, creators are descended from the Vanir goddess Freja, and sorcerers are descended from the Aesir god Balder. They're the source of our magic."

My mind caught on all the new information. "What the hell are Vanir and Aesir?" The word Aesir sounded vaguely familiar, but I couldn't place it.

"They're two different groups of gods. The Aesir is the main group, with the more known gods like Oden and Tor. The Vanir are associated with fertility, wisdom and precognition. The siblings Frej and Freja are Vanir."

That's why I recognised Aesir. We'd talked about the Aesir in school years ago, though we definitely hadn't learned about the Vanir.

I let it sink in, unsure if I was ready to believe in actual gods of mythology and overwhelmed by all this new information. "Okay." I drew the word out. "Let's say I believe you. How does this help me learn to control my magic?"

Erik smiled. "It can help you learn the limitations of magic. For instance, I believe that the gods took their magic from the earth, and that's why our magic uses the earth's resources to create or control the elements. I also think the limitations of the gods are our limitations.

For example, we can only create things that already exist, in some shape or form. We can't create a magical object that will reverse the Greenhouse Effect, because an object like that doesn't exist. Have you never wondered why, then, you can create a doorway to another plane, because that's certainly not how doorways usually work."

"I guess," I admitted.

"My theory is that we can use doorways because the gods can use doorways."

I thought about it for a moment. "So, what you're saying is, anything the gods could use – create? – we can also create?"

Erik nodded. "In essence, yes, that's what I think."

"But why aren't doorways more commonly used?"

"Because we don't know what kind of magic the gods have. They aren't exactly around for us to ask them, and not too many people would think of trying to create one when we know the limitations of our magic and don't think these kinds of doorways exist."

I'd need some time to really let that sink in. Magic was one thing, but gods? I wasn't sure I was ready to believe that yet.

Erik must've sensed my hesitancy, because he changed gears. "I want you to close your eyes."

I did as he instructed, and my heart immediately started beating faster. I tried to force my mind away from the tension in my chest and focused on the sounds of the leaves rustling in the wind, the feel of the soft grass and the mild breeze against my skin.

A tingle drifted over my skin, a barely-there sensation at first. It grew in intensity until it made me wriggle, but it wasn't a totally unpleasant sensation. A hum started in my stomach, stretching upwards and outwards, reaching towards the tingle.

My eyes flew open, and I watched in awe as water swirled in the air between me and Erik. I don't know how, but I knew, with absolute certainty, that we were doing that together. How we were doing it, I had no idea.

As I stared in wonder, the water stopped moving, and hung still in the air for a single moment.

I screeched as cold water drenched me, and I met Erik's gaze. "What the hell was that?"

He smiled a secret smile. "My magic was coaxing yours out. I created the water, and you did the rest."

How could I do something like that without even knowing it? "I... don't understand."

His smile didn't waver. "Magic calls to magic. If someone uses magic around you, you'll be able to feel it, and it will call to your magic."

A cool wind blew through the meadow, and I shivered. "So, wait, I can sense other creators and sorcerers?"

He shook his head. "No, not unless they're using their magic."

"Oh." I didn't know what else to say to that. I needed time to absorb all this new information; my head spun, trying to make sense of it all.

"Let's see if you can do it on your own." Erik pulled me out of my thoughts. "When you felt my magic, where did your magic rise from?"

Easy. "My stomach."

"Then that's where your magic rests. When you want to use your magic, you have to pull from there."

Umm... "Pull?"

Erik's lips twitched. "Metaphorically. When I used my magic, it awoke the magic inside you and you reacted instinctively. To do it on your own, you need to grab hold of your magic and coax it out. Some people imagine pulling their magic. Others coax it more gently. It's different for everyone."

When I still looked at him blankly, he grinned. "Close your eyes again."

I did without hesitation, and this time I could breathe easier.

"Good." I could still hear the smile in Erik's voice. "Now feel for your magic. Can you feel it resting in your stomach?"

I focused on the pit of my stomach, and to my surprise, instead of the usual hard knot, I only felt that hum, now nothing more than a barely-there whisper.

I nodded.

"Good. Now coax it to the surface."

Hmm. How could I coax that hum to the surface? I breathed out and imagined myself expelling all the magic, and opened my eyes, expecting... well, *something* to have happened, but nothing.

Erik's smiled widened, and the corners of his lips twitched, like he was trying not to laugh. "Try again."

I let out a frustrated sigh but closed my eyes once again and found that hum. This time, I tried a different approach, imagining the magic as a string. I carefully tugged on it, not wanting to accidentally cause a storm – again.

I opened my eyes and saw a leaf flutter in front of me, barely lifting off the ground before it sank back down.

I looked at the leaf. "That was... anticlimactic."

This time, Erik did laugh. My eyes left the leaf then, and I lowered my eyebrows and looked at him. He stopped laughing, but his eyes were alight with amusement. "You're going to need to do more than that."

I narrowed my eyes at him. "I realise that, but I didn't want to cause a storm or something."

He pursed his lips to keep from laughing.

I kept frowning at him. "Well, I might. Apparently, I already have."

He let out a soft sound. "Yes, but no one was hurt, right? And if you do cause a storm, I can always stop it, if you can't."

I bit my lip, still unsure, but finally relaxed my face.

"Let's try something else," Erik said. "With the lindworm, your intent came true, so maybe it can work again. I want you to find your magic again, coax it to the surface, but this time, I want you to imagine a wall of air in front of you. An impenetrable wall of air. Nothing can get through this wall, okay?"

I nodded my agreement and closed my eyes. Finding my magic was easier now, and I coaxed it to the surface faster. When I felt the magic beating under my skin, wanting to be released, I imagined the wall Erik described. I imagined the air in front of me thickening, hardening, becoming something solid. I held the image in my head and let go of the magic under my skin.

Magic rushed out of me, and I gasped. My eyes flew open just in time to see a stick flying towards my face. I flinched, but the stick never reached me. It bounced off an invisible wall only a breath away from my face, landing in the grass with a quiet *thud*.

I looked up at Erik and couldn't keep the grin off my face. "I did it!"

He smiled back, his eyes glittering. "You certainly did. Nice work."

We shared a smile. The leaves rustled gently in the wind, and the grass felt soft against my palms. I felt light, like my insides might just float away on a cloud.

Erik was the first to look away. "Let's call it a day. Can you meet me here again tomorrow?"

I started to nod, then remembered my plans with Noah. "Oh, um, tomorrow's not great. Actually, I was going to ask you if you could stay away from the meadow tomorrow."

Erik frowned. "Why?"

"Well..." I hesitated. "I promised my friend I'd show him the meadow, and, um..." I trailed off. How would he react if he knew I hadn't told my friends about him?

"You want some privacy?" His voice held a hint of emotion—hurt? Sadness? But before I could identify it, he went on, "Fine. I'll stay away." With that, he stood up, and when I blinked, he'd disappeared.

I stayed there for a long time, staring at the spot where Erik had disappeared through a doorway – a dark, almost black doorway, nothing like my bright, blue one. *What the freak just happened?* Obviously, he'd gotten mad, but about what? The fact that I didn't want to meet him tomorrow? Or something else?

What was it he had said? *You want some privacy?* In that hurt voice.

I froze as the realisation hit. Was that it? He was jealous? Of Noah?

A hysterical laugh bubbled up and burst out. And once I started laughing, I couldn't stop. The idea that Erik thought Noah and I were going to – what? Mess around? – was crazy. Especially considering I was pretty sure I didn't want to do that with anyone. Could you even do those kinds of things when you were asexual? Noah had said that asexual people could enjoy kissing, though, so maybe they could enjoy... other things as well.

I let out a frustrated shout and stared at my bouncing knee. Why did it have to be so confusing? I just wanted a clear-cut answer. Was that too much to ask for?

Sitting here and laughing hysterically wouldn't help me figure anything out, though, so I got up and left, ready to put Erik's mood swings – and my asexual freak-out session – behind me.

Standing back in my meadow, I tried to remember why I was there. I tried to remember going there, picking up my notebook and going there, and pulling up blank. Something was wrong. The trees didn't look quite right, and the colours were dulled, like there was a thin film over everything. But worse than that, the safety I always felt in my meadow was gone. Instead, it felt... wrong. Hostile. Like it didn't want me there.

I should get out of here. I hurried over to the spot where I usually left my notebook, underneath some shrubbery at the edge of the forest, and came up empty. My breath hitched in my throat. I always left my notebook there! Without it, I couldn't leave.

A strong wind picked up around me as my heart started beating faster, and I didn't know if I'd created it or if the meadow had.

The rustling of the trees in the wind didn't feel comforting anymore. It felt scary, like they might attack me, which was ridiculous.

I heard a high-pitched laugh somewhere, a childish giggle. But when I looked into the forest, I couldn't find anything other than trees.

A thick, greenish mist rolled in, and after only seconds, I couldn't see my feet anymore.

That giggle rang out again. I spun around, looking for the source, but once again, I couldn't see anything out of the ordinary. My heart beat way too fast, and my hands shook. I knew I needed to get my breathing under control, fast, or it would turn into a panic attack, but my attempts at deep breaths only ended in quiet sobs. I pressed my hand against my mouth, hoping to keep it in, but my panic quickly rose, my breaths coming in shorter and shorter breaths. The pressure on my chest made it feel impossible to breathe, even though I knew the pressure wasn't real. Or was it?

Another powerful wind tore through the place, hard enough that I stumbled a few steps to the side. Was I doing this? Was I destroying this one safe space I had?

Behind me, someone whispered my name, a deep, quiet voice. I spun around, and met dark brown eyes, one of them hidden behind a white mask. Through the fog, I could only see the white mask, the stark white standing out.

"Lia," Erik said again, surer this time. I reached out my hand, needing to hold onto something familiar, but I couldn't reach him. He was disappearing, and I couldn't breathe at all now.

CHAPTER 14
SHADOW

I woke up screaming. For a second, I thought I saw a shadow above me, but when I blinked, it was gone.

I gasped for breath, simultaneously pressing my hand against my belly, hoping it would help me breathe deeper, but my breaths were still too shallow.

I reached for my bedside table and managed to turn on the lamp. My eyes automatically found the painting above my desk. I tracked the outline with my eyes, but my heart still beat too fast, and I couldn't get my breathing to slow down. I gasped for breath again, and when I let it out, it came out a sob.

A knock on my door interrupted my spiralling. Before I could say anything, not that I could've if I wanted to, the door opened and my mom looked inside. When she saw me, she hurried to my bed, sat down next to me and pulled me into her arms. She didn't say anything, she just pressed me close and held me as I cried and gasped and sobbed. It took a long time, but I finally managed to force my breaths to become deeper and longer.

Mom didn't let me go. "Do you want to tell me?" she whispered against my hair.

I shook my head against her chest, forcing the images out of my head.

"Do you want me to stay with you for a while?"

I nodded, not trusting my voice to work.

Mom guided me down into bed again, then sat with me for a while. I must've fallen back asleep, because next thing I knew, the sun shone through my window. When I checked my phone, it said half past ten. I flew up from my bed. School started over an hour ago!

I heard a knock on my door, and Mom said softly from the other side, "Can I come in?"

"Um, yeah," I said. The door opened, and Mom stepped inside, closing it carefully behind her. "I'm really late for school, though," I told her and chewed on the inside of my cheek.

"You're not going to school today," Mom said decisively. "You need the day off, and we need to talk."

Something else hit me, and I frowned. "Shouldn't you be at work?"

She shook her head. "No. I'm staying home today."

"Can you really do that? I'm not a kid anymore."

"You're still my kid, no matter how old you get," Mom said, softening her voice. "And you're allowed to still need your mom, you know."

I didn't know what to say to that.

"Are you ready for some breakfast?"

At that moment, my stomach decided to grumble loudly. It wanted breakfast around eight, not eleven.

Mom laughed. "I'll take that as a yes." Her tone lightened a little, but it still held a note of worry. "Come downstairs when you're ready, okay?" With that, she left, closing the door behind her with a quiet click.

I sighed as a wave of guilt washed over me. The year before, when my anxiety had been at its worst, Mom had been so worried about me. While I loved her for caring about me, and she had helped me through it when I could barely get up in the morning, I hated worrying her. She already had enough on her plate without me adding to it.

I got dressed, but before I went downstairs, I texted Noah to let him know I wouldn't be able to meet that day, then I went downstairs, where Mom had gotten breakfast ready. She'd made toast, one of the few things I could eat when anxiety made my stomach clench, and a cup of tea.

I had just finished my toast and sipped my tea when Mom spoke up. "What's going on, Lia?"

I forced myself to swallow, then said, "What do you mean?"

"You're more stressed again, more anxious, and your nightmares are coming back." Mom shook her head. "Something is going on, or you wouldn't be getting worse again." She leaned forward, and her eyes were kind of glassy. My stomach clenched. "I want to help. Please let me help."

I took a shaky breath. I didn't want her to worry, but clearly she did that whether I talked to her or not. And maybe she could help me figure out this whole mess I'd somehow gotten myself into.

I let out a long breath, and then I told her about the strange things that had been happening for the last week. I told her about the storm in my meadow, meeting Erik and learning I might be not only a creator, but a sorceress, too. I told her about the freaky creatures that had appeared, the myling and the lindworm, and about Melinda's sudden appearance. The only thing I didn't mention was that I'd seen Erik a few more times other than that first time. I also didn't mention that, on top of all this, I was also becoming more and more certain that I wasn't straight. I still struggled with the realisation that a lot of the description of asexuality fit very well with me, and I wasn't ready to voice that. It didn't matter that Mom would probably be supportive. I just couldn't bring myself to say it out loud. Somehow, that would make it all the more real, and the thought terrified me. And I still felt like a fraud when I tried to use the label for myself. Like I was using a label I had no right to use.

When I was done, my tea had grown cold, and I put the cup down. I hated cold tea. Mom didn't say anything, her mouth pressed into a thin line and her eyes wide. I looked down at my hands, resting on the table in front of me, and picked at my nails. I started to regret telling her when she finally said something.

"No wonder your anxiety's been getting worse," she said faintly. "About this Erik guy…"

I interrupted her before she could lecture me. "I'm trying to stay away from him," I said. "I haven't been in my meadow since he showed up there."

Mom sighed. "Just be careful, okay? You don't know this guy, and I don't want you to get hurt."

I promised her I was being as careful as I possibly could, and she moved on.

"I'm more worried about these creatures that keep showing up," she said.

"Is there any chance that they are just that – creatures – or do you think they might be creations?" It felt nice being able to ask Mom about it. She probably knew more than I did, anyway.

Mom chewed on that for a while. "I've never heard of any creatures being real, but I don't want to say it's impossible. I mean, we create things from thin air, so clearly magic is real. But if they aren't creations, they probably would've started showing up earlier. Still, we can't rule anything out at this point."

We were quiet for a while, clearly trying to figure out this mystery that had landed in my lap. Like I didn't already have enough to worry about.

"I was thinking," I said. Mom looked at me and waited for me to go on. "I want to call Melinda. I'm..." I stared down at my hands and took a deep breath. "I think I'm in way over my head, and maybe she could help. Or maybe her coven could."

Mom nodded. "It's not a bad idea. Having a community of other magic-users can't hurt, and they might have more answers than I do. At the very least, it's worth meeting them. I also think it's a good idea for Noah to help you control your other magic. It would give you some extra protection, and I don't know anything about sorcerer magic."

I looked away, knowing what I needed to ask and yet hating the idea. Silence descended on the kitchen as I tried to bring myself to voice the question. "Do you know how..." I trailed off.

"How you have these powers?" Mom finished for me. "I don't. But I would guess they are from your father." She paused. "I'll see if I can find anything about his family, see if they can help cast some light on this whole thing." She sighed deeply. "I can't believe I never knew he was a sorcerer. I was honest with him about what I was. Why didn't he tell me?"

"I'm sorry, Mom." My voice tightened with the guilt choking me.

She looked up, shocked. "You have nothing to be sorry for," she said decisively. "And as much as it hurts to know he kept it a secret from me, I believe he must've had a good reason for not telling me."

What reason could be good enough to lie to the mother of your children? But I didn't say anything. If it made her feel better about it, I didn't want to burst that bubble.

Mom straightened in her chair and took a deep breath. "You said Melinda gave you her number, right? Let's call her together."

I nodded. "She did." I'd even added her number to my phone just in case I lost the note.

You could've heard a pin drop as we waited for her to pick up. *Beep.* Only the sound of the phone ringing broke the silence. *Beep.* I stared at the phone where I'd put it in the middle of the table, between Mom and me. *Beep.*

Then a quiet *click*, and a voice flowed from the phone. "This is Melinda."

I took a breath. "Hi, Melinda. This is Lia. We, um, we met at the library. You told me about your coven."

Melinda laughed lightly, the sound like bells. "I remember. Have you had a chance to think about it?"

"Yeah," I said. "Oh, my mom's on speaker, by the way. Is that okay?"

"Of course." The warmth in her tone soothed me, and I relaxed into my seat.

"Well, we were wondering if we could meet? With the coven, I mean."

"Of course," Melinda repeated. "Would Wednesday work for you? Around seven, maybe?"

I looked up at Mom, who nodded. "Yeah, that works," I told Melinda.

"Perfect. How about we meet at Almedalen?"

"Sure, that works," I agreed.

"Great! We will see you Wednesday, then." Melinda paused. "I'm glad you decided to meet us. The community is really great, and it's nice to know other people with magic who understands the struggles you face."

Hopefully, they can actually help with the struggles I'm facing, too.

I was in my meadow again. The lindworm slithered closer and closer, and I spun and ran. My heart beat so hard it hurt, and the lindworm hissed behind me. With a *whoosh,* it rolled in front of me, and I stumbled to a stop.

The lindworm hissed again, milky white spittle flying from its mouth. I jerked back, but it was too late. The foul-smelling liquid spattered into my eyes, and the world went dark.

I sat bolt upright, tangled in the sheets. Panic shortened my breath, and for a terrifying moment, I thought I was really blind. Darkness threatened to choke me, and I struggled to untangle my arms from the sheets wrapped around me. Finally, I reached the lamp on my bedside table and clicked it on.

Light flooded the room, and I blinked in the sudden light. I let out a choked sob of relief. Clutching the sheets tightly, I forced a breath. In—one, two, three, four. Hold—one, two. Out—one, two, three, four. Hold—one, two. I repeated the process until my heart finally slowed down. My lungs filled with precious oxygen.

I settled back against the pillows, too tense to fall asleep.

What is happening to me?

The next morning, it was almost impossible to get out of bed. Exhaustion after another night of nightmares made my body feel heavy, but I couldn't stay home from school two days in a row because of some bad dreams, so I forced myself out of bed. All day, I couldn't make myself focus in class, and I didn't take a single note. Clara noticed and asked about it, but I shook my head and told her everything was fine. Neither of us believed the lie, but I couldn't talk about it at school, or I'd risk breaking down in the middle of the hallway.

After school, I waited for Noah, who still had class for another half hour. When Clara noticed, she sat down next to me. "What's going on?"

I grimaced, but the look on her face made it clear that she wouldn't keep dropping the subject. "I've been having nightmares."

Clara's face softened. "Like before?"

I chewed my lip. "Yes and no. I wake up like before – which is why mom forced me to stay home yesterday – but the dreams are different." I told her about the two nightmares I'd had, leaving out all the fear and stress they had caused, shutting down all emotion. I couldn't deal with it right then. I told her about the shadow I'd seen both times – was it a figment of my imagination? Or was it another creature?

Clara looked worried. "Do you think this shadow thing has something to do with the nightmares?"

I shrugged. "I don't know. This whole situation is causing enough anxiety that it could easily cause nightmares on its own, but yes, this shadow thing is terrifying. Mom was on me like a hawk all day yesterday, but I'm going to do some research and see what I can find about it."

Clara nodded. "That's a good idea." She paused, clearly at a loss for words. "Are you going to be okay?"

I shrugged again. At this point I didn't feel like I could tell up from down.

Clara's eyes were shiny, and my stomach clenched.

Damn it. This is exactly why I didn't want to tell her.

Before I could start apologising, Clara sprung forward and hugged me, right there in the school corridor. My eyes watered.

Clara's voice came out muffled. "I know you want to apologise for worrying me or something, but don't you dare, or I will personally feed you to the next creepy creature that shows up."

I laughed through my tears, and there we sat, in the school corridor where anyone could walk by at any moment, hugging each other tight, laughing and crying. We must've looked insane, but at that moment, I couldn't bring myself to care.

I opened my mouth, ready to confess about having lied about Erik, but right then, someone cleared their throat next to us. "Am I interrupting anything?"

Clara and I pulled apart, slowly, and I looked at Noah. He looked like a mix between amused and worried. "Do you need a minute?"

"I'll be right there," I told him.

He nodded. "I'll wait downstairs."

Clara raised a brow at me. "What do you have planned?"

I narrowed my eyes. "Nothing like what you're thinking. We're going to practise magic, since I apparently have elemental magic too."

Clara smiled and her shoulders relaxed. "Good. That's really good. Well, don't let me keep you. But... call me tonight, okay? Let me know how it goes."

I promised to call, and then I went downstairs to meet Noah.

We collected our bikes from the rack at the school entrance before heading to my place. The sun barely peeked out through the heavy clouds, and the freezing air bit at my cheeks. The sun had already started setting as we took a quick walk with Kiwi before going straight up to my room. By the time I grabbed my notebook, only a small sliver of it peeked over the horizon. My stomach filled with giant mutant butterflies, and my mind drifted to my nightmare. What would we find once we went into my meadow?

No use dragging it out. I opened the notebook to my current place and started writing. Noah stood close to me, but not so close that we were touching.

My pen scratched over the paper, and the usual blue swirl appeared in front of me. I took Noah's hand, hoping that would be enough to take him with me. It usually worked with Kiwi, and I hoped it would work with him, too. Together, we stepped through the swirl.

I looked around, half expecting Erik to be standing there, but I found nothing except trees. I'd made it sunny today, hoping the sunlight would brighten my mood a little. I still didn't know quite what to think after Erik's extreme reaction the day before and the conversation with Clara. Despite her words, a knot of guilt had formed in my stomach.

Determined to not think about it, I looked at Noah. "Okay, so how do we do this?"

His lips quirked. "I've never seen anyone look so determined before." His voice held a note of laughter.

I scowled. "Well, I need to learn. Besides, how many eighteen-year-olds do you know who can't control their magic?"

"One, but I also don't know any eighteen-year-old sorcerers apart from you." He grew serious. "I think we also need to figure out where your magic comes from."

I looked at him with raised eyebrows. "Um, what?"

He grinned. "Well, all sorcerers are controlled by a certain part of their body," he said. "That's where their magic resides when it's dormant. That's different for all sorcerers, so that's usually what you learn first; to feel where your magic comes from, where it lives when you're not using it. Until you know that, it's impossible to learn to control it."

This all sounded a lot like what Erik had told me the day before. "Okay."

"The difficult part," he said, face drawn, "is to figure out where the magic comes from. The easiest way to find it is to trigger an outburst of magic when you're ready for it. That way, you can concentrate on the feeling when the burst is released."

I frowned. "The only times my magic has appeared was when I was really, really scared."

"Yeah, that's a problem," he agreed. "Because the easiest way to trigger your magic is probably to make you scared."

I chewed on my cheek. "Is there any other way? Because I don't really feel like creating a lindworm to scare me a little."

"Let's call that plan C," Noah said. "Usually any strong feeling works, and the most effective feeling is different for different people. Ella, for example, is most easily triggered by anger. Olivia, excitement.

You seem to be most easily triggered by fear."

I grimaced. "That's really inconvenient for someone who struggles with panic attacks." After all, panic attacks were really nothing more than physical reactions to fear – it's just that when that fear is, say, failing on a test, that physical reaction isn't as helpful as it was when the fear was being eaten by a bear about a million years ago.

Noah nodded. "That's why it's important you learn to control your powers. But before we start trying to trigger your emotions, let's try something else. It's a lot more difficult, but it's worth a try if we can avoid having to summon a lindworm." He grinned wryly, then abruptly sat down on the ground with his feet together in front of him. He patted the ground in front of him. "Sit."

I sat and mirrored his position. "Are we going to meditate? Because I should warn you, I am not good at it." I had tried meditation for my anxiety, but I always got stressed and impatient, and found myself more anxious than before I started.

He smiled. "Let's hope it goes better this time," he said. "Close your eyes."

I did as he instructed.

"Good. Now take a few deep breaths, yes, like that. Now, I want you to focus on how you feel. Work from the top down. Start with your head. How does it feel?"

I did, trying to relax as best I could. Closing my eyes always made my thoughts go crazy, but I tried hard to keep them under control. "What am I looking for?" I asked, hoping he wouldn't get suspicious.

"It should feel like a little tingling. It will probably be small since your magic is dormant right now, so you need to pay close attention or you'll miss it."

I pretended to focus on my head for a while, even though all I did was focus on breathing regularly and on the sensations all around me. Grounding myself was one of the best ways I'd found to calm myself from my anxiety.

After what I hoped was enough time, I focused on the feeling in my stomach, but this time I couldn't feel the hum over the knot of anxiety there. I frowned, frustrated that I couldn't feel the magic, and dug deeper, but all I accomplished was tightening that knot. My breath quickened as the pressure inside increased, and I bit down on my lip, hard, hoping to distract myself from the pain inside.

"Stop for a second," Noah said gently. "Don't open your eyes. Just focus on breathing for a minute, okay? That's all."

I forced a deep breath, but I couldn't keep my thoughts from racing. *What if I can't learn to control my magic? What if my stupid anxiety will always be in the way?* Tears pricked my eyes, and I dug my nails into my palms.

"Hey." Noah's voice lowered, softened, and I opened my eyes to look at him. "Don't get lost in your head. Take a deep breath, okay? Focus on feeling the warm breeze. Let your fingers sift through the soft grass. Take another deep breath. Feel the sunlight warm your skin. Listen to the leaves rustling in the wind. And another deep breath."

I did as he said, and for several minutes I let Noah ground me in the present. My panic slowly subsided, my breathing growing easier and easier.

"That's better," Noah said. "Now let's try again."

I did and found that the tension of anxiety had lessened. It wasn't completely gone, but it was less, and this time, I could see – feel – around it.

I gasped as I finally felt that hum – kind of like when a limb fell asleep after you'd sat still for too long, but much less.

My eyes flew open. "Wow." I couldn't keep the amazement out of my tone, even though I'd already experienced it before.

He smiled. "You found it?"

I nodded. "It was in my stomach, so it was hard to find – the anxiety is really overpowering – but it's there."

"Good. That's really good," he said. "But it does make our job a lot harder, because in order to control your magic, you will probably need to control your anxiety."

I sighed heavily. *Of course. Just my luck.* "I've been trying to control my anxiety for over a year. It's not as easy as all that."

Noah grimaced in sympathy. "I know. I'm not saying it is. But that's what we need to work on." He smiled a little. "And you did really well today. I know you started to spiral there for a bit, but you stopped it."

"I stopped it only because you distracted me," I said. "There's a reason I try to avoid thinking about that feeling in my stomach, because once I start, I likely can't stop, and then the anxiety just gets worse and worse."

"Well, I will be here to help you," he said. "You didn't think I'd leave you to fend for yourself, did you?"

I sighed. "No, it's just... frustrating. It couldn't be easy, could it?"

"It's never easy learning to control your magic," he said. "But you've already learned to control your magic once. I think that gives you a little bit of a head start."

I really hope that's true. Because if this situation gets any worse, I'll surely need it.

Before going to bed that night, I decided to do some research. Maybe I could find something about the shadow thing I kept seeing at night, or how to protect myself from it. A quick search for 'nightmare monster' brought me mara, mare in English, a creature that came in the night and rode people's chests, giving them nightmares, hence the name.

My chest tightened at the thought of a monster riding my chest.

I read on. Apparently the mare was created when a human mother-to-be crawled through the amniotic sac of a foal to ease her pain while giving birth, which was clearly some sort of dark magic. *Gross.* The child, if a girl, was born a mare, and would shift at night into this nightmare creature. (A boy would turn into a werewolf, apparently.)

I kept reading. Knowing what it was didn't help unless I could find out how to protect myself from it.

There! *The mare is obsessive and compulsive, so if you put flaxseeds around your bed, she will have to stop and count them all, and she won't have time to hurt you.*

I tiptoed downstairs, not wanting to wake Mom or Tilda, and looked in the pantry. I couldn't find any flaxseed, but I did find breadcrumbs that I used for baking, so I grabbed two handfuls of that and tiptoed back up. I spread them evenly on the floor around the entire bed, making sure to not miss a spot. When I felt sure there was no bare spot for the mare to sneak through, I crawled into bed and fell asleep faster than I had in a long time.

CHAPTER 15
THE COVEN

The next day, I felt surprisingly better. I'd slept fitfully, but I hadn't had any nightmares, and I hadn't woken up screaming, so I decided to call it a win. I gathered up the breadcrumbs, dug out an old jewellery box from my closet, and dumped them in there.

Wednesday was a late day at school, but it felt easier than it had in a long time. We had almost three hours of Communications, where we got to work on our project for most of the time. Clara, Alva and I found a room in the library where we sat and worked. We were planning a short lesson of twenty minutes about personalities according to Myers-Briggs, and we weren't quite sure where to start.

Alva sighed, bringing me out of my concentration. I'd been researching the different personality types, but I looked up from my laptop at Alva and found her staring at her screen.

She looked up over the frame of her round blue glasses and our eyes met. I must've looked questioning, because she quickly explained, "This is too hard. An actual lesson? What the heck are we going to do for an entire twenty minutes?"

I laughed. "It could be worse."

Alva frowned at me. "How could it possibly be worse?"

"We could be having a test on all this instead. At least this way we get to be a bit creative." I shrugged and looked down at my screen.

"Fair enough," Alva said, and I looked up again.

Clara pushed her laptop away. "I need a break or I might throw my laptop out the window, and I can't afford to replace it. Do any of you want anything from the cafeteria?"

I shook my head.

Alva opened her mouth, but before she could say anything Clara answered for her, "Latte, extra foam, extra hot."

Alva laughed and her eyes darted to me for a second before they landed on Clara again. "I'm that predictable, huh?"

Clara smiled wide and her eyes twinkled. Jesus, she was smitten. It was a wonder her eyes weren't heart shaped. "Maybe a little. Be right back!" And with that, she spun around and bounced out of the room. Yes, she actually bounced, like a five-year-old going to get candy for Saturday night.

Once Clara the chatterbox left, Alva and I sat in silence, neither of us sure what to say. The whirr of our laptops filled the room, and I flipped through a book just to have something to do.

Finally, when I was about ready to flee from the awkwardness, Alva said, "So, Clara said you two have been friends for a long time?"

I looked up at her. "Yeah, since we were seven."

Alva smiled. "That's nice. She's a really nice person." Her cheeks reddened and she looked away.

"She's the best," I said, trying to keep up some sort of conversation before we descended into awkward silence again. "So you've been hanging out a lot lately?"

Alva stared at her hands like they held the secrets to the universe. "Um, yeah. A bit, I guess." She looked back up at me. "She's so sweet and kind and selfless and, like, does she ever shut up?" Her voice grew animated.

I laughed. "Nope. No, she doesn't."

Before Alva could reply, Clara came back and handed Alva her latte. Then she put a cup in front of me and sat down with her own cup.

I looked at her and furrowed my brows.

"Green tea with mint," she replied to my wordless question. "I know you want it."

Well, who could resist a cup of green tea with mint?

As we started discussing the lesson plan again, I caught Clara sneaking glances at Alva as often as she could, which didn't surprise me in the least. It did surprise me that Alva snuck as many glances at Clara.

My stomach clenched with sadness. If I really were asexual, would I ever have that?

When I got home, Mom was already there. Tilda was at dance class, and it was just Mom and me. She had made tea for us, and sat in the kitchen, clearly waiting for me, so I sat across from her and sipped, enjoying the fruity blackberry taste.

"Is something wrong?" I asked when she didn't say anything for several minutes.

She shook her head and stared into her cup. I decided to let her take her time and focused on my tea. After several more minutes, she looked up. "I talked to your grandmother today," she said.

I frowned. My grandmother had died a couple of years earlier, almost ten years after my grandfather. Since Mom didn't have any siblings, it was basically just us.

"Your father's mother," she clarified.

Oh. "What did she say?" I asked, trying to ignore the anxiety that tightened in my stomach.

Mom smiled, but it didn't reach her eyes. "She was glad I reached out," she told me. "She didn't know we existed, but she insisted on coming here. And I don't think that's a bad idea, considering what's been happening lately."

No, I guessed it wasn't a bad idea. Especially if...

"She's a sorceress," Mom answered my unspoken question. "She said she might have some answers, but would rather talk in person."

I hesitated, but I had to ask. "Did... did she know what happened to him?"

Mom looked away, but not before I saw the flash of pain on her face. "She said he died." She sounded choked. "Almost fourteen years ago. He was killed."

Fourteen years ago. That would be around the time when he had left – except he hadn't left, had he? He'd died.

I took a deep breath, but it did nothing to calm the emotions that choked me. I couldn't understand it – I had no memories whatsoever of my father. I'd been only three years old when he'd left. Why did I feel so sad at the loss of a father I never knew? It made no sense. Whether he left by choice or not didn't change anything, did it?

Except it did. Because now I knew that he... he hadn't left because he didn't care about us. At least, it didn't seem like it. He'd been killed, and maybe he truly had cared about us like Mom always said.

My stomach tightened. All this time, I'd thought he couldn't have been as great as Mom claimed. If he really had been killed, that meant he didn't deserve my callousness.

I wanted to throw up as guilt ate at my insides. I'd been so bitter towards him, thought he couldn't have possibly loved any of us if he'd been able to leave that easily, when in reality he'd been forced to leave us. Not only that, he'd been *killed*.

And what about his mother – our grandmother? Was our grandfather still alive? Or did she live alone, suffering the grief of losing her son alone? We'd had no idea we had another grandmother – hell, I didn't even know her name.

My mind drifted back to the biggest bomb of all. The knowledge that he'd been killed only raised new questions. Who had done it? Why had he been killed? Had it been somehow connected to the magical world? But one question left me cold with dread.

Was his murder somehow connected to what was happening to me?

The moon shone, big and bright, over Almedalen that night. The night felt eerily still, the air crisp and biting. Not a soul was out, and the wind had died down hours earlier. Even the ducks were quiet. Only the sound of waves softly crashing against the shore in the distance interrupted the stillness as we stood by the city wall next to Almedalen.

I huddled into my coat and hid my face in my scarf. My nose had already started going numb.

Next to me, Tilda coughed into her own scarf. "Can someone please remind me why we live in Sweden? I've heard Spain is a really nice place to live."

Mom snorted. "And how are those Spanish lessons coming along?"

Tilda gave her a dark look. "They are going just fine, thanks for asking. I haven't failed the class yet, have I?"

"No, you haven't." Mom laughed and gave Tilda a sideways hug. "I'm proud of you. Learning a new language is hard."

"Exactly!"

I rubbed my hands together, smiling a little to myself. The smile quickly faded, though, when I spotted a group of people in the distance, heading towards us. *The coven.* My stomach clenched and I rubbed my hands faster, harder. Silence descended as we waited for them to reach us.

As they got closer, I recognised Melinda in the middle, dressed in dark jeans and a heavy coat. To her right were two older women, maybe around their fifties. The one next to Melinda had hair so light grey it was almost white, while the other woman had darker hair, black streaked with lighter grey. They wore all black, and even had witchy cloaks, because of course. To Melinda's right were a younger pair, a man and a woman holding hands. They both looked stereotypically Swedish with blond hair and bright eyes, though I couldn't tell what colour they were in the darkness of the night. They wore muted colours, the kind you'd expect to see on anyone in town. If you were looking for magic-users, they were the last people you'd ever suspect. The older women, on the other hand, you'd definitely point out in a crowd.

They finally reached us, and Melinda smiled. "I am so glad you wanted to meet with us." She looked over at my mom and Tilda. "This must be your family?"

I nodded, and they introduced themselves.

"It's so nice to meet you." Melinda's eyes seemed to twinkle in the moonlight. "I'm Melinda, and these are Maria and Lena," she pointed to the older women to her right, "and Emma and Filip." She pointed to the younger couple. "We call ourselves a coven, but it's not as witchy as it sounds, I promise." She chuckled.

Emma grinned. "Well, it's a little witchy."

Melinda shot her a look, but she smiled. "Okay, it's a little witchy. But mostly, it's a community for people with magic. It's a safe space where we can practise our magic without fear, a place where we can talk about it with others like us. It's a chance to learn from each other." Her smile turned wry. "Since there aren't too many sources on our specific type of magic, it's a chance to learn more about it, to understand our magic and ourselves better."

Maybe they *could* help us, then.

Melinda went on. "Do you have any questions for us?"

Tilda was quick as a whip. "What kind of magic do you have?"

Melinda blinked. "Well, I'm a creator."

"My sister and I are sorceresses." Maria, the dark-haired sister, smiled warmly.

"And we're creators," Emma replied.

"What kind of magic do you practise?" Mom asked.

"All kinds of magic." Melinda hugged her coat tighter around her. "It depends. Sometimes we practise the same thing – or, as close as we can get, considering we all have different magic – and sometimes we practise whatever we feel like, giving each other advice as we go. We're not very formal in that way, we can just do whatever we feel like each meeting."

This coven sounded better and better. Having a community of other magic-users, people to talk to about magic and learn from? That sounded really nice. Even if I had my family to talk to and Mom had taught me everything she knew about magic, I knew there was a lot we still didn't know.

"Have you ever heard of anyone creating... creatures?" mom asked.

"Creatures?" Lena frowned.

Mom nodded. "Creatures from mythology."

Emma gasped. Filip narrowed his eyes. "No. No one should be messing with magic like that. It's risky, not to mention *wrong.*" His voice was firm. "Why are you asking about mythological creatures?"

Mom looked at Filip, eyebrows pinched, before she replied, "Some... strange things have been happening lately."

"What kind of things?" Maria's voice was low.

"Strange beings showing up," Mom told her.

Maria and Lena shared a look of horror.

Emma shook her head. "It's not something we've heard anything about. But we'll keep an eye out."

Mom nodded. "Thank you."

Silence descended, until only the sound of waves could be heard. I shivered and huddled further into my coat, the breath in front of me turning into small clouds.

"Well." Melinda's steady voice broke the silence. "What do you say we go somewhere a little more private? I don't want to practise magic out here in the open."

Melinda led the way to one of the old church ruins within the city walls. On a November evening, most of them were completely abandoned, and the chances of someone going to visit were small. In the summer, they'd be packed with tourists.

We didn't talk much as we walked through the cobblestone streets of Visby. Some Christmas decorations already decorated the streets, giving the city an idyllic, cosy feel. Without the modern lights, walking through Visby truly felt like going back in time, the mismatched houses a remnant of the Middle Ages.

It only took a few minutes for us to get to one of the more well-kept ruins. We entered through a high arch and ended up in a large, shadowy open space. The structure of the church was mostly whole, with high arch windows everywhere, making it easy to imagine what it might've looked like when it was still in use. Only the moon and twinkling stars above lit the place.

Lena smiled and swept her hand out. The still evening was interrupted by the loud whistling of wind. Her hair blew around her face and the wind created a tornado around her.

I stared and my heart quickened. The amount of control she had over her magic was incredible. To be able to create such a strong wind and keep it contained… And here I couldn't even create a wind on command.

I looked over at Filip, who whispered to himself. Ivy shot up on the stone wall in front of him, growing higher and wider until it covered the entire wall. And still it kept growing, the dark leaves crawling over every available space.

My fingers tickled with the onslaught of magic, and I wished desperately for a pen and notebook. The magic whispered over my skin, the same faint electric *zing* I'd felt when Erik made the flower for me in my meadow. But we'd decided before we went that we wouldn't use any magic this time, only watch, and ask our questions.

On the opposite side of the room, Melinda mumbled to herself. Next to her, a tree plant rose. And rose. Branches grew faster than my eyes could track, leaves sprouting from them. The trunk thickened until Melinda had to move out of the way. Roots shot down into the ground and up, too big to be contained beneath the soil. The oak rose taller than the ruins now, the leafy crown still growing up and up and up.

My attention shifted to the trunk, which looked like it was being carved by nothing but air. A hollow grew in the trunk, along with other imperfections, giving the impression that the oak was hundreds of years and not only a few minutes old.

I gaped, breath hitching. I'd never seen anything like it. I'd created the trees in my meadow, sure, but they weren't even close to as impressive as that oak. Not nearly as big or as towering, and certainly not as detailed, either. To make something like this, with such intricate detail... the amount of skill required to do that stole my breath.

The growing tree finally slowed down, though branched still creaked and leaves still rustled.

"I'm going to go talk to her a little," Mom whispered to me.

Next to me, Tilda inched closer where she and I stood off to the side. "This is so freaking cool."

I leaned closer. "I know. Can you believe the amount of control it would take to do these things? It's insane."

Tilda stared hard at Filip's growing ivy. "I wish I could do stuff like that." Her voice held a wistful note.

I nudged her side. "I'm sure you'll be able to do it too someday."

"Yeah, right." Tilda snorted. "Did you see that oak over there? I can't even begin to fathom the amount of magic something like that would require."

Mom walked over to us, climbing over roots and ivy that had spread to the floor. "Are you ready to head home?"

Tilda looked around at all the magic around us again and sighed. "I guess."

Mom smiled. "Maybe we can join them some other time again."

I smiled back. Magic flowed over my skin, raising goosebumps in its wake, and for the first time in weeks, hope filled my chest.

CHAPTER 16
CREATURE FROM THE WOODS

After another night of fitful but dreamless sleep, I woke up feeling not quite refreshed but at least able to face the day. One look out the window, though, made my mood plummet. The sky, which had barely started lightening when I got up at nine, was full of dark clouds, making it clear that it would rain sometime during the day. When I stepped outside, my mood plummeted even further as I met an icy wind.

I burrowed into my jacket and had to walk my bike to school because of the strong wind. Maybe it would pick up to a proper storm. As if the imminent rain weren't enough.

By the time school ended, it was drizzling, and by the time Clara and I had gotten to the café, rain poured down. We hurried inside and ordered, and then sat in our usual spot, dripping wet.

Once we'd gotten settled, I told her about my grandmother who would be coming to visit on Friday. My voice shook a little when I got to the part about my father being dead.

"Oh, Lia, I'm sorry," she said, and before I knew it, she'd jumped up from the couch and hugged me. "I'm so sorry."

"I don't even know why I'm so sad," I said, pushing back tears. "It's not like it makes a difference in my life. I've never even known him."

"Still," Clara said. "He was your father. Of course you're sad that he's dead – and that he was murdered. There's nothing wrong with being sad about that."

"I guess," I said quietly, and blinked away the tears that pricked at my eyes. Wanting to change the subject, I said, "So what is going on with you and Alva?"

Clara looked up, startled, and her cheeks went pink. "Nothing," she said quickly.

"Come on," I said. "It's clearly not 'nothing'. I saw you two yesterday, and that was definitely something. I think she might like you back."

Clara choked on her tea. "What?"

I laughed at her reaction. "It's just the way she looked at you," I explained. "It was... well, it seemed to me that you two were making eyes at each other."

Clara didn't say anything. An older couple walked past us, their steps making the floor groan a little. They sat a few tables away, talking quietly.

When Clara spoke again, her voice had an edge. "I don't think she likes girls, though."

We sat in silence for a while, but that was okay. It warmed my heart that being her friend meant she would always be there for me, would always listen to me. Even just being in her presence, sitting in silence, was comforting. Some of the tension left my shoulders, and my breathing evened out.

"So," Clara said after almost ten minutes of silence, "how did it go with Noah the other day?"

I blinked. "Um, he says we made progress, but I don't know. I didn't actually do anything to try and control the magic. I just found where it, um, rested."

"That sounds like progress to me."

I shrugged. "Hey, Clara?"

"Mm?"

I hesitated. "How... how did you know that you're gay?"

Her eyes widened slightly, and it was clear that she didn't know what to say at first. Her mouth opened, but no sound came out.

Finally, she said, "Well, I guess I always felt kind of different. Or, maybe not when we were really young, but when other girls started having crushes, well, it was pretty clear to me that I wasn't interested in boys in that way. I didn't really figure it out until later, though. I sort of dated this guy back in seventh grade - remember Jonathan?" When I nodded, she went on. "Well, when he asked me on a date, I said yes because I genuinely liked him as a friend, and I thought maybe I'd start feeling something else if I gave it a chance. But then he kissed me, and it didn't really make me feel anything. No butterflies or fireworks or whatever metaphors books use. That's when I started seriously considering that I might simply not like guys like that. A few months later, I had my first crush – or, I think I might've had crushes before, but I just thought I wanted to be friends with them, you know? Anyway, when I met Alice, that's when I knew 100% that I was gay." She stopped then. I could tell she really wanted to ask, but she didn't.

"Oh," I said quietly. I didn't say anything else. Clara didn't say anything, just let me figure it out. "Um, I think I might not be straight," I said finally.

Clara nodded seriously. "Okay," she said, but nothing else. Not pushing me to tell her anything I might not be ready for.

"Not gay, either."

She just looked seriously at me, letting me get there on my own.

"Um, have you heard of the term asexual?" A nod. "Well, I think I might be that. I've been looking into it, because I, um, I'm not really interested in... kissing and stuff. I think." Oh my god, I couldn't have sounded more unsure if I tried. "And... well, I don't know yet, but it feels kind of right when I read about it. I've been reading about other asexual people's experiences, and it sounds like me." I paused, chewing my lip. "I don't know, though. I feel like... like I have no right to use the label. I feel so unsure about it all, and I feel like a... a fraud."

"Okay." She gave me a small smile full of encouragement. "It's okay if you don't know yet. It's okay to be unsure. You don't have to figure it all out right away, or even at all. You know, labels aren't meant to be tests, checklists that have to fit perfectly. They're meant to be tools, to help you express yourself and find people with similar experiences. If it feels right to you, that's all that matters. And besides, there are so many different queer experiences, even among people with the same label. There's no right way to be queer, no one universal queer experience. You don't have to prove to anyone that you're queer." She reached out to take my hand and squeezed. "Just tell me if I can do anything to make it easier for you, okay? I know questioning can be hard and confusing, but I'm here for you."

The knot of anxiety in my stomach loosened. I hadn't realised how stressed I'd been over telling her until then. I blinked away a few tears. "Thank you," I whispered.

"Don't thank me for that," Clara said. "I know what you're going through. If I can make it any easier for you, of course I will."

I felt lighter than I had in a long time.

The next day, I walked Kiwi just as the sun started setting. Which was before three in the afternoon. But at least we caught a few minutes of sunlight. Sigh. We walked over a small field, and I waited for Kiwi to do her business when I saw a light in the air. I narrowed my eyes, trying to make it out, but it was too far away. But there were definitely spots of brightness there.

"If they're fairies, I'm quitting, okay?" I said to Kiwi. She finished her business and started walking again – straight to the little floating lights.

When we got closer, I saw that they were, indeed, fairies. They were tiny and shiny, with a bluish tint to their skin, and they had no wings, so they just basically floated right there.

Sure, why not? The world was clearly going crazy, anyway, why not add some wingless fairies to the mix. Beyond that, I couldn't really tell much about them. There were several of them, but they were moving around so quickly I couldn't count them properly. I heard a quiet buzzing sound. Then, one of the fairies – because they really couldn't be anything else, could they? – broke away from the rest and stopped right in front of my face. Now that the fairy was close, I could tell that it had long, white hair. Other than that, it had no features that marked it as male or female.

Hello, Lia.

I jumped as I heard them, but they hadn't spoken out loud. No, I heard them inside my head.

Oh, goody.

We need your help, the fairy continued in my head. *Someone is disturbing the balance in the universe.*

I tried to think back, *Um, okay?*

The other fairies buzzed louder. *We need you to help set the balance right, before it's too late.*

That sounded ominous and vague. *What exactly do you want me to do about it?*

You must fight the creature from the woods.

Okay, sure, let me get right on that. After all, I have nothing better to do with my life.

The buzzing grew even louder, and I could feel their disapproval. Had I thought that to them? Oops.

You must save this world before it's too late.

Now wait a minute. I had not signed up for any world-saving. I was just trying to graduate from the gymnasium without another breakdown, for god's sake!

It's our only chance.

Yeah, okay, how exactly am I supposed to save the world? I couldn't even control my magic, how was I supposed to fight a creature from the woods – whatever the heck that even meant?

You have to save us all. With one last judgmental buzz, the fairy floated back to their friends, and then they disappeared.

I sighed heavily. "What is my life becoming, Kiwi?"

Things didn't improve when I got home, because as soon as I closed the door behind me, Mom stuck her head out of the kitchen and told me my grandmother had showed up. And sure enough, there she was, sitting at our dinner table with a cup of tea. Opposite her sat Tilda, who looked pale.

She looked surprisingly young for a grandmother. Short, white hair fell in light waves, and wrinkles covered her face, but her eyes were alert. My other grandmother had been tired and definitely not as refreshed.

She stood up when she saw me and smiled. Kiwi rushed past me and started barking, but after I said her name sharply, she shut up and carefully walked up to my grandmother, sniffing the air as she went. She was usually very suspicious of strangers. My grandmother bent down slightly to let her sniff her hand. Apparently, she smelled okay, because Kiwi lost interest soon after that.

My grandmother stood again and looked at me for a long moment. "You must be Lia," she said.

I nodded, even though it hadn't been a question.

"I'm Eva. I'm so sorry I haven't been in your life," she said, "but if you'll let me, I'd like to be."

I chewed my lip. It had been just Mom, Tilda and me for so long that it felt strange to have this other relative. "I guess," I said finally. When I looked up, I met Tilda's eyes. She offered a small smile and I smiled back and took a deep, cleansing breath. At least we always had each other. In all the craziness of the past few weeks, I'd totally forgotten about that, but if anyone could understand all of this, it would be my sister. My sister, who was as much a hybrid as me.

I promised myself that we would talk, the two of us, soon, but right then, we had a grandmother to get to know.

We all sat down, me next to Tilda and Mom next to Eva. We talked for a while, Tilda and I asking about other family – there was none – which felt different, to say the least, until Tilda finally asked the question we were all wondering about. "How could you not have known about us?"

Eva stilled. "About twenty years ago, Johan left our home just outside of Stockholm. He kept in touch, called us – me and his father – once every week to let us know he was safe, but he never told us where he went or what he did. Only that he was happy. Then five years later, he called and said he was coming home. Something had happened, though he wouldn't say what it was, and he needed our help." She paused, and she blinked several times. "That was the last time I heard from him. It wasn't until several weeks later that they found him dead. Murdered. A hiker stumbled over his body. They never found out who did it."

Oh my God. That was all I could think for several minutes. Once I got past the initial shock, one question popped into the forefront of my mind. What had happened that made him want to go back home to his parents? And was that what had gotten him killed?

Mom shook her head and pressed her hand to her lips. "He told me he was going to visit you. I was so happy. I'd wanted to meet his family for so long – wanted you to meet Lia and Tilda – but he convinced me that he needed to meet you alone first. And then he never came back. I reported him missing, but then he was seen a couple of days later somewhere near Stockholm, so everyone assumed that he left of his own accord." She paused. "I tried to find where he might go, but he had used a different surname and I couldn't find anything, so I just accepted that he didn't want anything to do with us. It wasn't until a few days ago that I remembered him mentioning your name once. That's how I finally found you."

Mom looked at Eva. Her eyes were glassy. Eva had a drawn expression on her face, like she was holding back her emotions.

I looked at Tilda. This felt like a moment that needed to be between Mom and Eva. Tilda nodded slightly, and we both stood up and went upstairs, followed by Kiwi. We'd let them talk about Johan, catch up with each other, and then we'd join when we were needed.

We went into Tilda's room, which was bright and purple, with flowery walls. The bed had a sheer, white canopy. It was girly and cute and fit Tilda perfectly. She was what most people would consider a girly girl; she liked make-up and fashion, she loved dancing, and she was slender, but short like me.

"So," she said. "This is weird."

I snorted. "Weird doesn't begin to cover it."

Tilda mulled this over. "I think there's a lot more to this story than what I've been told," she said, raising an eyebrow at me.

I sighed, but it was about time she found out what was going on. After all, it might very well affect her too. So I told her. Everything. And she didn't say anything through the whole story, just listened.

When I finished, she said, "Wow. That's insane. And those fairies told you that you need to save the world?"

"Yep. Actually, they told me I need to save this world. Suggesting there are others."

"I don't even have the brainspace to deal with that right now," Tilda said.

I sighed. "You and me both. Apart from that, they didn't say anything really helpful."

Tilda snorted. "Well, of course not. They're fairies – you didn't really expect them to be straightforward, did you?"

I raised my eyebrows. "I didn't expect them to show up in the first place. I mean, come on, fairies?"

"Fair enough. Wow. I can't believe this is our lives. Forget the Kardashians – you could make a tv-show of our lives and it would be far more interesting." She paused. "Okay, anything would be more interesting than that, but still."

I laughed. "Trust you to make jokes in such a hopeless situation."

"It's not hopeless." Tilda grimaced. "It's just... a little bleak."

"Uh-huh." My voice was dry. "Sure. Yeah. Bleak is a good word."

Tilda hit me in the arm. "Shut up! Bleak is a perfectly fine word." Then she grew serious again. "We should be careful, though. I have a feeling this is only the beginning."

If only I'd known then how right she was.

CHAPTER 17
ICY BLUE EYES

Tilda and I went back downstairs a little while later. Both Mom and Eva had tears in their eyes, and I wanted to go over and hug Mom. I resisted the urge – there'd be time later for comfort – and Tilda and I sat down at the table again.

Eva looked at me, Tilda and Mom in turn. "Why don't you tell me what's going on?" The words came out even, but her eyes were still glassy.

I started from the beginning. I told her about the creatures, meeting Erik, and the sorcery. I told her about Melinda approaching me, and meeting the coven. I only left out the fact that I had seen Erik more than once – that I kept seeing him regularly.

When I was finished, I fell silent, waiting for a reaction. This had to be a lot for her to take in. A few days ago, she hadn't even known she had grandkids, and now she had two. It couldn't be easy to learn that your only son had a whole secret family – and that's not even considering all the crazy stuff that was happening.

Silence settled over the table. Eva stared unseeingly at something behind me. I didn't blame her – what the hell was there to say at this point?

Finally, she said, her voice a little faint, "Well, that is certainly a lot.

I don't... I'm not sure what I can do to help, but I'll see if I can find out what's going on. I'll... yeah, I'll see what I can do."

She left shortly after that. She hadn't said much after my story, hadn't seemed to know what to say, and neither did we. I wasn't sure what to feel about the fact that I had a grandmother I'd never known about. She hadn't been there for the first eighteen years of my life, but then, I could hardly blame her for that. She hadn't even known we existed – hadn't known that our father had a family of his own.

Why hadn't he told her? From what I'd seen, my grandmother had loved him, and the wistfulness in her voice made it clear she still missed him. Was there something more to their relationship that she wasn't telling us? A reason why our father hadn't wanted to introduce us to her? Or was there another reason why he kept us secret? More important, could we trust her?

There were too many questions and no answers.

The next day, I met up with Noah at Almedalen. As convenient as my meadow was, he said, it existed in a sort of vacuum, and it would be easier to practise my power over the elements in the real world. Or so he thought. I figured he'd know more about it than me, so I took my bike and went into the stormy weather outside.

The ride to Almedalen took twice as long because the wind beat at my face. The wind cut right through my warm jacket and straight into my bones, making me shiver and question my sanity. And since Almedalen was down by the harbour, the wind was even worse when

I got there.

At least it wasn't raining.

We'd decided it would be safer to practise after dark, to hopefully avoid anyone seeing us use magic, and by the time I got there, only a few lamp posts around the park lit the place. Perfect for a clandestine meeting.

To the left, the playground hid in the shadows, and in the middle, the pond glittered in the night. We'd always feed the ducks who lives there when we went there as kids. Around the pond, walkways slithered in between grassy hills and bushes and trees. If it had been summer, there would be colour everywhere, pink cherry blossoms and blue flowers and vibrant, green grass. This time of year, not a soul disturbed the quiet evening.

Between the playground and the pond stood a willow, and that's where we went. It didn't offer much cover, not as much as it would've in the middle of summer, but it was something, and Noah promised he would make sure no one saw us.

"Right," Noah started. "Let's do this before we both turn into icicles. First, I want you to find your magic again."

I closed my eyes and shifted my focus inward, to my lower belly. I looked for that small tingling sensation, but a hard wind bit at my cheeks and I shivered. I burrowed deeper into my coat and tried to focus again.

There! My magic, a small tingling in my lower belly, lying there, waiting to be used.

"Found it?" When I nodded, Noah continued, "Now I want you to bring it to the surface. You don't need to try and do something specific, just guide your magic to the surface somehow."

I opened my mouth to tell him I'd already done that, then shut it. Instead, I focused back on my magic, imagined the little string, and I grabbed it with invisible hands and tugged, *hard.*

The tingling spread and spread, until I tingled all over, like I'd had a tiny electrical shock. I gasped and my eyes flew open.

Noah gaped. I think I did, too. For a moment, there seemed to be water everywhere, floating in the air around us. Then it splashed back into the pond. The ducks squawked and fled, and I shrieked as the water drenched me.

"Oh my God," I murmured. "Was that *me?*"

Noah stared wide-eyed and slack-jawed at the pond. "How the hell did you do *that?*"

I started giggling. I couldn't help it. Noah's face, combined with my shock at my own powers, combined with the waterworks we had witnessed proved to be too much, and I broke down in a fit of giggles. Noah watched me for a moment, then he started laughing too, and for the longest time, we laughed at the absurdity of the situation.

"So, did I do it right?" I asked once we finally calmed down.

Noah huffed. "I'll say. Though next time, you might want to try something a little more discreet. Emptying Almedalen of water seems a little extreme."

I clamped my lips shut against another wave of laughter. "I wasn't even trying to do anything," I explained, shivering. Now that we'd regained our senses, a freezing gust of wind reminded me that it was the end of November, there was a storm raging, and disgusting water from the pond drenched me. The greenish-tinted water smelled like something had died in it. "I just tried to tug at my magic, and then, well, that happened."

"Yeah. That happened." Noah looked at me, and his eyes glittered. "I'm going to go out on a limb here and say that you are an extraordinarily powerful sorceress."

I didn't know what to say to that, so I looked away.

Neither of us said anything for a while, until Noah finally suggested we end the lesson there and try and find some warmth, which sounded like a splendid idea to me.

Mom had the Sunday off work, so when I got back from my lesson with Noah, she, Tilda and I spent the day together. We took a long walk in the forest with Kiwi, made dinner together and played Monopoly. That night, Eva called with some news.

Mom put her on speakerphone, letting Tilda and me hear what she told us.

"I found someone who met Johan," she started. "Just a few days before he disappeared. A skogsrå who talked to him."

"Hold on a minute." Skepticism coloured Tilda's voice.. "What's a skogsrå?"

"Skogsrå is a creature in Scandinavian folklore who takes care of the forest and everything that lives in it," Eva explained. "She's a sort of nature spirit, meant to protect the forest from those who might wish to harm it. In recent times, that is often humans cutting it down. They are rare now, too much of their homes have been cut down, but they still exist in certain places where the forest is thick and big enough. Gotland has a few forests that are big enough for a skogsrå."

"And Dad went to see one?" I asked, then paused as two sets of wide eyes looked at me. I'd never called him Dad before – I always said 'my father' as a way of keeping a distance, but now that I knew he hadn't left because he didn't want us, I was done with that. I might not have gotten much time with him, but clearly he had loved us.

"Yes," Eva said after a long minute. "He did. I found her, and convinced her to talk to me, and she told me that he came to see her to ask for a favour. He wanted her to bind your powers. Both of your powers, until the time came when you needed them. But only your elemental magic. Your creative powers were left alone."

Tilda and I looked at each other. That explained why we'd both been able to use our creative powers since we were kids, but my elemental powers had only started appearing now. Question was, why hadn't Tilda's powers surfaced yet? Would they also appear in a few years, when she was older?

"Okay, so she bound our powers?" Tilda asked. Eva confirmed. "But why? Why did he want our powers bound?"

"She wouldn't tell me that." Eva's voice rose in frustration. "She only said that he wanted to protect you from something. But she wanted to meet you."

Tilda pouted. Like a little child. "Well, that's super helpful." I huffed out a short laugh, and she continued. "Are all magical creatures this helpful?"

She had a good point.

I remembered something. "I have another question. These creatures that seem to follow me around, are they actual mythological creatures or are they created?"

Eva mulled this over. "Either is possible. But it seems highly coincidental that they have only started appearing now."

"How can you know that the skogsrå wasn't created, then?" Tilda asked.

"Because," Mom jumped in, "creating animal-like creatures is one thing. Even a myling is simple enough, as they aren't really sentient beings anyway. But creating a human-like skogsrå, able to talk and think, that's a completely different thing. Creating people is simply not done."

Creating mythological creatures seemed like something that was not done to me, and yet this person had clearly done that, but I kept my mouth shut. I knew she was right. Creating an animal was hard enough – the only reason why Kiwi had turned out so well was that I had studied Shih Tzu puppies in detail, and even then, it was probably a big heaping of luck, too. Not to mention she was a bit different from the race standards – she was a bit bigger, her snout a little too long, her fur a little too soft. The biggest tell that she was different, though, was her eyes; bright, almost icy blue with a dark blue ring in the middle. Anyone who looked closely at her eyes would realise they weren't natural.

Creating a person ought to be next to impossible, considering that.

"Exactly," Eva agreed. "There are no official rules that govern creators and sorcerers, although some local covens may have some rules, but there is an understanding that people are not created. It would be wrong in so many ways, I can't even count them."

"Right," I said. "But if we agree that these creatures were most likely created, then the question is, who is creating them?"

"I don't like it," Eva said. "You need to be careful, both of you."

It looked more and more like careful might not be enough.

The next day, Mom dropped me and Tilda off at Högklint after school – the nature reserve just outside the city where Eva said the skogsrå lived. She didn't like leaving us there, but according to Eva, it would only talk to me and Tilda.

Högklint took my breath away every time. You could see all of Visby from the cliff. You could also see the prettiest sunsets from there, and surrounding the cliff sprawled a lush forest. I'd never really been in the forest before, though we'd visited Högklint several times before with Mom.

Tilda and I started walking into the forest. We kept close to each other, hoping it would discourage creatures from attacking us – or, rather, discourage whoever controlled the creatures. Maybe it was naïve to hope – after all, Erik and I had been together when the lindworm had attacked – but it felt comforting to stick close to each other. We didn't talk at all, just listened to the sound of the trees rustling in the wind and our footsteps crunching the leaves.

I took a deep breath, trying to calm my nerves, and breathed in the fresh scent of pines. Conifer made up the entirety of the forest – mostly pines, but a few firs and junipers, as well.

I breathed in the moist air, and I knew it wouldn't be long before it started to rain.

After a few minutes, two small creatures appeared right in front of us, waving their hands. We had to halt to keep from stumbling right over them. They looked almost like tiny people – they didn't even reach my knees – except they had greenish grey skin, and their eyes were so huge they seemed to take up most of their faces. They were wearing something that looked like a brown sack, but they were so small I couldn't quite tell. They said something, but their voices were too squeaky to make it out, and they kept waving at us.

"Um, do you want us to follow you?" I asked.

They both nodded and started walking. For such small creatures, they moved fast, and we had to hurry to keep up.

The sound of soft footsteps on leaves made us both freeze. I looked around, trying to find the source, and saw a young woman walking through the trees. She wore a soft green dress that flowed around her, and her light, almost white hair looked tangled as it fell almost down to her waist. She wore nothing on her feet, and she wore only a thin, short-sleeved dress. I shivered just by looking at her. It was almost below freezing, and windy. How she could wear so little and look like the wind didn't bother her in the least was beyond me.

She stopped a few metres away from us and smiled, a small, secret smile. Her beauty stole my breath. Something about her felt soft and sweet, and I couldn't help but trust her right away.

"Hello, Lia, Tilda." The words came out soft but clear. "It's been a long time since I last saw you."

"Who are you?" Tilda asked loudly, and I winced.

That small, secret smile didn't waver. "My name is Ivy. I take care of this forest and everything in it."

I found that a little funny, considering the official plant of Gotland was, in fact, ivy.

"What were those little creatures?" I asked curiously. "Trolls?"

Ivy laughed. "No, though they are somewhat similar to trolls.

They're called di sma undar jordi in Gutnish – de små under jorden. They're a kind of goblin that lives only on Gotland. They used to live on farms, and some of them still do, but many of them have moved to forests because of the things humans put in the soil. The fertilizers make it impossible for them to live on farms anymore. Nowadays, many of them live in forests where there's a skogsrå, since we take care of the earth in a way humans don't anymore."

Di sma undar jordi. The small ones underground. That was kind of cute.

"Are they created?" Tilda asked.

A look crossed Ivy's face, but it disappeared before I could figure it out. "No," she said firmly. "None of the creatures in this forest were created. Those abominations are not welcome in my forest."

I frowned. "Abominations?"

"Yes," Ivy said, voice hard. "Those things are not natural. Living beings are not meant to be created. It is wrong and unnatural. Mindless things. One cannot create a mind, conscience, what you humans would call a soul."

Oops. Let's not tell her about Kiwi.

She continued, shaking her head. "And using these creatures for violence... We were all meant to live in peace with each other and nature."

"Do you know who is creating them?" I asked, forcing my mind away from Kiwi before it developed into a full-scale panic attack. *Kiwi's okay. Somehow, she does have a mind of her own. Maybe I just have strong creative magic or something.*

Ivy shook her head again. "I wish I did. But that's not why I asked you two to come here."

I frowned. "It's not?"

She smiled again. "No, although it is connected."

"Okay," Tilda said, drawing the word out. "Then what are we here for?"

"The one who is creating these creatures, they're upsetting the balance in nature. I can feel the earth shifting more and more every day, and soon it'll be irreversible. It needs to be stopped."

Tilda planted her hands on her hips. "Let me guess; you want us to stop it?"

Ivy didn't rise to the challenge in her voice. "Yes. You need to stop whoever is creating these creatures before the change becomes irreversible and Ragnarök is upon us."

Ragnarök? I didn't know much about Ragnarök, but I did know it was basically the end of the world in Norse mythology. *I'll have to research that later.*

"Can't anyone else do it?" I asked. "We don't even know what to do. Surely there must be someone else."

"No," Ivy said. "You were chosen by the gods when you were born with the ability to create – and the ability to control the elements. A prophecy was told that two sisters, born of both worlds, would be our saving grace – or the end of the world as we know it."

Tilda pursed her lips. "Well, if we're meant to somehow save the world, it would be helpful if I could access my magic. *All* of it."

Ivy froze. For a long time, she didn't seem to move at all, not even to breathe. "Your magic hasn't unlocked?" I barely heard the whispered words over the howling wind.

"Mine has," I said, remembering the freaky afternoon in my meadow, when I'd unwittingly started a storm and scared the crap out of myself. The first time Erik had been there. "But not Tilda's."

"Can you unlock it?" Tilda asked.

"No," Ivy said, and for the first time, she looked worried. "My spell was clear and strong. The only thing that can unlock your magic is your needing it. Until you really need it, it will be kept locked within you."

"But I do need it!" Tilda exclaimed. "You basically said so."

Ivy shook her head. "No. If it hasn't unlocked yet, you don't need it yet."

I jumped in. "Okay, but what exactly are we meant to do to stop the end of the world?"

"I don't know," Ivy said. "But I think stopping the person who is doing all this would be a good start."

"So all we need to do is stop someone from ending the world? Someone we don't know, who is sending creatures after me to kill me? Sure, sounds simple enough."

"That is all I can say," Ivy said. "Now, di sma will help you find your way back."

Tilda opened her mouth to say something, probably to tell her how very unhelpful she'd been, but Ivy was gone.

"That was frustratingly unhelpful," Tilda said when we got back home. Mom had to go to work for an emergency, so we were alone for the rest of the evening.

"Yeah," I agreed. "We still have no idea what to do about any of this."

"So, what do we do? I have to say, it's kind of tempting to just ignore the problem and let them fix it on their own."

I raised my eyebrows at her. "Yeah, like we're actually going to do that."

She smiled angelically. I wasn't fooled for a second. "I didn't say we should do that. Just that it's tempting."

I snorted, then bit my lip. "I think we need to meet with the coven again. Maybe they really don't know anything, but at this point I'm willing to try anything. We should probably see what we can find out about Ragnarök, too."

Tilda nodded. "Let's start there."

I went upstairs to grab my laptop, then we sat in the living room to research the hell out of Ragnarök, me with a cup of tea, Tilda with a hot chocolate – yes, with marshmallows. Kiwi stretched out next to me, belly up, and I scratched it absentmindedly.

What if Ivy is right – what if it's impossible to create a functioning mind? The thought snuck uninvited into my head, and I pushed it away. Kiwi had been fine for almost a full decade. Surely we would've noticed already if something wasn't right.

Wouldn't we?

Don't think about that. I forced myself to focus on the webpage in front of me.

"Ragnarök," I read out loud. "The word comes from Old Norse and means Fate of the Gods. In Norse mythology, it is the end of the cosmos, and everything in it, including the gods themselves. It will start with the Fimbulwinter, a winter that will last for three winters and will plunge the world into never before seen cold, as the warmth of the sun will fail. The wolves Skoll and Hati will at last catch their prey, the sun and the moon, and the stars will disappear." I paused and let my eyes roam over the page. "Okay, so this is basically a prophecy of everything that will happen once the Fimbulwinter starts. The tree

Yggdrasil will tremble, bad beings will be released from their prisons, gods will die. At the end of it all, the world will sink underneath the water... Oh, but a few gods will make it and a new, beautiful world will rise." I paused, remembering what the fairies had told me earlier. "The end of the world as we know it... Not the end of the world, but the end of the world as we know it, and the start of a new one. Well, it could be worse. It could be the actual end of all time."

We let that sink in for a moment. "Okay," Tilda finally started. "Provided we believe in – I can't believe I'm even saying this – the ancient Norse gods, that means they will all die if Ragnarök happens."

"Wouldn't that make them invested in making sure it doesn't happen?" If all this was true, and the gods would die, then why on earth would they leave their fate, and the fate of all of mankind, up to two teenagers? It made no sense. Unless the gods were all suicidal, but I doubted that.

Tilda groaned. "My brain hurts. And all of this doesn't help us at all. We still don't know how to stop it."

Dread settled in my stomach like lead. "Well, according to this site, it can't be stopped. This is all a prophecy – it tells us what's going to happen, not what might happen. It's not a question of if the world will end, it's a question of when."

CHAPTER 18
DEAD AND MISSING

"Have you seen the news?" Clara asked as I picked up the phone, blinking sleep from my eyes. Her voice shook.

"No," I said, dragging the word out. "Why?"

Clara sniffled, and just like that, I was wide awake. "They found him. Axel... they found him."

My first thought was to ask why she was crying – that was good news, right? It'd been almost two weeks since his disappearance, so him being found was good. Then it started sinking in. "He's...?" I couldn't finish the question. My stomach clenched and I swallowed hard.

"They found him dead up at Högklint," Clara said after a long moment.

My heart skipped a beat. "Högklint? That's where Tilda and I met Ivy yesterday." After we got home the day before, I'd called Clara and Noah to tell them what we'd found out.

Clara didn't say anything for such a long time that I thought she might've hung up. Only excited chattering outside of my window interrupted the silence. It made me want to open the window and shout at the people there. How could they be excited when something so horrible had happened? "This thing is really bad, isn't it?"

I hadn't understood the seriousness of the situation until then. I mean, the end of the world obviously sounded serious, but it was all abstract up until that point. But one of the kids at my school turning up dead? That was anything but abstract. That made everything feel very much real.

"Yeah," I said when I realised Clara was waiting for me to say something. "Yeah, it's bad."

I met Clara outside of school an hour later. The sun shone for the first time in what felt like a year, and sweat covered my forehead when I got to school. It was so wrong – a teenager had just been found dead. The weather should reflect that. It shouldn't be bright and sunny and happy.

It was about an hour before we needed to be there, but neither of us wanted to be alone at home right then. After Clara and I hung up, I called Noah, and he was meeting us at the library, where we could all sit in one of the study rooms and have some privacy.

"I can't believe it," Clara said as we walked towards the library. "Who would want to kill a seventeen-year-old kid?"

That was the question that I kept coming back to. And I had no answers. Murders did happen on Gotland. No one could argue that after someone was murdered in the middle of the city, in the middle of one of the busiest weeks on Gotland. The strange timing tickled at me, but it wasn't outside the realm of possible.

But the fact that he'd been found on Högklint the day after Tilda and I were there looking for answers was a very big coincidence if it wasn't all connected.

I groaned, too many thoughts and too many questions crowding inside my head. We desperately needed some answers, but no one seemed willing to give them to us.

And seriously, Tilda and I were just two teenagers. Sure, we had magic, but we were still kids. Did no one understand the stupidity in leaving the fate of the entire world up to a couple of kids?

My heart started beating fast, and I had to blink away tears. Clara stopped walking abruptly and grabbed my hand, pulling me into a restroom just as I broke down into hyperventilating sobs.

Clara locked the door behind us and then she didn't say anything, knowing exactly what I needed.

My chest rose and fell rapidly with my shallow breaths, and tears streamed down my face. I held my breath to keep a sob from escaping, but it was no use.

I focused on following the contour of one of the tiles with my eyes, breathing in time with the movement. It took a few minutes for me to calm my breathing, but when I did, I grabbed some paper towels to dry off my tears.

"You know you don't have to do this on your own, right?" Clara said. "I know things seem hopeless right now. But whatever the hell is going on, you don't have to do it alone."

I nodded, blinking away some more tears. "Thank you," I said and hugged her tightly.

I took a few more moments to gather myself, then we went to find Noah at the library. He sat in one of the study rooms, much to my relief. He didn't comment on my swollen face, for which I was grateful. Talking about it would've likely sent me into another panic attack.

"We need to come up with a plan," Noah said. "I don't know whether the murder is connected or not, but either way, we need to figure out what's going on and, more importantly, what we're going to do. If this is the start of the end of the world, we need to do something, and fast."

His determined tone made me feel a little better. A proper plan of action would make me feel even better.

"Right," I said. "Any ideas?"

"Not quite, but I do have some musings." Noah closed the book he was reading, and I saw the title. *Norse Gods* by Johan Egerkrans. Of course. Because that's what our lives had come to. "So far, we've been dealing mostly with creatures from Scandinavian folklore, so I figured Norse mythology might be a good place to start researching. You've heard of Ragnarök, right?"

"Right," Clara said. "It's basically the end of the world according to the Vikings, right?"

Noah nodded. "Yes. From what I read, there are some different accounts, but basically, the gods will fight the trickster god Loke, the giant wolf Fenrir, and the fire-giants, and lose. The world will end, although some sources claim that some gods will survive, along with a man and a woman, and they'll repopulate the earth."

"Right." I dragged the word out. "Tilda and I read about this the other day, after we met with Ivy. But the gods don't exist. Or, if they do, they haven't been heard from in hundreds of years. How does this help us?"

"I think maybe someone is trying to lure the gods out and then start

Ragnarök."

I was about to start screaming in frustration. "Okay. How does one start Ragnarök?"

Noah grimaced. "Well, that, I couldn't find. All I can find is that it'll start when the spinners of fate decide."

My head started to pound. "So how exactly does this help us?"

"I don't know, exactly," Noah said. "Maybe it doesn't help at all. But at least we know, if we're right, things are about to get a lot worse, if someone is trying to convince the gods Ragnarök is a necessity."

"Yeah, I'd think they wouldn't be too keen to have Ragnarök start, since they're all meant to die," Clara said.

"Okay, so how do we find this person?" I asked. "Tilda and I are going to try and visit with this coven again, see if they might know anything at all. Do you have any other ideas on what to do?"

Clara shook her head. "No, but I think Erik definitely has something to do with it. Are we sure he's not the one doing it?"

My stomach clenched. I really wanted it to be someone else, but all evidence – which, admittedly, wasn't a lot and mostly circumstantial – pointed towards him. Erik had somehow broken into my safe space, he'd been there when the lindworm showed up, and he kept showing up everywhere.

"I don't know," I said finally. "He does seem suspect. But even if it is him, what do I do about it? Just ask him about it outright?"

Clara and Noah both shook their heads.

"Too dangerous," Noah said. "He might hurt you if he thinks you suspect him. Just keep avoiding him, okay?"

I nodded, hoping they couldn't tell how conflicted I was about it. They were right; the timing of Erik's sudden appearance was suspicious at best, and trusting him could prove to be a big mistake. But then there was the fact that he'd been there when the lindworm showed up. He wouldn't make it attack himself, would he? Or did he do it to cast suspicion off himself?

I didn't want to believe he could be the one behind everything. Despite my better intentions, I'd started caring about him. And I felt so much grief when I thought of everything he'd been through. Was my compassion for him clouding my judgement, keeping me from seeing his true colours?

I had no answers, and smart or not, I knew with absolute certainty that I would see him again, and I still hadn't told my friends about him.

Noah spoke up. "I want to look up skogsrå, see what I can find about it. I'd feel better if I knew exactly what Ivy is, if we're going off her word and nothing else."

I nodded and opened my laptop. When it started, I opened Google and typed 'skogsrå' into the search engine. I clicked on the first result and read out loud, "The skogsrå is in charge of protecting the forest. Skogsrå is always a beautiful female, but dangerous, too, especially for men. She is known for getting men lost in the forest and taking them for herself, from where they'll never return. And if they do, their soul will stay with her, they'll become introverted and quiet, and they'll always long to go back to the forest and her." My heart skipped a beat and I looked up and met Clara's wide eyes.

"Do you think..." Her breath caught. "Axel?"

My breath froze in my lungs. "I don't know," I whispered. Could Ivy be responsible for Axel going missing?

"Let's not go there yet." The firm words reassured me, some of the tension leaving my shoulders. "We don't even know if his disappearance is connected to everything that's going on."

He was right, of course. Still, the thought didn't quite want to let go of the grip it had on my insides.

Clara chewed on her fingernail. "What else does it say?"

I looked back to the screen. "Apparently she's a beautiful woman from the front, but her back is hollow and bark-like, like a tree. So if you want to expose her, just look at her back."

"Is there any way to ward her off?" Noah asked.

"Hmm." My eyes tracked over the screen. "Well, if you want to avoid being taken by her, you can turn your shirt inside out. And she can be killed with a silver bullet – okay, really? Is she a werewolf?"

Noah snorted. "Well, the silver bullets thing is totally unhelpful, but just to be safe, we should turn our shirts inside out if we go into the forest, just until we know what we're dealing with here."

I agreed and then threw a look at the clock in the corner of my screen and jumped up. "Okay, that's a start. Clara, we really need to go or we'll be late."

We hurried to get our books and get to class. As we waited outside the classroom with the rest of our class, no one spoke, seemingly deep in thought. I think we were all pretty shaken up about the guy who had died. Some of my classmates might have even known him. On the small island – and at our small school – it often seemed like everybody knew everybody.

Our teacher, Sandra, showed up and let us in. She didn't smile at us like she usually did, just hurried to the desk to put down her things. Then she sat in the chair behind the desk, something else she didn't usually do, not at the start of a lesson.

We all sat down in silence. Clara and I shared a look.

"Most of you have probably heard by now what happened with one of our students last night," Sandra said solemnly. "I know some of you might have known him. Even if you didn't, this is difficult for all of us. We understand if some of you might not feel up to being at school today, and it's okay if you feel you need to go home. Our school counsellors and the school psychologist will be here all day if you feel like you need to talk to someone, and of course you can talk to any of your teachers, too." She paused, and no one said a word for a moment. "It is important that we all have empathy and respect for one another today. Everyone deals with crises in different ways, and we need to respect that. I expect all of you to take care of each other today."

Everyone nodded.

"Good," Sandra said. "I figure no one will be able to focus on the essay writing today, and I know this is your first class of the day and you all must have a lot of questions. I'll answer as best I can."

A girl to my right put her hand in the air. Sandra gave her a nod, and she asked, "Do you know how it happened? How he was killed?"

I flinched.

Sandra's lips tightened. "No. The police haven't told the public yet."

Another hand in the air, this time a guy from the back. "Do they have any suspects yet?"

"Not that I know of," Sandra answered. "The police haven't told the public much. All I really know is that he was found on Högklint last night and that the police are investigating it as a murder."

"So they know he was killed? It wasn't an accident?"

"No, it seems like it was a murder."

A third hand rose, and Alva asked, quietly, "Is it true that someone else has gone missing?"

You could hear a pin drop in the deafening silence that descended upon the room. It was clear this wasn't something the rest of the class had been aware of.

Sandra's eyes looked shiny. "Linus hasn't been seen since yesterday morning."

CHAPTER 19
CHOSEN BY THE GODS

The rest of the day went by in a kind of blur. I was grateful Mom worked the evening shift, or she definitely would've gotten worried over my state of mind. When I got home from school, I immediately got out the ingredients to make mint chocolate chip cookies, desperate for a distraction. Kiwi sat down next to the counter and stared up, waiting for crumbs to fall down for her to eat.

I chopped up a bar of mint chocolate, then put it aside to wait. I measured up all the ingredients, whipped up the butter and sugar, and added the dry ingredients. When I started to mix together the last of it, though, my mind drifted.

One boy dead, another missing. It didn't escape my notice that they had both been boys – the preferred prey of the skogsrå. Could it be Ivy? I'd felt like we could trust her, but we didn't really know her. What we did know was that the skogsrå liked taking men, though according to myth they almost never resurfaced. Axel had turned up dead. Did that mean it wasn't a skogsrå? After all, humans could be just as horrifying as mythological creatures, if not worse. It wasn't out of the realm of possibility for a human to kidnap and kill teenagers.

I separated the cookie dough into smaller pieces and rolled them into balls. Making sure to keep them apart to give them space to grow in the oven, I placed them on a baking sheet.

Thinking about this wasn't giving me any answers. It only served to give me an ulcer, so I pushed the thoughts away and focused on what to do next.

I put the cookies into the oven, determination filling me. Picking up my phone, I found Melinda's contact and called.

She picked up after only two rings. "This is Melinda."

"Hi, Melinda. It's Lia. Listen, I was wondering if I could maybe come to your next meeting with the coven?"

Silence. Then, "Of course. We meet on Thursdays, in Stenkyrka. Right near the Virgin – you know where it is?"

I paused, my hand on the doorknob. *Thursday? That means cancelling on Clara.* My heart squeezed with guilt, but could I really miss this opportunity to maybe – hopefully – get some answers?

I must've been quiet for too long, because Melinda's voice sounded through the phone. "Is there a problem?"

I shook my head, then remembered I was on the phone, and she couldn't actually see me. "No, no problem." *Clara will understand.* Somehow, that thought only made me feel worse. I didn't deserve such a good friend as Clara. "What time do you meet?"

There was the sound of rustling on the other end of the phone. "We meet at six, and the meetings usually last for around two hours. You can leave whenever you want, though – you don't have to stay for the entire meeting."

"Sounds good," I said. "I'll see you tomorrow, then."

The thought of cancelling on Clara made tears prick at my eyes, but we had a deadline now, if we wanted to avoid any more murders. I was apparently destined to save the world, chosen by the gods I didn't even believe in. I would have to change my priorities, as much as the idea of cancelling hurt. If we waited another week, there was a chance there would be another dead teenager.

Tilda and I made dinner and ate in silence. She'd heard on the news about what had happened, and neither of us really knew what to say. While we were cleaning up, my phone rang.

"What are your plans tomorrow after school?" Noah asked.

I opened my mouth to tell him coffee and movie with Clara, and remembered I'd have to change those plans. My heart clenched and I paused with my plate halfway into the dishwasher.

"I'm going to meet the coven again," I said finally.

Glass clinked as Tilda put hers down forcefully above my head. I looked up to find her glaring at me.

"Not alone, you're not." Noah's firm voice brooked no room for argument. "I'm going with you."

My heart squeezed. "I should go alone. It might not be safe." *I am not putting my friends in danger.*

Tilda narrowed her eyes at me from the other side of the dishwasher, where she was now putting the glasses in. "No way you are going alone. I'm coming. You might as well let Noah come, too. The more the merrier, right?"

I sighed. "I'll be going to the forest at night. The way things are going, I wouldn't be surprised if I'm ambushed by creatures. I don't want to put either of you in danger."

Tilda frowned. "I'm already in danger. Or did you forget that the both of us are meant to save the world? Not you alone. You can't do this alone, Lia. And honestly, I think we need any help we can get."

I chewed my cheek for a minute. The last thing I wanted was to put my friends, my little sister, in danger. But I knew better than to argue with Tilda once she set her mind on something. I'd never met anyone more stubborn than her. And Noah was the only one of us who could control his sorcery. Tilda didn't even have access to all her powers, only her creative powers, and I was about as skilled at controlling it as a ten-year-old.

"Fine. But you," I directed this at Noah, "get to explain to Clara that she cannot go."

Noah's tone was amused. "I can do that."

We made plans to meet up right after school the next day, before we'd take the bus to Stenkyrka, and then we hung up, which left me with the task of explaining to Clara that I wouldn't be able to make it to the café the following day.

Tilda and I finished loading the dishwasher, and I walked up the stairs to my bedroom, my stomach cramping painfully. The last thing I wanted to do was cancel on Clara, but could I really pick coffee with my friend over figuring out who murdered a guy at my school?

Without thinking too much about it, I picked up my notebook and opened the portal to my meadow, needing the comfort of my safe space. I stepped through the blue swirls and sank into the grass.

I buried my hands in the grass and dug my fingers into the dirt, grounding myself in the moment. My hair blew in the wind, but I barely noticed the anomaly through the inner turmoil I felt. I shook, no, the world shook, and then I felt a pair of strong arms around me, pulling me into them. I started struggling, but relaxed when I heard Erik's voice.

"Breathe, Lia."

I gasped in a breath that ended in a sob.

"Breathe with me," Erik said. "In." He took a deep breath and held it for a few seconds. "Out." He slowly let it out. I took a shallow breath and held it, counting to three like I'd learned. Then I let it out.

After several minutes of breathing like that, my heartrate slowed down and the shaking stopped. Erik carefully let go of me to look at my face. "Are you okay?"

I started nodding but stopped as my eyes caught on something. I let out a sound that couldn't be human. "What happened to the trees?" My voice rose high and thin.

Erik didn't even turn around to look. "The price of magic."

I blinked. "What magic? I didn't use any magic!"

His eyes narrowed. "Didn't use any magic? Lia, the whole place was shaking when I got here. You created an earthquake. When you use sorcery, you pull your magic from the surrounding environment."

My stomach clenched as I stared at the dead trees. I'd done that. I'd destroyed those trees, like I'd destroyed part of the forest when I created my meadow. I'd sucked the life out of them, leaving them nothing but husks. How was I any better than the big companies who chopped down rainforests and destroyed the environment?

I shivered. *Maybe the world would be better off if humanity was eradicated.*

I shook my head, dispelling the thought. No. I needed to get better at controlling my magic. And humans weren't perfect, but that didn't mean every single person on the planet deserved to die.

Oh, the irony, that the person meant to save the world wasn't even sure humanity was worth saving?

Determination filled me, and I looked back at Erik. "I need to practise."

He shook his head. "Not today. You're clearly upset about something, and you used a ton of magic starting that earthquake. We can practise tomorrow."

I started nodding, then shook my head. "No, tomorrow doesn't work. We're going to Stenkyrka to talk to this coven, see if they know anything about what's been happening lately."

A worried look flashed across his face, but I blinked and it was gone. "Be careful."

When I woke up Thursday morning, instead of the usual excitement I felt, dread curled in my stomach. Melinda had seemed nice enough when we met, but she had strange timing, and we really had no idea what we'd be walking into.

Clara had been understanding about me cancelling our plans, which only made me feel worse. I really didn't deserve a friend as amazing as her. She'd always been there for me, always understanding and helping, and here I was, cancelling on her. Five years, and we'd never missed a Thursday. The routine always comforted me, and cancelling felt like letting Clara down.

The dread only grew as the day went on, and by the time Tilda,

Noah and I got on the bus, my heart beat hard and my usual breathing exercises did nothing to calm my nerves. I prayed I wouldn't have a panic attack.

Tilda squeezed my hand and offered me a supportive smile, but it only resulted in reminding me that I might be leading my baby sister into danger, which only made my heart beat faster. I tried to take a deep breath, but it got stuck. I curled my fingers into my palm and pressed my nails into it. The biting pain helped me focus on the task at hand, distracting me from the pain I felt inside.

"At least we all have our shirts on inside out," Tilda tried to comfort me. "It'll keep us safe from the skogsrå."

Except skogsrå clearly isn't the only creature out to get us, I thought. I didn't say anything though, not wanting her to worry too much.

The bus ride felt like an eternity and at the same time not long enough. Tilda didn't let go of my hand once, not even when we disembarked in Stenkyrka and started walking. We had to walk for quite a bit to reach the forest where the coven was supposed to be meeting soon, and once we reached the forest, our climb began. The coven met at the cliff, where the Virgin stood.

The sun had set several hours earlier, leaving the forest dark. Clouds covered the sky, not letting even the smallest ray of moonlight through. Thankfully, we'd had the foresight to bring a flashlight, but the tall pines left dark shadows everywhere.

Despite the warm evening air and the trees protecting us from the worst of the wind, I shivered. The air smelled freshly of pine, and an eerie silence settled over the forest. Only the sound of dry leaves crunching underneath our shoes interrupted the quiet.

My mind drifted to the poor virgin who had supposedly fallen to her death at the cliff. Would that be us by the end of the evening?

Tilda squeezed my hand, and this time, I wasn't so sure it was for my benefit. The still darkness of the forest crept up on all of us.

I reached out to grab Noah's hand.

We climbed the mountain for another eternity, until the ground finally evened out. I shivered and my heart raced. We had to be close to the cliff. I could hear the waves crashing and the wind howling.

Tilda swept the flashlight in front of us, and I froze as I thought I saw a shape in the trees. I let go of Noah's hand, pointing. "There!"

Tilda turned the flashlight where I pointed, I saw nothing other than trees. I forced a breath and reached out to find Noah's hand again. When I couldn't, I looked to my left, but he wasn't there.

At this point, my heart beat fast enough that I started seriously worrying about a panic attack.

"Noah?" I called softly, not wanting to alert the coven of our presence. "Are you there?"

Tilda dropped my hand and sneezed. I spun around, not wanting her to disappear, too, but it was already too late.

I was on my own.

Chapter 20
Lost in the Forest

The forest plunged into pitch darkness, the light from Tilda's flashlight gone along with her. I couldn't see so much as a step in front of me.

"Tilda? You there?"

But silence reigned in the forest. Not even the rustle of leaves in the wind or the crunch of shoes on dry leaves disturbed the air.

I shivered and forced myself to breathe, even though I hadn't been able to take a deep breath for hours, then I pulled out my phone from my pocket and turned on the flashlight function. I spun in a slow circle, looking for some sign of Tilda and Noah, but found nothing except trees.

My breath caught, and I swallowed a sob. *They just got lost in the forest*, I tried to tell myself to no avail. *We'll find each other.*

I heard a rustle in the leaves, and I spun around, sweeping my phone around. There. A shadow in the trees.

"Hello? Is anyone there?"

Nothing.

I turned in another circle, my breaths quicker now, and caught sight of a tiny little light to my right. I focused on it, and my heart slowed, and I forgot all about my anxiety. My legs started toward the light before my mind really caught up to what I was doing.

I stumbled through the forest, never once taking my eyes off the little light floating a few metres in front of me. I fell and got up without looking away from the light. My legs ached from exertion, and I breathed heavily, but I barely noticed it.

I looked around, blinking, disoriented. I was out on the cliff, teetering off the edge.

I drew in a sharp breath and stumbled back. *How did I end up here? I was in the middle of the forest only a blink ago.*

I shivered. Out on the cliff, the strong, icy wind gripped me, threatening to send me over the edge.

The leaves behind me rustled, and I spun around. To my surprise, I found my phone still in my hand. I swept it around, looking for the source of the sound.

There. A shadow emerging from the trees. Only, as it stepped out of the forest and onto the cliff, the form didn't solidify. It stayed a tall, dark shadow, somewhat resembling the shape of a person. Two small orbs – the eyes, I assumed – shone bright white in the darkness, and sharp teeth flashed in the light of my flashlight.

"Oh my God," I gasped, stumbling back a step. I tripped on something and fell on my butt, and pain shot up my spine. That would hurt tomorrow.

Provided I lived that long.

The tall shadow moved towards me, and as it got nearer, I saw the outline of long, sharp nails – or claws.

My heart raced and I shook like a leaf in the wind as I tried – and failed – to stand. My knees shook too badly to hold my weight. I fell again, and something caught my attention at the edge of the forest. I tore my gaze away from the approaching shadow and saw a flash of dark hair against stark white, but then the shadow lunged towards me, and the world went dark.

I blinked my eyes open and met a forest green gaze. I drew in a sharp breath and sat up, and Melinda somehow drew back fast enough to avoid being head-butted.

I looked around, surprised to find myself in a brightly lit room. "Where am I?"

"My home." Melinda swept her arm out. "This is my living room."

I realised I lay on a soft couch. The soft beige and dark green shades in the room gave it a soothing atmosphere that I couldn't appreciate. There were plants everywhere, a small table next to the couch and a lamp in one corner that cast the room in a bright light.

"Where are Noah and Tilda?" My voice sharpened with panic.

Melinda gave me a reassuring smile that did nothing to calm my racing heart. "They're here. I found you and your friends on the cliff. Your friends had just found you passed out. I took you all here to make sure you weren't hurt."

I opened my mouth to reply, but a squeak rang out, and then arms swept around me. "You're awake!" My sister sounded breathless.

"Yeah," I squeaked out as she crushed me to her. She was surprisingly strong for such a small girl. "I can't breathe."

Tilda released her death grip but didn't let go completely. She looked freaked out, her eyes wide and lips trembling. "Sorry." She took a deep breath, obviously trying to gather herself. Then she hit my arm. Hard. "You scared me! Don't you ever do that again!"

I rubbed my arm. "Ow!"

She didn't look apologetic in the slightest. "That's what you get for scaring me like that. What happened?"

I shivered as I remembered the creepy shadow. I looked over Tilda's shoulder and met Noah's worried gaze. "I don't know. I... I don't know how I got to the cliff. I was in the forest, where you guys disappeared, and then I was on the cliff. There was this shadow thing there – with sharp teeth and I'm pretty sure it had claws and the eyes were like two white orbs and it was walking towards me, and I stumbled, and then I must've passed out."

Melinda mumbled something too quiet for me to hear. The three of us turned towards her, and I spoke. "What?"

"A gast," she repeated. "It's a type of malevolent spirit – a ghost, if you will. They are the spirits of truly evil people."

A ghost? I'd been attacked by a freaking ghost?

"If mythological creatures must come to life, why couldn't it be a unicorn?" I muttered.

"Or, better yet, a hot fae prince," Tilda added with a grin. "Preferably with an equally hot older brother. Wouldn't that be perfect?"

I laughed, and it released some of the tension in my shoulders. Nevermind that I didn't think I wanted a hot fae prince.

Noah piped up. "The gast – or ghost or whatever – wasn't there when we got there, though. Any idea why an evil spirit would up and disappear?" He directed the question at Melinda.

She shook her head. "Maybe it heard you two coming and left. I don't know. It is odd behaviour for sure." She paused. "Maybe you should tell me what's going on."

I bit my lip. "Well, some really weird things have been going on lately, and we were hoping you might have an idea what it could be."

Melinda frowned slightly. "I don't know, but why don't you tell me what's been happening? I'll see if I can shed some light."

I explained about the creatures that had started appearing every-where I went, and the guys that had gone missing. I told her about meeting Ivy, and what she told us about being chosen by the gods.

Melinda listened quietly, not looking away from me for a second while I explained all that had happened lately. When I finished, she didn't say anything for a moment, absorbing everything I had said.

"Well," she finally said after what felt like an eternity, "all that is definitely suspicious. You have no idea who could be behind all this?"

The three of us shook our heads.

"Actually," Tilda piped up, "there is this one guy who appeared right around the time all this started happening. He ambushed Lia in a meadow where she hangs out sometimes and seemed to know a lot about her. But you haven't met him since, have you?" She looked at me.

I shook my head, and my stomach clenched. "I've been avoiding that place. His appearance was really coincidental."

Melinda's eyes narrowed in thought. "What did this guy look like?"

I shrugged. "Well, he was wearing a mask that covered half his face, and he had dark hair and dark eyes, but he was really pale, too."

Melinda's eyes widened slightly. "I know who he is. I met him around the same time as you must have. I'd never seen him before, but he asked to join our coven, said he'd been abandoned as a kid and had no one else. I felt bad for him, and we created the coven to make sure that no creator or sorcerer would have to feel alone and out of place with no one to turn to, so I let him join. He's a talented creator, for sure."

"Could he create these creatures?" Noah's voice lowered.

Melinda looked serious. "If anyone could, it's him."

My insides clenched, and I had to force myself to not shake my head in denial. Erik was moody, for sure, and he acted strange sometimes, but I'd started trusting him over the last couple of weeks, and almost considered him a sort of friend. And he'd helped me. I didn't want to believe he only did that to use me.

I blinked rapidly, hoping no one would notice the tears that filled my eyes.

"You should keep avoiding him," Melinda told me. "I will see what I can find out, but I'll have to be careful as to not raise his suspicions. Then I can contact you in a few days to let you know what I find." I nodded, and she continued. "Well, it's getting late, and I'm sure you all need to get home."

I looked at my clock and gasped. It had been almost three hours since we'd stepped off the bus. Thank God Mom was working late that night, or she'd be freaking out.

We exchanged phone numbers, and then Melinda followed us to the bus, and we thankfully didn't have to wait long for it to come. None of us said anything as the bus carried us back into Visby, and I didn't relax completely until the streetlights from Visby finally surrounded us again.

As we disembarked, I called Clara, who had agreed to stay home on the condition that we call her as soon as we got home again. She decided to come over and brought one of our favourite comedies, and then the four of us spent the rest of the night huddled on our couch, neither of us willing to talk about the freaky events of the evening.

Clara and Noah stayed over on the couch, too freaked out to brave the night and walk home. We all got ready in silence and Clara hugged me tight before I went upstairs to go to bed. I spent a long time freaking out in the darkness of my bedroom, certain I wouldn't be able to sleep at all that night, when my bedroom door opened and Tilda peeked inside. "Is it okay if I stay in here tonight?"

I whispered yes and moved aside, and she put her pillow on the opposite side of the bed and crawled under the covers. We hadn't slept like that in years, but having the company made me feel a little lighter.

"Why are there breadcrumbs around your bed?" Tilda's voice held a hint of amusement.

"Um... Well, I think I've been visited by this, hm, nightmare monster, and apparently she's very obsessive and compulsive and will have to stay and count every breadcrumb, so it keeps her away."

Tilda snorted. "Wow. Who thinks up all this stuff?"

"No idea. But it helps, and I'm not one to look a gift horse in the mouth."

We were silent for another long moment, long enough that I thought Tilda had fallen asleep. Then, "We're really going to have to fight this... whoever is doing this, aren't we?" Her voice whispered out, but I heard it in the otherwise deathly silent room.

"Yeah," I whispered back as dread curled in my stomach. "Yeah, I think we are."

She didn't ask how we'd manage it, and I was grateful, because I didn't know the answer to that question.

As I started falling asleep, my mind reminded me of something I'd seen right before I'd passed out – the contrast between dark hair and stark white reminded me of how Erik's hair looked against his mask. But what had he been doing in Stenkyrka? And, if it really was him, did he have something to do with the gast?

CHAPTER 21

BURNING

On Friday, after Clara and Noah went home, Tilda and I decided to skip school. I had never missed this much school, but the end of the world put things in perspective. What did it matter if I failed in school if the world ended tomorrow?

This didn't keep me from stressing out, but I shoved that to the back of my mind. We had more important things to worry about.

Mom had already gone to work by the time Tilda and I woke up and had left a note for us: *Had to cover a shift today for a sick colleague, but I'll be home for dinner.*

We made breakfast together and sat in the living room, and I told Tilda what had happened after she and Noah had disappeared. I told her how I'd somehow found myself at the edge of the cliff, how the shadow thing – the gast – had shown up, and how I thought I'd seen Erik right before I passed out.

Once I finished talking, Tilda swallowed. "Okay, first of all, that's too freaking creepy. Evil ghosts? Sign me off. And second, and I hate having to say this, but Erik being there is really suspicious."

I didn't like it either, mostly because I couldn't keep myself from feeling sympathy for him, but I couldn't ignore the fact that the signs pointed to him being behind at least some of the freaky stuff that was going on because I felt bad for him.

I sighed deeply. "I know. What do you think about Melinda?"

Tilda squished her mouth to the side, her usual tell that she was thinking hard about something. "Well, the timing of her appearance if a bit convenient, but she's done nothing but try to help us. I see no reason why we shouldn't trust her. She didn't even hesitate to help you yesterday, and she even offered to try and get us some answers."

I bit the inside of my cheek. "You're right. She hasn't actually done anything suspicious. I'm hesitant to trust anyone right now, but she hasn't given us any reason to distrust her."

We talked a little more, but we were both still tired and shaken from the night before and decided to watch some sitcom to distract ourselves. I had trouble focusing on what was happening in the show, but it comforted me to have it on in the background and spending the entire day with my sister.

My mind kept drifting to the events of the last few weeks, though. We were supposed to save the world, but we had no idea how. If we assumed Erik was the one trying to set Ragnarök in motion then we needed to stop him, but how? We had way too little information to go on, and our only lead had been unwilling to tell us much.

I sighed, and Tilda looked at me, curiosity crossing her face. "I think we need to ask Melinda for help." We couldn't keep waffling over this, especially as time was running out for Linus.

"I agree," Tilda said, "we need to call her. Because we are *not* going back to Stenkyrka. And if you suggest we do, I swear I will tie you up."

"That's not as deterring as you think it is," I said dryly. "I'd rather be tied up than have to deal with this crap. Can you tie me to my bed?"

Tilda snorted. "Fair enough. We'll tie ourselves up and let someone else fix this."

Oh, how I wished we could do that, but that option had flown out the window when someone – please don't let it be Erik – had started killing kids in my school.

I refocused on the task at hand. "We're not going back to Stenkyrka. Honestly, if I never step foot on northern Gotland again, it'll be too soon. We'll just have to wait for Melinda to call, and if she doesn't, we'll call her." I paused. "I also need to confront Erik."

Tilda sat up straight. "Are you out of your mind? That's the last thing you need to do right now. Seriously. You need to avoid him like he's freaking Jack the Ripper reincarnated." I opened my mouth to interject, but she shushed me. "I'm serious, Lia. I know you want to fix all of this by yourself, and keep the rest of us out of it, but if the time comes that we have to confront Erik, we will do it together. Get that into your thick skull."

I blinked, surprised. Tilda rarely lost her temper – she was sarcastic at times, sure, but she didn't freak out like that.

"Promise me, Lia," Tilda said, meeting my eyes and refusing to look away.

I sighed. "Fine. I won't confront him on my own." She narrowed her eyes. "I promise."

Tilda watched me for a long moment, then nodded slightly, dropping it.

We spent the rest of the day watching television, until Noah called after school and asked if he could come over. I told him yes, and he showed up ten minutes later. I opened the door, and he looked me over, his eyes glimmering with humour. "Cute shirt," he said, laughter in his voice.

Right. I still hadn't changed out of my pyjamas, featuring a white, oversized shirt with a sleepy unicorn on it and a pair of pink sleep shorts.

I blushed. "Shut up."

He chuckled. "So," he said as I led him into the living room, "I think it's time we hurry up with your training a little."

I nodded. "Agreed. At this rate, I'll need it sooner rather than later. As cool as writing magic is, it's virtually useless in a fight."

"Do you have time now?"

I blinked, then looked at Tilda. "Are you okay to be home alone for a while?"

"Actually," Noah piped in, "I think it might be a good idea for her to come with us. I know her sorcery hasn't been unlocked yet, but maybe if she sees you training, she might be at least somewhat ready when her powers are unlocked."

Tilda jumped off the couch like a crazed rabbit. Seriously, she practically bounced on her feet. "Give me five minutes to get dressed." She didn't look the least bit embarrassed at being caught in her pyjamas.

We both hurried up the stairs to get changed into something a little warmer, then hurried back downstairs. While we were bundling up, Noah said, "After our last practise, I figured a more, hm, secluded space might be an idea, so I asked my mom if she had any ideas. She offered to drive us, I hope that's okay?"

I snorted. "What, you don't want to explain to a bunch of humans why the water in the pond is suddenly floating in the air? Weird." I pulled on my wool mittens. "It's fine, Almedalen was probably a really bad idea anyway."

Tilda gaped at me. "You practised magic in the middle of Almedalen?"

I shrugged. "It was rainy and dark, and nobody was around. The only really private place I know is my meadow, and the elements work kind of funny there. Not the best place to practise sorcery."

"You thought Almedalen was a good idea?" She looked incredulous. "I don't know if I should laugh or tell mom you almost showed your magic to humans."

"You better not tell mom," I said as threateningly as I could, which wasn't very. I pulled my knitted hat down low enough that it almost hid my eyes, and Noah laughed.

"You sure you don't want to dress more warmly?" he asked sarcastically.

I rolled my eyes. "Shut up. It's cold as a witch's butt today." I had almost frozen my toes and fingers off when I'd taken Kiwi for a walk – a really quick one.

"A witch's butt?" Tilda murmured. "You have a lot of experience with that?"

I punched her arm. "Shut up."

"Snappy comeback."

I punched her in the arm again for good measure.

Noah's mom drove us outside the city, and dropped us off at a large, empty field in the middle of nowhere. There were no houses, no people, no nothing, for several kilometres. Nothing but the semi-frozen field and a copse of trees as far as the eye could see.

And nothing to protect us from the icy wind.

I sighed and shivered. Winter had seemingly appeared overnight, and I wanted to hibernate.

At least no one would accidentally walk by and see us practising magic.

"Sorry I can't stay," Noah's mom said. "But the twins are home with the chicken pox, and Jenny has a work meeting she really can't miss. Just call when you're done, and one of us will pick you up as soon as we can, okay?"

"Alright," Noah said as his mom drove off. "Last time we practised you found a way to use your magic deliberately. Today, I want you to do that, but much, much less. I'd really prefer it if you didn't blow me and Tilda back into the city."

"Right. Any advice on how to do that?"

"What did you do last time?"

I thought back. "Hmm. I imagined my magic as – a thread, of sorts. And then I just tugged."

Noah smiled faintly. "My guess is you tugged hard and all your magic responded. So what I want you to do now is exactly that. Find that thread again, and tug on it, but don't tug as hard this time. A little should be enough. The magic is there, ready to be used. It wants you to use it, so that should be enough."

I closed my eyes and focused on the feeling of my magic again. This time, when I found it, I didn't tug, I just nudged it a little. At first, nothing happened. I nudged again, and the violent wind stopped.

I opened my eyes. Tilda's hair still blew in the wind, but it didn't touch me at all.

She gaped at me and the stillness that surrounded me. "Okay, now I'm jealous. I want my sorcery to be unlocked, too."

I laughed, and my concentration broke. A particularly nasty wind made me sway.

"Much better," Noah said. "Now that you've managed that, you need to learn to pick which element to use. If it comes to it – which I hope it doesn't – some elements are more useful in battle." I thought back to the lindworm I had set on fire. Yes, that seemed useful in a fight. "Being able to pick what element best suits your needs is key."

I started tapping my foot.

"I find the easiest way to do this is to imagine what I want to happen. If I want to start a fire in the fireplace, for example, I imagine the wood burning, and then I gently nudge my magic - very gently, because I don't want to accidentally set the house on fire."

That's what I'd done with the lindworm – I imagined it catching on fire, and it did.

Noah asked me to imagine the hard ground under my feet melting, and I did. I imagined the warm, soft soil under my feet and reached deep down for my magic. Nothing happened. I nudged a little harder, and still nothing happened.

I frowned at Noah, frustrated.

"This is usually the part that takes time to learn," he explained. "I'd be surprised if you succeeded on your first try. Try to imagine the feel of the soil, the scent, the way it looks. Use all your senses."

It took another half hour before I managed to melt the soil – I did, however, manage to accidentally throw Noah several metres with a particularly strong wind and set fire to the few blades of grass that had survived the cold, which Noah doused with water – but I finally managed to melt the soil.

By the time I managed that, we were all freezing, and Noah called his mom to pick us up. The sun had sunk almost halfway through our training session, and I was half convinced my butt would fall off at any moment from the cold. We climbed into the heated car, and relief eased my aching muscles.

"How did it go?" Noah's mom, Nina, asked.

"It went well," Noah told her.

I frowned at him. "It really didn't."

He gave me an encouraging smile. "It did. I told you, the hard part is learning to control the magic and make it do what you want. Honestly, I'm impressed you managed to do it so soon."

Nina met my eyes in the rearview mirror. "This takes years for sorcerers to learn."

I sighed. "Maybe, but most sorcerers learn it when they're ten. I'm almost eighteen."

"You didn't have your magic when you were ten," Noah said. "Considering the circumstances, you're doing remarkably well. Stop being so hard on yourself."

That was easier said than done, but I dropped it and let Nina pull me into a conversation about school. The frustration stayed with me, though, and a terrifying thought snaked its way into my mind.

How can I save the world from Ragnarök if I can't even melt semi-frozen soil?

Darkness surrounded me. An unnatural darkness, thick and pulsing with malice. I shivered, cold to the bone. I'd never felt cold like that before. Even the coldest winter night didn't hold a candle to this cold.

I will never see the sun again. I will never feel warm again.

A voice whispered my name in the dark, and I fumbled around, trying to find them, but there was nothing but cold, empty air around me.

Another whisper, closer this time, and I shouted out. "Hello? Is anyone there?"

No answer.

A flash, and the world was on fire. Sickening heat replaced the bone-deep cold, and blue flames replaced the darkness. The scent of burning flesh reached my nose, and I opened my mouth to scream, but no sound escaped.

I burned, burned, burned.

Chapter 22
Frozen

I woke up in a sweat, my heart beating wildly. For a second, I thought I saw a shadow above me, but I blinked and it disappeared.

I squeezed my eyes shut and shook my head, trying to forget the nightmare that had woken me up. The memory of the darkness and the cold of the room made me shiver, and I pulled the comforter tighter around me.

I reached out to turn on the lamp on my bedside table, and soft light flooded the room, but even the light of the lamp and the warmth of the comforter couldn't erase the memory of the dream.

My eyes caught on the string of breadcrumbs surrounding my bed, and I frowned. Why hadn't they worked this time? They'd always worked before.

I stood and looked around, trying to figure out what had gone wrong this time. It didn't take long before I saw the problem; there, a small hole in the line of breadcrumbs, no bigger than a centimetre, but obviously big enough for the mare to get through.

I quickly fixed the trail and double-checked the rest. No more holes.

It still took a long time for me to calm myself down enough to try and get some sleep, and even then, I left the light on.

The next morning, I woke up bleary-eyed, feeling like I hadn't slept at all. I considered burying my head under my pillow, but I had things I needed to do – a world to save, and I couldn't afford to spend my Saturday in bed, no matter how tempting it was.

Shivering at the memory of the nightmare, I picked out my cosiest knitted sweater with a turtleneck I could burrow into.

When I went downstairs, Tilda already sat in the living room, looking at something on her phone. When she heard me coming down the stairs, she looked up.

"Good morning," I said, and frowned when she didn't say anything. "What's up?"

"They found him," she said, and her voice shook. "The guy who was missing? They found his... body."

My knees folded, and I was thankful I'd reached the couch or I would've ended up on the floor. Kiwi jumped onto the couch and licked my face. "He's dead?"

That meant two dead guys, in only a few weeks. My stomach roiled.

Tilda nodded. "Do you think this is connected to Ragnarök?"

"I don't know," I said helplessly and petted Kiwi's head absent-mindedly. "It feels like a strange coincidence, but then again, things like this happen in the whole world. Just because we don't see a lot of serial killers on Gotland doesn't mean it can't happen here. I don't know."

I focused on Kiwi's furry face. It was easier than feeling everything.

I felt so many things that it all blurred together into a knot in my stomach. "I don't know," I repeated. "And speculating about it isn't really helpful at this point. It doesn't really change anything, does it?"

Tilda sighed. "I guess not."

"We need to do something."

Tilda narrowed her eyes at me. "If you even suggest you confront Erik again, I swear to god I will strangle you in your sleep."

"Do you have any other ideas?"

"Actually, yes. I did some research on Norse mythology – I figure if Ragnarök is real, and all these creatures are real, then why not the rituals and stuff?"

I wanted to protest, but then, two weeks earlier, I would've said the end of the world was nothing more than superstition, at least until us humans destroyed the planet. Why not ancient magic rituals?

"I really hope you're not about to suggest we sacrifice a goat or something," I said wryly.

"No, we need to sacrifice a lamb," Tilda deadpanned.

"That's not even funny right now." I wrinkled my nose.

Tilda laughed. "Sure it is. But no, we are not sacrificing anything. I read about sejd, which was apparently used for divination and stuff. It was some kind of magic that some of the gods could use. Maybe we could try that and see if we can get some answers."

I nodded thoughtfully. "Sure. Except we don't have sejd. We have creative magic. And control of the elements. No divination."

Tilda sighed. "What if we create something that will give us answers?"

"Like what? The creative magic is really limited. What we create has to exist in reality, at least somewhat." We could create a pink phone, for example, if that phone existed in another colour, but we couldn't create a whole new phone, or a magical object that could solve all our problems.

"I don't see you coming up with a better idea."

I sighed. "I don't have a better idea. For now I'm going to practise my newfound magic and hope a great idea hits me like lightning from clear skies."

Tilda grinned. "I'll practise my creative magic, too, since my sorcery is nowhere to be found. I had this idea I want to try, anyway. I figured if it comes down to a fight, I can be prepared with some objects – trinkets and stuff – to give my magic something to destroy. It's not a guarantee it won't pick a forest to destroy, but it's something, right?"

After walking aimlessly for a while, I ended up in Almedalen. The quacking of the ducks disturbed the otherwise quiet park. After making sure no one could see, I closed my eyes and focused on the magic resting in my stomach. I took a deep breath and carefully coaxed it out, picturing what I wanted to happen. I made sure to only let a tiny bit of magic out.

At first, nothing happened, and I pushed my frustration down. I pulled on a little more magic and held my breath.

The ground shook. Not as much as it had in my meadow, but it definitely shook.

A particularly loud quack made me look towards the pond, and I saw a dark shape appear in the water.

As it emerged from the water, I saw a sleek, black horse. As the horse strode towards me, seemingly walking on water, I forgot all about the cold. I took a step forward and reached out a hand, stroking its muzzle. I drew in a surprised breath as I found the hair soft and warm and somehow not at all wet.

How was it not wet if it had just emerged from the water? The thought almost sobered me up, but then the horse pushed its muzzle into my hand and I forgot all about it. I had never seen such a gorgeous horse before. And to think, I'd been scared of horses before! That seemed utterly silly now.

I think I heard someone say my name, but it sounded so very far away, and it didn't matter, anyway. I needed to ride, so I went to the side of the horse, stroking my fingers through its thick fur. It must've bent down for me, because I didn't struggle at all getting on the back. The horse turned toward the water and started walking slowly, and I sifted my fingers through its soft, thick mane.

Before I knew it we were halfway into the pond, and I had water up to my waist, but it didn't feel cold. Another few steps and we were entirely underwater.

That's when the horse changed. The mane grew tangled, the fur lost its shine, and the eyes turned into pure white, lit by a crazy gleam. When it opened its mouth to try and bite me, the teeth were sharp. I wrenched myself away, or I tried to, but the horse caught my jacket with its teeth. I kicked until finally my jacket ripped and I got away from the horse, but I couldn't find the way up, and my lungs were starting to burn.

I started swimming blindly, desperate to get away from the horse, but something grabbed hold of my foot, and no matter how I kicked and kicked, I couldn't get away. Something was pulling me further down into the pond, and the urge to breathe was almost impossible to resist now.

I kicked again, but my attempts were getting weaker and weaker. I couldn't resist dragging in a breath, and water flowed into my mouth and lungs.

Something yanked me away from the horse and away from the water. I broke the surface and gasped for air, but only ended up coughing up water.

Strong arms wrenched me up onto land and then my saviour tugged themselves out of the water just as the horse nipped at their heels. I blinked, trying to focus my vision to see who had saved me, and dark hair and a white face came into focus for a second before my vision darkened.

Next thing I knew, I lay on something soft – a bed – and I couldn't move. I shook and shivered, and then I saw someone standing next to the bed. I blinked to clear my vision, and dark hair and a white mask came into view. A quick glance around showed me a dark room, lit only by the flickering lights of candles. A piano stood in shadow, pushed against one wall, but other than that, the room was mostly empty.

My eyes flicked back to Erik, and panic hit me. Where had he taken me? But before I could say anything, my vision swam, and darkness claimed me.

CHAPTER 23
ERIK'S LAIR

The next time I woke up I felt a little better. I had stopped shaking and shivering, though I still felt cold, but really, that was no different than usual. No light lit the room, and when I checked the time, it said 02:27. I must've been out for hours.

I was also in my own room, my own bed, and turning a light on confirmed that Erik wasn't there. Had I dreamt the whole thing? I mean, I saw – or thought I saw – Erik pull me out of the water. Maybe that had inspired my dreams?

I sat up in bed, careful to keep the comforter tugged to my chin. Apart from a little cold, I felt alright. A little tired, but otherwise alright.

I looked around me, and the familiarity of my room comforted me. The same white desk and matching bookshelf that had been there for years, the closet where the portal to my meadow always appeared, the worn, beige armchair I liked to read in. My bedside table, with the alarm clock and a book carefully placed upon it. The window with my latest created plant, overlooking our little garden and the road. My navy blue comforter, and my knitted light pink blanket placed on top of it.

I relaxed. It must have been a dream, waking up in that strange room with Erik. And it probably hadn't even been him who pulled me out of the water. Why would he have been there? No, it was probably a stranger who walked by and saw me flailing in the pond. And my oxygen-deprived brain had conjured an image of the person who occupied my thoughts so often right before I passed out. Yes, that must be it.

Deciding that I was probably not going to die from hypothermia, I lay back in bed and went back to sleep. And for the first time in weeks, I didn't dream. Maybe the nightmare monster thought I'd had enough of monsters for one evening, or maybe I was too exhausted to dream, but either way, I felt more well-rested when I woke up the next morning than I had in weeks.

I also woke up starving, so I wrapped myself in a fluffy blue blanket and walked downstairs. Tilda sat at the dining table, but she jumped up when she saw me and sprang forward. Her arms wrapped tightly around me, and shock kept me from moving. I breathed in the familiar scent of Tilda's shampoo – fresh apples. Then I unfroze and hugged her back.

"Don't scare me like that again." With her face buried in my shoulder, her voice came out muffled.

I didn't answer, just hugged her tighter. We stood there, quietly hugging each other, for several long minutes, until Tilda sniffled and let go. She hesitated, then grabbed my arm and pulled me to the couch. She forced me to sit down, and I must have still been a little out of it from my near-drowning accident, because I let her without protest.

"Sit. Stay." She tried to sound stern, but her eyes glittered with unshed tears.

I opened my mouth to say something sarcastic, then changed my mind and closed it, and Tilda turned and walked away.

I stayed.

A few minutes later, she came back with a steaming mug and handed it to me. I wrapped my hands around it and enjoyed the heat.

A flash of black mane floating in the water.

I jerked back with a gasp, and boiling hot tea sloshed onto my hands. Tilda sprung forward and took the cup from me and pulled me into the kitchen before I could even reflect on the pain.

Tepid water hit my scalding hands, and I stared at it, trying hard not to think about the freezing water of Almedalen. My heart pounded in my chest and my hands shook under the steady stream.

"Are you okay? Lia?"

I blinked out of the daze and met Tilda's worried gaze. "Yeah," I said, shaking my head to dispel the memories. "I'm good. Sorry."

"Don't apologize." Tilda's eyes were once again shiny.

"I'm okay," I repeated, but I don't think I convinced anyone.

I jerked at the harsh sound of the doorbell.

"Keep your hands under the water," Tilda instructed and went to answer the door. I heard murmuring voices in the hall, but I got lost in the streaming water again and they faded into the background. Then someone exclaimed my name, and I jerked and spun towards the sound just as two arms wrapped around me for the second time that day.

"Oh my God, you scared us," Clara said and her voice shook. "Don't ever scare us like that again!"

I didn't bother telling her Tilda had already demanded the same and hugged her back.

A knot worked its way up my throat until I couldn't breathe, and tears filled my eyes. I gasped for breath, and Clara hugged me tighter.

"Deep breaths," she whispered, and breathed in deeply. "In." She let the breath out. "And out. Come on, breathe with me."

I took a breath that got stuck halfway and sobbed. Clara took another deep breath and I tried again. And again and again, until the tears slowed and my breaths deepened.

Clara pulled away and looked at me. "You okay?"

I nodded, not quite trusting my voice to work.

"We'll figure this out," Clara told me.

I doubted it but didn't say anything.

"Are you ready to join Tilda and Noah? I'm sure he wants a hug, too. And we have some things we need to discuss."

I nodded again, and we joined them in the living room. After another crushing hug, we all sat, and determination filled me.

I looked at Tilda. "I don't understand. How did I get home?"

Her eyes widened. "You don't remember? Erik brought you here. He must've created some kind of doorway, like you do with your meadow, because he appeared all of a sudden with you in his arms. I thought for sure you were dead." Her voice hitched. "He told us this horse creature had... had tried to drown you, and then he left you here."

My hands shook as the realization hit. Had it really been him who'd pulled me out of the water? Did that mean that I'd really woken up with him, too? No, that must have been a dream. Still... "He must be the one who pulled me out of the water." How the hell had he known where I was? "Do we know what that horse creature was?"

"A bäckahäst," Noah said. "It's a horse-like creature that lives in ponds, brooks, rivers, and any smaller collection of water. They basically trick children to get on them and then drown them."

"I think I've heard about that somewhere," I said. The thought of one such horse living in the pond in Almedalen with the ducks had never crossed my mind, though. "Do you think someone created it?"

"Kids run around that pond feeding the ducks all the time," Clara said. "If there really was a creepy murder horse living in Almedalen there would be tons of stories about children going missing. It had to have been created."

I shivered. Lovely.

Noah spoke up. "Is it just me, or is it really suspicious that Erik's been there two of the times these creatures have come after you?"

Clara nodded. "Suspicious at best. How the heck did he know where you were? That's too much of a coincidence."

I chewed on my cheek. They were right, and I could hardly believe the good timing, but he'd saved me. And he'd helped me fight the lindworm. Why would he do that if he was the one trying to hurt me?

"Why would he save me from the bäckahäst if he was the one sending the creatures after me?" I asked, voicing my doubt for the first time.

Noah and Clara exchanged a glance. "Maybe to get you to trust him?" Clara suggested. "Since you've been avoiding him, maybe he was trying to get your attention, and your trust."

Except I hadn't been avoiding him. Guilt churned in my stomach. I could understand what it must look like from their perspective, knowing Erik had shown up with the gast and now the bäckahäst, but it wasn't enough for me to tell them the truth about him.

Still, they had a point. Him being there for two creatures – three, counting the lindworm, which they didn't know about – was a really big coincidence, and I wasn't sure I believed in those. There seemed to be too many of them at the moment.

Were my friends right? Was he suspect and I was letting my feelings cloud my judgement? It certainly wouldn't be the first time. Hell, dealing with anxiety, that was the norm.

I wanted to groan out loud, but I didn't want my friends to know how conflicted I felt. Instead, I sighed. "We should call Melinda."

Tilda looked at me sharply. "Not today, we shouldn't. Today, you're going to stay in bed, buried under as many blankets as I can possibly find, drinking hot tea and eating whatever food I can scrounge up, or I'm going to call Mom and tell her you almost drowned yesterday."

If Mom found out any of the stuff that had happened the last few days, she'd lock both of us up and stand guard herself if she had to. Not that I would blame her if she did.

I sighed. "Fine. But tomorrow, we're calling Melinda."

Tilda smiled beatifically. "Tomorrow, we can call Melinda."

Clara and Noah went home, and Tilda did as she promised and buried me underneath a mountain of blankets. When she went downstairs to make me some food, I quickly threw the blankets aside and grabbed my notebook.

Erik already stood in the meadow when I got there. At this point I was almost certain he hung out here as much as I had before he showed up.

He sat in the middle of the clearing with his eyes closed, but he didn't appear relaxed. No, his whole body seemed tense, and his face contorted in anger and... fear? No, that couldn't be it.

The minute I stepped through the doorway, his eyes flew open, and he jumped up. "Are you okay?" His voice came out low, full of genuine fear. Fear, for me?

I nodded. "I'm fine."

He frowned. "You sure? You almost drowned yesterday!"

"I'm okay. But... how did you know I was there?"

"I didn't. I was there, and I saw you practising magic, and I was going over to talk to you, and then I saw the horse drag you under. I tried to get you as fast as I could, but I thought... I thought I'd been too late."

I narrowed my eyes in disbelief. "What were you doing in Almedalen? It was pouring rain."

He snorted. "You were there, too, remember? And... I use the underground tunnels to travel through the city. It's easier that way. No one has to get uncomfortable by looking at me. One of them happens to open up close to Almedalen."

"Oh." *Oh.* My heart hurt for him, but I steeled myself. *What if he's just using you, Lia?* "Do you know what's going on? Who's creating these creatures and why?"

He stared at me. "I wish I did. I wish I could help you, but I don't know."

"Are you doing it?"

His eye twitched, the only reaction I got. "No."

"No?"

He shook his head and disbelief crossed his face. "No. I wouldn't do anything to hurt you. You... you're the only person who's never been bothered by the mask."

I wanted to believe him, and he'd saved me, but I just... "I don't know what to think," I admitted.

He stepped forward and raised his arms as if to grab me, hug me, but then he let them fall. "You truly think I would hurt you?"

I shook my head. "I don't know."

Hurt replaced disbelief on his face, and he backed away. "Let me make it easier for you." The coldness in his voice broke my heart.

"Erik..." But he was already gone.

I spent the rest of the day in bed, like Tilda had told me to. I tried to focus on reading, on watching television, but my mind kept drifting to the look on Erik's face before he left. He'd been hurt, really badly, and I hated that I'd been the one to hurt him.

The pain I felt reminded me of the heartbreak I'd read about in books. But how could I be this heartbroken over a friend? Because that's what Erik had become. Sometime over the last few weeks, I'd started considering him a friend, and the knowledge that I'd hurt him *hurt*.

That night, I didn't have any nightmares, and the next day, I woke up with more energy than I'd had in a long time. Determination filled me.

I'm done waiting for someone else to fix this mess for me. It was obvious no one would. It was time to end this.

I called Melinda. "Did you find anything?"

"Hello to you too, Lia," she said. "Yes, actually. I was just about to call you. I've found out where Erik lives."***

We ended up going to a café to talk. Tilda and I didn't feel comfortable letting Melinda into our home, and we were reluctant to trust anyone. Still, if Melinda had answers about Erik, we had to give her a chance. Besides, what was the worst that could happen?

Well, the world could end. Literally.

Not helpful, brain.

"Talk," Tilda said, voice uncharacteristically hard.

Melinda flinched. "Well, I talked to this Ivy, who said you girls were chosen to stop Ragnarök from happening. She said we need to stop whoever is doing all of this."

"We know," Tilda said. "She gave us the same speech. You said you know where Erik lives?"

"Yes, I do."

"Where?" I asked, finally piping in.

"Did you know there are extensive tunnels under Visby?"

I nodded slowly. Erik had mentioned something about tunnels the day before, and I remembered something vague from History class about tunnels running all over underneath the city.

"Tunnels?" Tilda said. "That's kind of creepy."

Melinda nodded. "Yes. The military dug and used them back when they had more of a presence on the island. Erik lives down in those tunnels."

Tilda grimaced. "That's definitely creepy. He lives underground?"

"Yes," Melinda said. "I think we should go there and look for him."

I narrowed my eyes at her. "Two things. One, how do you know where to find it? And how did you find Ivy, for that matter? And two, if he's the one doing all this, he's dangerous. I'm not sure going to look for him is such a great idea."

"Did you know that creators are supposedly descended from the goddess Freja?" Melinda asked. "Well, Freja had this magic, sejd, which is a kind of divination. I can't tell the future, but I get these *feelings* that always lead me in the right way. That's how I know where to find Erik. And how I found Ivy."

Tilda looked thoughtful. "I mean, if we go looking for him, at least we have the element of surprise on our side. I like the idea of going into those tunnels as much as I like the idea of stubbing my toe every day for the rest of my life, but we do need to do something and this way we can be prepared and we can do it on our terms."

"I guess," I said, hesitating. "I just..."

I'm not ready. I wasn't ready to face Erik again. I wasn't ready to let go of that tiny hope that he wasn't the one trying to end the world.

I wasn't ready to face someone hell-bent on ending the world. I could barely thaw the ground when I concentrated all my efforts. How could I fight Erik, if it came to that?

"We'll be careful," Tilda said, voice soft. "We won't do anything stupid. You said it yourself – we need to do something other than sit on our asses. And we have a lead on Erik – one that will give us the advantage."

I let out a long breath. "Fine. We'll go."

The entrance that was supposedly closest to where Erik lived was in the House of Paintings, an old house that had been built into the City Wall and had stood abandoned for ages. Melinda walked confidently up to the entrance and opened the door, like she did this all the time. Tilda and I shared a wide-eyed look, and I fidgeted, but we followed her.

Inside, an old, worn staircase lead up. Melinda walked right past it and only stopped at the opposite wall. She bent down and felt around on the floor, and my stomach clenched. Tilda gave me a reassuring smile, but it didn't make me feel any better.

Melinda pulled at what appeared to be a trapdoor, but it didn't budge. She pulled harder, her face going red from the exertion, and still nothing happened. My stomach sank, but I couldn't tell if it was from disappointment or relief.

Melinda muttered something under her breath, and a crowbar appeared in her hands. I jolted in surprise, but really, I shouldn't be. We'd already seen that Melinda was adept at using magic. Of course something silly like a stuck trapdoor wouldn't keep her from her goal.

It didn't take much prying to finally get the trapdoor open. Melinda turned to look at us, then quickly lowered herself into the tunnel. Tilda and I hesitated for a moment, then went after her.

The tight, damp tunnel made my heart beat harder. I breathed in the faint scent of mould. But my shoulders relaxed a little as the air grew warmer, far less cold than I'd expected.

Still, pressure clamped my chest, and I had to blink away tears at the thought of Erik going home this way.

Stop it. He tricked you. Stop feeling bad for him.

Tilda dropped down behind me, and I reached out to take her hand. Losing each other down here would be really bad.

Quietly, we started following Melinda. The light of her flashlight bounced between stone walls.

It was slow progress, and the tunnel didn't widen. I wasn't claustrophobic by any means, but I felt like the walls were closing in on me and the pressure on my chest increased until I could barely breathe. I squeezed Tilda's hand, and she squeezed back, but it didn't make me feel any better.

A loud scratching interrupted the quiet of the tunnels, and I jumped, my head banging off the low ceiling. I yelped and rubbed my head.

"You okay?" Tilda squeezed my hand.

"Fine." My voice came out nothing more than a whisper. "Just banged my head. What is that scratching?"

"Probably just some mice." Melinda's voice rang out.

Tilda shuddered. "Maybe this wasn't such a good idea."

"Too late to turn back now."

The tunnel started narrowing and narrowing, until we had to walk sideways to fit. My breath came in short bursts, and my palms grew damp. I clutched at Tilda's hand and she squeezed back.

Finally, I saw a warmer light at the end of the tunnel, different from the flashlight. Relief made my hands shake, until I realized that probably meant we were getting close to Erik's quarters. My stomach clenched, and I took a long breath to keep from hyperventilating, but I still felt like no air got into my lungs. I wasn't ready to confront him.

The tunnel ended abruptly, not even widening before opening up into a large chamber. Recognition made my heart beat faster as we stepped into the room. Stone walls, and everywhere we looked, there were candles – candelabras with black candles casting a flickering light over the chamber. There was also a fireplace – or something somewhat close to a fireplace – but no fire to heat the room.

At the far wall stood a bed with dark sheets, but other than that, it was sparsely decorated. A piano stood to the right, and to the left of the bed stood a small bedside table, the white paint standing out against the dark colours of the rest of the chamber. A book rested on the table, and that was it.

This was the room from my dream. Except, it couldn't have been a dream, could it? Erik must have brought me here before he took me home, and I'd woken up briefly before falling unconscious again.

My breath caught. He'd had me in his... his... lair? Room? House? He'd had me, unconscious in his lair, and he could've done anything. If he wanted me gone, if he was the one sending these creatures after me, he'd had the perfect opportunity. But he'd saved me from the bäckahäst, and he'd taken me home.

My heart squeezed with sympathy for Erik. Stupid, stupid heart. But I couldn't stop thinking about how lonely he must be, living alone in the cold tunnels below Visby.

If Erik wasn't the one doing this... I studiously didn't look at Melinda. Why was she trying to cast suspicion on Erik? Could she be the one sending the creatures after me?

"Well," Melinda said slowly, looking around in disappointment. "That's a bit of a let-down. But we could stay here and wait for him."

Tilda walked further into the room, inspecting every surface. "Oh no, I'm not staying here a minute longer than necessary. This place gives me chills."

It gave me chills, too. It reminded me of something straight out of a horror flick. And who knew how long it would take before Erik came back? What would happen if we were here when he came back? I wasn't ready for a confrontation, not when I'd just started to figure things out.

Melinda gave a long-suffering sigh. "Then what was even the point of coming here?"

Tilda shrugged. "At least now we know where to find him. We can come back some other time when we're more prepared."

Melinda frowned and sighed again. "Fine. Let's go, then."***

Once we got out of the tunnel, Tilda and I ditched Melinda and went home. It was still pretty early, around lunch, and the sun still surprisingly shone, the air warmer than it had been in a long time. After the tight tunnels, the relief of being out in the open again eased my mind.

"Well, that was a bit of a bust," I said, beginning the long process of getting out of all the outerwear.

Tilda grinned. "Not entirely." She reached into her coat and produced a small book – the book that had been on Erik's nightstand. She handed it to me. "I'm not sure what it is, but I thought it could be a notebook or something. It might be too much hoping for it to have all his nefarious plans, but it's worth a try, don't you think?"

I nodded and opened the book. Tilda was right; the book seemed to be a notebook of some kind. I leafed through the pages. On closer inspection, it looked like a journal. Each page had a date written in tidy handwriting. I found my name in there, and Melinda's, too.

This was my chance to find out, once and for all, what his motivations truly were. I looked up at Tilda. "I'm going to start reading this and see what it says. It looks like a journal or something."

She nodded. "I'll take Kiwi for a walk. You're not going to do anything stupid, right?"

"I'm just going to read."

Chapter 24
Nothingness

I curled up in bed with the journal and started reading. The first entries were from over a month earlier, before I'd met him. I skimmed over those parts and looked for mentions of Ragnarök or creating creatures. There was nothing helpful, until I got to November, a couple of weeks before I met him.

I met another creator today. Her name is Melinda, and she told me she's part of a coven of creators and sorcerers here on Gotland. She said their purpose is to make sure no descendants of the gods have to feel out of place or alone in the world, and she invited me to come to their meeting tomorrow and see if I want to join.

It's a bit weird that she showed up out of the blue, but she gave me this feeling of calm and security. I'm not sure, but I'm going to see the coven tomorrow and see what happens. It would be nice to have a community of people to be able to rely on, but will they accept me despite

the mask? Melinda seemed unbothered, but that doesn't
mean they all will be.

I frowned. Melinda hadn't mentioned that she had been the one to
approach Erik. Still, I supposed it made sense that she'd approach all
the creators and sorcerers – descendants of the gods? I didn't have the
headspace to even start to deal with that – on the island.
I continued.

> *I met with the coven today. They were nice and didn't*
> *seem at all bothered by the mask. They didn't actually*
> *do much at the meeting, just talked about their magic*
> *and their experiences living and hiding among humans*
> *and practised a little magic. I made sure to only use my*
> *creative powers, because who knows what they'd try to*
> *do if they found out I'm both creator and sorcerer. It*
> *wouldn't be the first time someone tried to use me for my*
> *powers, and I can't let myself become someone's thing*
> *again.*

My heart ached. I didn't know all of what had happened to Erik, or
exactly how he had been used in the past, but it was clear as day that
this was a lonely guy who didn't have anyone he could trust. If he was
really the one trying to start Ragnarök, I almost couldn't blame him
for wanting humankind dead.

Here, the journal skipped ahead a few days, and he wrote about how
Melinda had asked him to approach me and told him how to reach

my meadow. How he hadn't been able to say no after she saved him from the loneliness he'd lived with for so long, having no one around to talk to for years. She'd given him a community of others like him who didn't judge him, and although they were wary of the mask and what hid underneath it, they didn't outright shun him.

My eyes filled with tears, and I quickly dried them, not wanting them to spill onto the pages of the journal. He'd lied to me. That knowledge hurt worse than the thought that he might be the one trying to hurt me – not that I'd found anything in the journal to suggest he was. And still, seeing how excited he was to finally have a place to belong, even though the people in the coven still thought less of him because of the mask, it made my heart ache for him.

I kept reading until I reached the part where he met me for the first time.

I met Lia today. Melinda didn't mention that the meadow where I could find her was Lia's own creation. Her sanctuary. We didn't talk, she left as soon as she noticed me, but she started a storm before she left. It had to be her, because the place was so saturated with her magic that it would take a lot of concentration for me to be able to do something big like that. Could she be a hybrid, like me?

After she left, I stayed for a long time. Her magic is incredible. It felt like being enveloped in a warm hug –

not that I've ever felt a hug, but what I imagine a hug would feel like. And yet it set my nerves on edge. I've never felt anything like it. Never felt that kind of solace, of calm. I have to go there again, to try to explain myself but also to feel that again.

He kept talking about how safe and secure he felt whenever he visited my meadow – the same feeling I got when I went there. Apart from the lure of my magic, which freaked me out a little. I read on.

Lia and I talked for the first time today. She was scared – I guess I can't blame her for that. I intruded on her safe space, but I can't stay away. Not from her meadow, and not from her. But even though she was scared, she didn't seem too bothered by the mask. She was curious, but she didn't flinch when I told her it wasn't pretty. And she promised to meet me again! I can't wait! She's just so nice and sweet and amazing, and maybe... maybe she wouldn't care about my scars... No, that's too much to hope for. I can never let her see my scars. It was so nice to be able to talk to someone who didn't seem to mind the mask for once. Even the coven is still wary of me, doesn't go too near me or look directly at me, but Lia didn't seem to mind.

And as time went on, as we met for our lessons, the feelings he started having for me became clear as day, even though he never outright mentioned them. The way he wrote about me, like I was some kind of angel who could do no wrong, snuck into my heart, and I couldn't dry the tears fast enough. Especially when I read the entry from the day we faced the lindworm – the day he'd almost taken his mask off for me.

I told her today. How not even my parents had been able to love me, how my mother left me, how I was paraded at that circus. I told her everything, and she wasn't disgusted. She felt bad for me, for all I've been through! She truly is amazing. I've never met anyone like her, anyone so compassionate and kind.

I almost took my mask off for her. She looked so earnest and she said it wouldn't bother her, but I know it would. It bothers everyone. Even the nurses and doctors flinched when they saw me. How could she not? I'll have to be very careful around her, and not let myself get ensnared again and risk showing her my face. I couldn't bear to have her look at me with disgust, the way everyone does once they see what's underneath the mask.

I'm worried about her. A lindworm attacked today, and though she set it on fire, she could've gotten hurt. I'll have to keep a look out, make sure she isn't hurt. And I have to figure out who is creating these things that keep attacking her. I can't let her be hurt!

I'd never considered myself a very good person. I mean, I tried to be nice, but I knew I was a burden to the people who loved me. Seeing someone who clearly thought the world of me, it reached inside me and squeezed my heart.

I cared about Erik. I wasn't attracted to him, not the way he was to me, but I cared for him a lot. I couldn't deny that now.

I jumped up from my bed, hit by the sudden urge to see him, *right now.* I didn't stop to think that it might not be safe – the way he cared about me made me certain in the knowledge that he would never hurt me. Certainty settled inside me.

He's not the one sending the creatures after me.

He'd had plenty of chances to hurt me, if that's what he wanted, but instead he'd saved me. He'd helped me fight the lindworm, and he'd risked himself saving me from the bäckahäst. He'd had me in his place, and he could've easily killed me at that point, but he'd just taken me home.

If I were to trust Erik's notes, then Melinda clearly couldn't be trusted. She'd orchestrated the whole thing from the start. Erik had helped her, but how much did he really know about what she was doing? She was clearly trying to recruit people, and she had first shown up right after the creatures started showing up. She was the one insisting that we go look for Erik. And no one could deny that she was powerful enough to manage it. Not after what we'd seen her do at the meeting with the coven. Could she be the one sending the creatures after me? Erik couldn't know that – if – she was sending the creatures after me, or he wouldn't have helped her, of that I was sure. But did he know she was trying to start Ragnarök?

I had promised Tilda that I wouldn't do anything stupid, but I had to talk to Erik.

Without thinking it through, I picked up my own notebook and started writing. Before long, the blue swirls of my doorway appeared where my wardrobe usually stood, and I grabbed Erik's journal and stepped in without hesitation. It was time for a confrontation.

I didn't have to wait long for Erik to appear. It couldn't have been more than a few minutes before he showed, the white mask a stark contrast to his dark clothes and hair as usual.

He looked shaken and flushed. Had he already noticed his journal missing? He opened his mouth to say something, but then his eyes found the notebook in my hand and his eyes widened.

The sky above us rumbled, and dark clouds blocked out the sun. The meadow was answering the chaotic mess inside of me.

"So that's where it is." Erik sounded resigned. "I thought I was going insane." His eyes met mine, full of anger and *pain*. "So you read it then?"

I nodded. "I'm sorry."

His eyes flashed. "You're sorry? You stole my journal, invaded my privacy by reading it, and *you're sorry?*" His voice rose.

My hands shook. "I didn't know what else to do! I needed answers and you keep evading my questions."

He drew in a sharp breath. "Because I'm trying to protect you!" Breathing hard, he looked away from me, gaze locking on the trees behind me.

Taking advantage of his apparent disquiet, I spoke up. I should ask him about Melinda, but that's not what came out of my mouth. "What do you want with me?"

Erik flinched, and his eyes flashed back to mine. "I... I don't know." His voice lowered.

"Why were you in Stenkyrka?"

His voice hardened, and he gestured to the notebook in my hand. "If you read that, I'm sure you can guess."

"To see Melinda?" I was surprised when my voice didn't shake or crack with all the emotions roiling inside. Too many feelings to pick one out. A big, fat raindrop hit me. "Did you have anything to do with the gast?"

He shook his head violently. "No! I swear I didn't! I wouldn't hurt you."

Real pain coloured his tone, and some of my resolve cracked. All I wanted was to go over there and hug him and tell him he never had to be alone again, but I needed answers.

"Do you know who it is?"

"No." His voice broke. "But I wouldn't hurt you. If you read that journal, you should know that."

"I don't know what to believe," I said, throwing my hands up in frustration. "Nothing makes sense and everyone seems to have an agenda. How can I trust you?"

Erik flinched like my words physically hurt him. He opened his mouth to say something, then seemed to change his mind. He spun around and rushed into the surrounding forest, and I hurried after him. I would not let him run away, not now.

The sky opened up, and rain pelted me, but I barely noticed, too caught up in the storm inside to care about the storm I created.

Stumbling into the trees, tripping over stray roots, I called out his name, but he didn't reply.

Stay away from the forest. I don't know if it was a conscious thought or pure instinct, but every cell in my body screamed at me to turn around, to get back to safety. My heart raced and fear made me shaky, but I pushed through it.

I saw a shadow move and hurried after it, calling out again, and then the ground disappeared from under me and I fell into nothingness.

I think I screamed, but I heard no sound. I couldn't see, couldn't feel, couldn't hear. Like all of my senses had just... disappeared. Just darkness all around me as I kept stumbling forward, waving my arms in front of me, hoping to touch something, anything, but nothing. I gasped for a breath that ended up as a cry, but no sound left my mouth. Or maybe I'd gone deaf.

Please, please, please, no.

I stumbled on nothing and fell to my knees. I tried to scream but I still heard no sound. Even the ground beneath me felt like nothing, like I knelt on air. I threw my hands around my stomach, instinctively trying to squish the internal pain that gathered there, as I kept gasping for breath.

When I thought I might die from lack of oxygen, I felt something hard touch my back, then grasp my waist, and I was tugged backwards.

I blinked into the sudden brightness and looked around wildly, finding myself surrounded by bright green trees. I gasped for breath, my heart still beating hard, and felt a whiff of fresh air. On instinct, I dropped my hands and touched soft grass. I grasped at it, panic still clutching my insides tight, and ripped a few strands of grass off, but I barely noticed. Even the familiarity of my meadow couldn't ease the terror I felt.

I tried to gasp in a breath, panic rising once more. Was that what existed outside the boundaries of my meadow? Just... nothing.

I gasped for breath again, to no avail. The hand that held mine pulled again, turned me around, until I met Erik's horrified gaze. We were drenched, and rain still poured from the sky, the wind whistling in the trees.

"It's okay, I've got you," he whispered.

My eyes widened as I slowly realised his mask was off. It must've fallen off while he was pulling me out of the nothingness.

He must've realised at the same time, because he dropped my hand and pulled away, turning his face from me, but I'd already seen. Burns covered half his face, raised skin almost purple in colour.

"What..." My voice broke, and I tried again. "What happened to you?"

Erik didn't look at me as he replied. "Fire." His voice rasped with held-back emotion.

I reached out, and he flinched, but I didn't let it deter me. I raised my hand to his face, then froze centimetres away. "Does it... does it hurt?"

He stared at me with wide eyes and shook his head no.

I let my fingers touch his burned cheek, softly, carefully. The skin felt uneven and tough, almost leathery.

Erik drew in a breath so sharp it must've been painful.

"I'm sorry." I didn't look away from him for a second. "I'm so sorry for what you must've gone through."

He kept staring at me, and I didn't know what else to say. What he must've been through to have that kind of scarring... no words in the world could make that kind of suffering better.

"You're not disgusted?" He sounded surprised, and it made my heart ache for him.

I didn't answer him with words. At this point, I wasn't sure he'd believe me if I told him no. Instead, I dropped my hand and sprung forward, throwing my arms around him and hugging him tight.

For a long moment, he didn't move a muscle. He was so stiff it felt like hugging a statue. Then his arms went around me, and I felt him shuddering. I didn't let go when I heard his quiet sobs, or when he squeezed me tighter, or when his tears drenched my shirt.

We stayed that way for a long time, until he finally pulled away. His eyes were red and swollen, and my stomach clenched.

"I'm sorry." I kept my voice low. "I'm sorry I read your journal. I just... I don't know what to think anymore. Who to trust. And I'm... I'm scared." I gasped for breath. "I'm terrified of what will happen. I'm terrified that my sister, my friends, might get hurt, and I'm still barely in control of my magic. I'm scared that I won't be able to protect them. And I don't know what to do. Hell, I barely know what's going on half of the time! I just needed some answers."

Erik squeezed my hand. "I guess I can understand that. I just... I wish you could trust me. But I can see why you can't." He frowned, and I opened my mouth to say something, but he spoke again. "How did you get the journal, anyway?"

Here goes nothing... "Um, Melinda showed me and Tilda where

you... live. Tilda grabbed it before we left."

He cursed. "Why the hell would Melinda do that?"

I pursed my lips. "Well, she said it was to help us, but I'm starting to think it was more of a ploy to get us to trust her." I took a breath. "Speaking of Melinda, what is she doing?"

Erik hesitated.

"Look," I said. "I don't know if you're actually working with her or not..." Probably should've finished reading that journal. "And I guess I can't force you to tell me anything. But the cat's pretty much out of the bag now."

"I did work with her," he started. "But I didn't agree to hurting you. I didn't know Melinda was sending those creatures to hurt you – if she is, but I don't know who else it could be. After the lindworm attacked us, I went to her to ask for help, but she didn't seem surprised. She told me, then, that she wanted to start Ragnarök. I should've figured it out then, but I truly thought she wanted to recruit you. She said someone else sent those creatures after you, to stop you from joining her, and she asked me to keep an eye on you. Though I'd already decided to do that."

I believed him. Maybe because of what I had read, or maybe because of the desperate look in his eyes.

"When I saw you in Stenkyrka the other night, with that gast, I realised she hadn't told me everything."

"Hold up," I said as he confirmed my suspicions. "So Melinda really is creating all these creatures?"

Erik nodded.

I paused as I realised what else he'd said. "She's trying to start Ragnarök."

Chapter 25
Kidnapped

The air was still and silent; even the trees in the meadow seemed to be waiting. "How? I mean, why would creating creatures from Scandinavian folklore start Ragnarök? That's what I don't get."

Well, it was one of the things I didn't get.

"I'm not entirely sure," Erik said, "but what she told me was that Ragnarök should've happened ages ago, but the gods – yes, the actual gods – isolated themselves in Asgård, their own realm, effectively preventing it from happening. What she wants is to make herself a big enough threat that they can't keep ignoring it and will come to stop her, in which case she believes Ragnarök will start pretty much automatically. My guess is, she thinks sending her creatures after the gods' chosen one will get them to step in, to enter Midgård – that's the human realm – again. And once they come back, Ragnarök will start, long overdue."

If Ivy had told us that, it would've made everything much easier. Now, at least, I knew what we needed to do to stop the end of the world.

"Okay," I sighed and picked at the grass. A soft wind blew through the trees, and the leaves rustled. "So we just need to stop her from creating any more creatures. How the hell do we do that?"

"She's not going to stop." Erik leaned forward. "She's determined to make it happen."

"I suppose reasoning with her isn't going to help?" Hope lifted my tone.

He shook his head. "Not a chance."

"Well, I need to go back and talk to Tilda about all this." I pushed myself up from the grass-covered ground.

"Wait!"

I paused and waited for him to go on.

"Will you come back?"

I didn't hesitate. "Yes. Tomorrow?" That should give me enough time to overanalyse our entire interaction. And it was time to come clean to my friends.

He nodded. I picked up my notebook and quickly opened the doorway back to the regular world. I looked back at Erik for a second, and then I stepped through the swirls.

As soon as I got back to my room, I called Clara and Noah and asked them to come as soon as they could. In less than an hour, the four of us – me, Tilda, Clara and Noah – were gathered in our living room. Clara and Noah looked confused, and I couldn't blame them. The day had been eventful, and they had no idea what could've happened since we last saw each other.

I started by telling them about Melinda, finding Erik's place, and reading his journal. I didn't go into detail about what I'd read, feeling like that would be betraying Erik's trust. When I told them I'd gone to meet Erik, Tilda narrowed her eyes at me. I skimmed over some of the details, like my trip into nothingness, but I told them what Erik had told me about Melinda, and how I'd been meeting with him for the past few weeks.

When I finished, no one said a word. Only the whistling wind outside disturbed the silence. Then Tilda spoke up. "You trust him?" Disbelief and confusion coloured her tone.

I nodded without hesitation. "I do. Reading that journal, it was obvious that Melinda has been manipulating him, and he sounded honestly regretful when he talked about it." I really didn't think he'd been faking that. If he did, he was the best actor I'd ever seen.

Tilda didn't look convinced, but Clara spoke up. "I think it's time we met Erik."

My first reaction was to refuse. Our interactions felt so private, it felt wrong to introduce my friends to him. I didn't know why, but I wanted to keep Erik to myself. He'd been my secret for such a long time. But it was the smart thing to do. Maybe they'd be able to be more logical about it than me, because I was obviously too invested in Erik to see things clearly. And if he was telling the truth, like I believed, then we'd all need to work together to stop Melinda before it was too late. Before she managed to convince the gods she was a big enough threat to require their immediate interference. Whether she was right or not, I had a feeling it would be a really bad thing if the gods came out of hibernation.

I nodded. "I promised I'd meet him in my meadow tomorrow, so you guys can all come."

I pushed down my unease at letting even more people into my safe space. Our survival – the survival of the world – was more important than me keeping my sanctuary private.

We decided to meet the next day after school to go together and talk to Erik. The thought of bringing others there made me want to break into hives, but I reminded myself it was my choice to take them there. They weren't going into it uninvited. The thought didn't make me feel any better, and I pushed it down and refused to acknowledge it. We'd have to make sacrifices to save the world, and if that meant sacrificing the privacy of my meadow, then so be it.

We made plans for the next day, and then Noah had to leave, since he'd promised his parents to babysit, and Tilda had some schoolwork she needed to do – something I probably needed to do, too, considering how I'd been neglecting school recently, but it was hard to feel like school was important right then – so it was me and Clara alone, for the first time in a long time.

"Well," Clara said, uncertain. "At least we can't complain this semester was boring."

I burst out laughing, and the tightness on my chest relaxed slightly for the first time in what felt like months. I'd missed this – just Clara and me hanging out. She was my best friend for a reason, and I loved her like a sister.

"You know, I'd actually prefer another boring semester over this," I said.

"Me too." Clara forced a smile. "Well, since it's just us, why don't we put on a film or something? Something funny to distract us a bit. There's nothing we can do right now anyway, so we might as well try to relax. I feel like I haven't done that in months."

I agreed, and we picked out some comedy film we'd watched a

million times before, something about a family with really bad luck for a day.

I went to get some snacks for us, and Clara followed to help out.

"Hey, have you thought any more about the asexuality thing?" she asked as I found some chips in the pantry.

I froze, and anxiety tightened in my stomach. I wanted to listen to Clara's words after I'd come out to her, that I didn't have to prove to anyone that I was queer, but I still felt like maybe I didn't have the right to call myself asexual. Still, something about it just felt right, like it just fit. Maybe it didn't have to be more complicated than that. Maybe... maybe I could accept that, someday.

"A lot," I told Clara.

"And how do you feel about it?" She picked at some imaginary lint on the counter. "We don't have to talk about this if it makes you uncomfortable."

I shook my head. "No, it's okay," I said, surprised that it actually was. "I've been thinking back and forth about it, and I'm still not sure, you know, I bet I still have a lot of overthinking left to do before I can feel really at peace with it. I still feel like maybe I don't have the right to use the label, like I'm not... asexual enough, I guess. But it feels... right, somehow. Maybe that doesn't make any sense, but..."

Clara smiled, her typical bright smile that I hadn't seen in way too long. "It makes perfect sense! It was kind of like that for me, too, when I figured out I was gay. I mean, I always knew I wasn't interested in guys the way all the other girls seemed to be, but it didn't hit me until later that I was actually interested in girls instead. But when I started thinking it, I couldn't stop thinking about it for such a long time. It just felt right, like you said, like it fit. It was such a nice feeling."

She reached out to squeeze my hand. "And you are asexual enough. I know it's not totally easy to make yourself believe it, but you are queer enough. You never have to prove to anyone that you are queer enough, because you are."

Admiration filled me. Clara had always been proud of herself, of her identity, and I found it incredible. She never seemed to doubt herself the way I couldn't stop doubting myself. "How do you do it?" The question slipped out.

Clara blinked. "What do you mean?"

"How can you be so... confident in yourself? In your identity?" It seemed crazy to me, how someone could feel so secure in themselves, when I couldn't stop overthinking every single detail of my life.

Clara smiled, a sad smile that was uncharacteristic for her. "I decided a long time ago that I wouldn't let anyone decide who I should be."

I frowned. "What do you mean?"

Clara hesitated for a moment. "I don't want to burden you with this right now. You've got so much going on already, I don't want to add onto it."

My frown deepened. "You could never burden me, Clara," I said, my voice brooking no room for argument. "You're my best friend. I won't make you talk about it if you feel uncomfortable, but I want you to know I'm always here for you, even though I haven't been that good at it lately."

With my anxiety, our friendship had become so much about me, and guilt churned in my stomach. I hadn't even noticed Clara had her own issues. She was always such a good friend to me, and I was a sucky friend to her.

Clara narrowed her eyes. "Don't you dare."

I looked at her with confusion. "What?"

"Don't you dare feel guilty. You have nothing to be guilty about. You have your own issues, and I knew I could talk to you if I needed to. I know you're here for me when I need you. It was my decision to not open up, okay? Don't put that on yourself."

I tried to let her words sink in, but I struggled with letting go of the guilt. *She's such an amazing friend to me – I should be a better friend to her. She deserves a better friend than me.*

Clara sighed. "When I was younger, I was bullied. You know, kids aren't that accepting of people being different, and even though I wasn't openly gay back then, I was very energetic and, I guess, kind of all over the place. You know, loud and annoying and I loved being the centre of attention. Well, the other girls found me really annoying, and I guess I can't really blame them. But when I figured out I liked girls, I decided I would be proud of being different. I didn't want my bullies to force me into the closet, to make me feel ashamed of who I am. I refused to let the bullies win, to let them succeed in pushing me down, so I decided right then that I would just be myself and everyone else could go to hell."

If she meant to make me feel less impressed with her, she failed. The strength it had to have taken for such a young girl to use her gayness as a weapon against her bullies was unbelievable. I told her as much.

Clara shook her head, but I jumped forward and hugged her to shut her up. The hug lasted for what could have been an eternity, until Clara whispered, "Thank you," and pulled away, discreetly drying her eyes. I smiled at her, and she smiled back. Then, I grabbed a bowl and poured some chips into it, handed it off to Clara, grabbed some chocolate from the fridge, and we went back to the living room to distract ourselves with other people's bad luck.

As the evening neared, Clara had to head home. I prepared dinner, meatballs with potatoes, ready for when Mom got home from work. That evening, we played games and watched television – a new episode of our crime show had been released – and laughed together.

When it got time for bed, I hesitated to say good night to everyone and go upstairs. Something in me knew that this would be the last normal evening we'd have in a while, and I didn't want to let go of the moment. I hugged mom longer than normal, breathing in her familiar scent and letting it soothe me.

While Tilda and I were getting ready, my phone rang, showing an unknown number.

I picked it up. "Hello?"

"Lia?" asked a somewhat familiar voice. It sounded like it belonged to a middle-aged woman – a frantic woman.

"Yeah?"

"This is Nina, Noah's mom."

My stomach clenched in dread. "What's wrong?"

"Have you seen Noah tonight?"

I frowned. "No, not since he left our flat this afternoon. He said he had promised to babysit."

"He did," Nina said. "But he never came home this afternoon."

My heart started racing. "Did you try calling him?"

As soon as the words left my mouth, I wanted to shove them back in.

"Yes." Nina sounded choked. "You're sure you haven't heard anything from him? It's not like him to not check in like this."

"No, nothing."

"And you have no idea where he might be?" My heart broke at the fear in her voice.

"I'm sorry," I told Nina, though I had a suspicion what might have happened to him.

"It's okay," Nina said, though it clearly was far from okay. "Let me know if you hear from him, please?"

"Of course," I promised. "I hope you find him soon."

Nina thanked me for my help and hung up. I turned around and met Tilda's worried gaze.

"We need to meet Erik right now," I told her, and my voice shook. "That was Noah's mom. He never came home today."

Tilda's chest rose unsteadily. "He's missing?"

I nodded, tears filling my eyes.

"But we have no idea where to even look for him." Tilda's voice shook.

"It's got to be Melinda. She's the one who's been sending the creatures after me, she's the one trying to start Ragnarök – she has to be the one kidnapping these guys, too." It was too much of a coincidence, especially now that Noah had been taken.

"But what does she need them for?" Tilda asked, putting my exact thoughts into words.

I shook my head. "I don't know. But we can't wait anymore, and risk her hurting him." What could she possibly be needing these guys for? Maybe Erik had some answers, maybe he didn't, but either way, we had to do something now. We couldn't risk waiting until the next day when it meant Noah might be hurt... or worse.

245

CHAPTER 26
FIRE

As I started writing, fear and worry for Noah distracted me from the fact that I was bringing someone with me into my meadow. My heart raced, and my chest hurt from the lack of a proper breath.

Opening the portal took several tries. My writing was so scribbled because of the way my hands were shaking. Finally, my handwriting became legible enough to open the portal, and blue swirls appeared in front of us.

I grabbed Tilda's hand, and together, we stepped through the swirls.

Tilda looked around her in awe, eyes wide and mouth slightly open. I smiled, a small smile, at her, and then I turned to look into the trees, searching. It never took long for Erik to show up.

I waited, two, three, four heartbeats. *Maybe he's asleep? Maybe he won't show up? What will we do if he doesn't show?*

We were woefully unprepared to face off with Melinda, and without Erik, we wouldn't stand a chance, but everything inside me rebelled at the idea of waiting until the morning to save Noah.

My heart beat so frantically it hurt. I gasped for breath, in desperate need of oxygen. Then, I felt a flicker in my stomach. Erik emerged from the trees, looking dazed with sleep. When he saw us, his eyes sharpened.

"What's wrong?" he called across the clearing.

"Noah's gone missing." My voice shook. "I think Melinda's taken him."

Erik frowned. "How do you know it's her?"

"The guys that have been disappearing all month, only to show up... dead." I choked on the last word and took a second to push my tears down. I didn't have time to break down now. "It started right after Melinda appeared and all these creatures showed up. It can't be a coincidence."

Erik mulled this over. "Maybe, but even if it is her, what do you propose we do? Just show up and fight her? She's an incredibly powerful sorceress who wants to start the end of the world. If she's taken your friend, she's done it for a reason, and she won't let him go."

"I'd figured that much out already, thanks." Sarcasm dripped from my tone. "But we can't do nothing! We have to save him."

Erik pursed his lips. "But how? We can't storm Stenkyrka forest and hope for the best. She'll kill us all in a heartbeat."

"Maybe not." I bit my lip. "She still thinks Tilda and I trust her. Maybe we can use that to our advantage."

Erik nodded and he looked into the distance. "Maybe. I have an idea."

We had a plan. We'd go to Melinda's house, hoping she'd be at home, and ask for her help finding Noah. Tilda and I would go in alone, since we were supposed to think Erik was the one behind everything. Once in her house, we'd lull her into a false sense of security, make her believe we truly thought she was on our side, and then we'd knock her out and search her place for clues on where to find Noah. And in case she woke up before we were done, I would create an impenetrable shield of wind around her to keep her stuck there. Erik had explained how to do that.

Okay, maybe it wasn't a great plan, and a lot of it depended on my magic, which was risky at best, but we couldn't think of anything better at the moment, and we didn't want to wait and risk Noah being hurt. There was only one tiny issue left...

"How do we get to Stenkyrka in the middle of the night? There are definitely no buses past midnight."

Erik raised an eyebrow. "You take us there, of course."

I blinked and raised both my eyebrows. "I take us there? How do you suggest I do that? I can't teleport, if that's what you're suggesting."

Erik snorted. "You create a doorway. Like the one that takes you here."

Why didn't I realise that earlier? If I could make a doorway back to my room, then there was no reason I shouldn't be able to make it open up somewhere else, like Stenkyrka. "Are you sure that's possible? I mean, the doorway shouldn't be possible in the first place, should it? It doesn't exist."

"You wouldn't have been able to get to the meadow if the doorway didn't exist. Remember my theory? I think the gods used doorways similar to this, and that's why we can create them. It's not commonly used because obviously we don't know exactly what kind of magic the gods used, since they've been gone from this realm for so long."

Excited, I grabbed my notebook and pen. Then I looked at Tilda. "Are you sure you want to come? This will be really dangerous and you don't have your sorcery yet."

She looked like she wanted to stomp her foot. "The prophecy is about the both of us. I'm sure. Besides, I'm prepared." She shook her hand, making the charms on her bracelet tinkle.

"What are those for?"

Tilda grinned. "Since creating destroys something else when used, I figured I'd prepare with some trinkets I don't use. I told you I wanted to try this. That way, I hopefully won't destroy something important."

I stared at my sister, impressed. So much had happened that I'd forgotten all about her little theory. Still, I hesitated, not wanting my sister in danger but also knowing there was no way I'd be able to convince her to stay behind. Not to mention, I needed her. She may not have her sorcery, but she was great at using her creativity, and since she could speak her commands and didn't have to write them down, she'd be a lot faster than me.

Finally, I nodded, though worry for my sister still made me hesitant. I started writing quickly, and before long, the blue swirls of the door-way appeared in front of us. I put the notebook in my jacket, grabbed Tilda and Erik's hands, and stepped through.

The cold, dark forest sent shivers down my spine. Wind tore through the trees, making them shake, and I held tighter to Tilda and Erik. The wind howled through the trees, and the scent of wet pine tickled my nose.

I remembered that Erik had to hide, to make sure Melinda trusted us for a bit longer. I released his hand.

I looked to my left and met Tilda's wide eyes with equally wide eyes of my own, then I gave a small nod, hoping to assure her, even though I wanted nothing more than to run and hide. Instead, I held on as tight as I could to Tilda's hand, remembering what had happened the last time we were in Stenkyrka, and together we walked towards Melinda's house.

It didn't take long before we saw her house – though it was more of a little cottage, with dark brown wooden walls, surrounded by an overflowing, yet somehow organised, garden. With nothing but a little moonlight trickling through the trees to light it, the garden was mostly cast in shadow, shadows that seemed to almost move. Next to us, the flowers rustled, and I jumped. When I swept my gaze over the garden, though, I found nothing. Nothing but plants everywhere.

I took a deep breath, squeezed Tilda's hand, and together, we walked up to the door. I knocked two, three times, and then had to keep myself from throwing the door open.

Footsteps padded through the house, and the door opened a little, then more, to show Melinda in a long, pink nightgown, looking groggy. "Lia? Tilda? What are you girls doing here? It's the middle of the night!"

I smiled shakily at her. "I know. I'm so sorry for waking you, but our friend, Noah, has disappeared and, well, I hoped maybe you could help us look for him? Last time we met, you mentioned this magic, um..." I searched my memory.

"Sejd," Tilda finished.

Melinda's face was the picture of innocent worry, but I didn't buy it for a moment.

"Of course. I'm sorry about your friend. I'm sure you must be worried considering the other missing boys. I'll see what I can do."

She stepped back and opened the door wider, letting us through. I didn't want to put my back to her but had no way of preventing it without making her suspicious. I pushed Tilda in front of me, putting myself between her and Melinda, in case she tried anything.

"Let's go into the kitchen," Melinda said from behind me, and Tilda headed left into the kitchen. Once we were in, I turned quickly to look at Melinda, and she waved for me and Tilda to sit. We did, without saying a word. I said nothing, too scared of giving us away by accidentally saying the wrong thing.

Melinda prepared some tea, all the while making sure not to turn her back to us. My palms started sweating. Did she suspect something?

Once she was done, she poured the tea – it smelled strongly of mint – into three teacups and handed me and Tilda a cup each. Then she sat opposite us and watched us for a long moment, not saying so much as a word.

I squirmed, uncomfortable, and looked at Tilda. She looked as nerve-wracked as I felt. I just hoped Melinda would chalk our nervousness up to us being worried about our friend and nothing else.

Melinda closed her eyes and breathed in deeply. I wrinkled my nose slightly at the intense scent of mint, and then the world disappeared. Images flashed before my eyes... the dark forest... a path... the Virgin... the cliff...

I blinked and I sat back in the warm, brightly lit kitchen.

Tilda squeezed my hand and looked at me, a question in her eyes. I shook my head ever so slightly, telling her without words to not worry about it.

When I turned my gaze back to Melinda, her eyes flew open, suspicion clear in them. I drew in a sharp breath, and she threw out her hand to attack. Tilda and I were thrown backwards.

I hit the wall headfirst, and black spots swam in my vision. I blinked, trying to clear my vision, and struggled to get up on shaking legs. I tried to get my magic to answer, but I couldn't find my magic through the ball of anxiety, the fear that lodged in my throat. I tried to do what I'd done with the lindworm, tried to will something to happen, but I couldn't focus for the black spots that still danced in my vision.

Flames engulfed the little kitchen, all of it, except a small circle around Tilda and I. Melinda screamed and spun around, leaping through the flames and fleeing the kitchen.

I finally managed to get my legs to hold my weight and stumbled to my feet. I looked at Tilda, confused, because I definitely wasn't controlling the fire, but she stared into the blaze and didn't look at me.

The heat burned my face, and sweat broke out on my skin, even as the flames seemed to withdraw from me and Tilda. Flames lit the entire kitchen.

I grabbed Tilda's hand and pulled her out of the kitchen. The fire parted, leaving us a trail to follow out of the cottage. The door flew open, and I dragged Tilda through it, into the cold night air.

Sweat immediately cooled on my skin as the wind bit at my cheeks, making my eyes tear up from the force of it. I shivered at the sharp contrast and huddled into my scarf, which had halfway fallen off in our hurry from the cottage and blew behind me in the wind. Still, I didn't want to let go of Tilda to grab it and wrap it around me.

We stumbled through the garden, and Tilda tripped and fell, her hand torn from my grasp.

I stumbled to a stop and turned around, pulling Tilda up, but I froze as I saw the cottage, caught up in flames. I gaped as heat once again blasted my face.

"What the hell?" I exclaimed. "What was that?"

Tilda looked at the cottage with wide eyes full of fear. "I... I think it was me," Tilda said in a small voice.

I looked at her, surprised. "You think your sorcery unlocked?"

She nodded, still wide-eyed and fearful. "I felt this really hard tug in my stomach, and then it released when Melinda attacked, and suddenly the room was on fire."

I blinked. "Yeah, that sounds like sorcery. Because I definitely didn't do that." I drew in a breath that ended up in a cough. "Come on, let's get out of here. Even if the flames won't touch us, the smoke definitely will."

Holding on tight to each other, we hurried into the surrounding forest, until we couldn't see the cottage or the flames anymore.

We slowed down to catch our breath, and I finally remembered my vision from before.

"I think I know where Noah is." My eyes widened. Could it be that easy?

Erik showed up next to Tilda. I jumped. It was like he appeared out of freaking nowhere.

Tilda squeaked. "Holy crap! Give us some warning next time!"

"Show the way." Erik smiled a little at Tilda's reaction. As we started walking, he asked, "What the hell happened at Melinda's?"

"Um..." I said. "I think Melinda figured out that we were trying to trick her, because she tried to attack us, and then Tilda kind of... set the place on fire. By accident. Totally saved us, though."

I found the small trail I'd seen in my vision and started running. After only seconds I was gasping for breath, but I kept going. Noah was still in danger, he had to be freezing, risking hypothermia if he was outside... hundreds of different scenarios flitted through my mind, and I hurried. *Please, gods, please let Noah be okay*, I prayed silently to the Norse gods I'd doubted my whole life.

CHAPTER 27

FOREVER CLOSED

We reached the cliff where the Virgin was located, but I didn't see Noah. I looked around wildly, shouting his name even though my lungs burned from a lack of oxygen.

"Noah?" My voice grew high-pitched. "Noah!"

Erik grabbed my hand to get my attention and pointed to a small wooden structure at the edge of the woods.

It was small enough that it would barely fit a grown person, but I sprinted towards it. My foot got caught on a wayward root, and I fell. My hands and knees burned, but I barely noticed it. Hands grabbed me around the waist and Erik set me back on my feet. I didn't even stop to thank him, just kept running.

We reached the door, and I frantically searched for a doorknob with frozen fingers. I felt something and I pulled at it. Nothing happened. I pulled harder. The door still wouldn't budge.

"Noah?" My heart still raced from the sprint, making my voice breathless. "Noah, are you in there?"

Nothing.

I pulled at the door again and again. My breath came in short bursts, but I couldn't stop. I had to get the door open!

Hands wrapped around me from behind. I swatted at them, but

they wouldn't release me.

"Lia!" Erik's voice rang out, loud in my ear. "It won't open."

I sniffed and gasped in a breath. "It has to open! It has to..." My voice broke.

"We'll get it open," Erik promised. "We just need a little bit of magic."

Of course, dummy. You have magic, remember?

Not the time.

I met Erik's eyes. "Do you have any ideas?"

He smiled. "I do. Wood is affected by earth magic. We'll just splinter the door."

I pulled on my magic. "How?"

Erik flicked his eyes to the door. "Just focus all your magic on the door. Remember, intent is key."

I tugged my magic to the surface and looked at the door. I didn't want to make the whole building explode with Noah in it, so I pushed my magic towards the door slowly, carefully.

Nothing happened.

Tears filled my eyes. My hands shook, but I kept pushing and pushing. My insides tugged, but I ignored it and imagined the door splintering into nothing.

Tilda grabbed my hand and squeezed, and I pushed harder.

The sound of wood cracking, and the door splintered. My eyes widened, and I stared at the thousands of little splinters hovering in the air where the door used to be.

Now I just need to let them fall.

I let my magic go, but it didn't go quite the way I expected. Magic burst out of me, and the splinters came racing towards us. I screamed, but the splinters met a wall of solid air just a breath away from my face.

"Holy crap!" Tilda's voice rose in a mixture of excitement and terror. "Does it always feel like this, using your sorcery?"

I looked at her. "You did this?"

She shrugged. "The wall of air thing, I think. I imagined it to happen, and it did."

Maybe it'll be easier for her to learn to control her sorcery, then.

I didn't reply, though. I ran through the now obliterated doorway. Erik shone a flashlight into the structure, and I saw Noah, tied to the floor. He was unconscious but looked mostly unharmed. There were a few scratches and bruises, littering his face and arms, but there were no other visible injuries.

I rushed forward and fell to my knees next to him, checking his pulse. My heart beat hard as I waited, holding my breath. One second, two... There! A faint fluttering, but it was there. I shook him and yelled his name. He blinked his eyes open, frowning.

"Lia? What... what are you doing here? What's going on?"

I sobbed in relief and hugged him tight. "You... you were taken," I forced out between sobs. "You don't remember?"

He pulled away, still frowning.

"No." He rubbed his forehead. "I only remember leaving your place to go home. I was walking through that little forest on the way home, and then... I don't remember anything."

"Oh," I said faintly. "Well, I guess it doesn't matter. We should get you to the hospital to make sure you aren't hypothermic or somethi ng..."

I heard a laugh in the distance. I looked over my shoulder and saw Melinda standing there. Her clothes were in burnt tatters, but she looked otherwise unharmed.

"Did you really think a little fire would kill me?" she cackled. "Did you really think it would be that easy?"

I stood up and reached into my jacket, finding my notebook and pen. "One can always hope." I forced confidence I wasn't feeling into my voice.

Melinda smiled wide, and it sent shivers down my spine. I couldn't believe I'd ever thought she could be trusted. Being in her presence made me want to turn and run and never look back. My legs itched to run, and my insides felt frozen, yet my hands felt clammy. My stomach clenched, and no matter how much I tried to take deep breaths, I couldn't get enough air into my lungs.

I saw Tilda from the corner of my eye, standing up straight next to me. Behind me, Noah still sat on the ground. And Erik... Erik stepped forward, until he partly covered me.

I have to fight.

I couldn't let the anxiety get the better of me. My sister, my friends, needed me. Maybe I wouldn't survive the night, but if it meant saving the people I loved, I would risk it. I would do whatever I had to in order to save them.

There are worse ways to go than fighting for those you love.

Besides, I shouldn't have expected to save the world without making some sacrifices.

"The boy belongs to me." Melinda looked straight at Noah. I spun around and saw his eyes glaze over. He took a step forward. Erik grabbed him, but Noah fought, kicking and screaming and trying to get closer to Melinda.

"Stop!" I screamed at her. "Leave him alone! Stop it!"

Melinda laughed. "Sweet child," she chided. "Once a boy comes with me, he belongs to me, to the forest, forever. You cannot take him back. He will always miss the forest, until he wastes away to nothing."

What the hell? Who did this woman think she was? People weren't belongings, for gods' sake. "Let him go," I said, voice hard.

Melinda's smile widened. "What are you going to do about it?"

Before I could reply, Erik stepped in. His voice was strained as he said, "Why take the boys, Melinda? I understand why you created all these creatures, I can even understand why you wanted to start Ragnarök, but what part do the boys have?"

"You figured it out, did you?" Melinda turned her blazing green eyes to Erik, who was still struggling to hold on to Noah. "The boys are for me, sweetie. For my entertainment. Living in the forest can be quite dull, you see. The trees aren't much company, and neither are the squirrels. But the boys... oh, how sweet their devotion was. Their life force, too."

This woman had to be crazy. That was the only explanation.

Then it hit me. A woman who lived in the forest, kept company only by the trees and the animals that inhabited the forest, and who took boys to keep her company... "Let me see your back," I told Melinda.

Her eyes glinted as she looked at me. "Someone did her research," she cooed.

Noah stilled.

I hardened my voice. "Show me your back."

She smiled and spun elegantly, showing off her back. Except it wasn't a human back. It was hollow, with bark where skin was supposed to be. Like a tree.

Ivy wasn't the one kidnapping the boys, after all. Though I'd been partially right; it was a skogsrå behind the kidnappings.

Erik drew in a sharp breath. "Skogsrå."

She finished her spin and faced us again, looking only at me. "Took you long enough to figure it out."

"Why do you want to start Ragnarök, though?" I asked. "Wouldn't that mean you would die, along with everyone else? Aren't you supposed to protect your forest?"

Her eyes flashed and she snapped. "Yes, I'm supposed to protect my forest! And that's what I'm doing! Don't pretend you don't know what you humans are doing to the forests. To the planet! I will not stand by and watch humans destroy my forest. *This* is me protecting it."

"But Ragnarök is the end of the world!" Tilda exclaimed. "How can that be protecting the forest?"

"It is only the end of the world as we know it." Melinda snorted. "Of course you humans would never be able to see past your own little noses, but it is for the greater good. The world will be submerged underwater, gods and humans alike will perish, and then the world shall reemerge from the ocean and will have a second chance. The world is dying, and Ragnarök will be a second chance for it to live."

She has a point. Maybe the world does need a reboot. I shook my head to dispel those thoughts. Yes, humans were destroying the planet, but saving the planet by killing off every single human was wrong. We had to find another way.

"Killing off the human race is not the greater good," I told Melinda. "There has to be another way to save the planet."

"It will not be killing off the human race, sweetie," she explained.

"It will simply be giving humanity a chance to evolve, once again."

She was crazy. How exactly would humanity evolve by dying?

She smiled sadly. "I'm sorry it came to this, but you leave me no choice. Perhaps when I kill their two chosen champions, the gods will finally show up and put a stop to the humans' mistreatment of the world. They have left the world in the hands of humans for far too long – now it's time they face the consequences!" She threw out her hand, but this time I was ready, and threw mine up in time. My shield of water extinguished her flames easily.

Erik pushed Noah back into the wooden structure now missing a door. With a sweep of his hand, he created a wall of air to keep him inside. "Only to keep him out of the way," he explained when I gave him a hard stare.

Good idea. We wouldn't want Melinda to somehow use him against us.

Melinda wasted no time and sent a wave of water towards us. My water shield couldn't protect us from water, and we were thrown back by the wave.

I had an idea and looked at Erik. He met my gaze, and I mouthed to him. *Distract her.*

Then I scrambled back, hiding behind the wooden structure, hoping that Tilda and Erik would be able to hold Melinda off for long enough.

I hesitated. To create something new, I'd have to sacrifice something that already existed, and I knew exactly what would be destroyed if I proceeded with this.

Melinda cackled. "Hiding, little halfling? Are you really going to let your little sister fight your battles?" I heard something crack and prayed to every god I didn't believe in that Tilda and Erik were okay.

I started writing.

> *Birch trees are everywhere, the branches full of bright green, thick leaves. The ground is covered in soft grass, and the air smells of wet grass. The sky can barely be seen through the foliage, but it's blue without a cloud in sight. In the forest, there's a small meadow, and in it is a small cottage made of dark wood, surrounded by a garden with flowers of all different colours; red, blue, purple, pink, white, yellow, orange. The garden is surrounded by a white picket fence, and the sunlight is streaming through the thick foliage. A soft breeze blows through the meadow, sweeping a few leaves with it.*

There. That would have to do.

I stood up and stepped out from behind the structure, and saw Tilda throw some kind of heavy object through the air. Melinda ducked out of the way, but not quick enough, and was hit in the arm. Melinda threw her arms out, and a hard wind swept us off our feet. I landed hard on my butt but jumped back to my feet and attempted to set fire to Melinda. She screamed in pain, but quickly doused herself in water, killing the flames.

"Distract her!" I yelled to Tilda, who muttered something, probably to create something. I didn't watch to see what she created though – I had to trust her to take care of herself. Once again I started writing.

*A doorway that leads to the magical forest. Blue swirls
that appear right behind Melinda. Once the doorway
closes, no one will be able to enter or leave the forest.*

The doorway appeared right behind Melinda. I threw all my magic at her, wind, fire and water flying through the air. The ground rumbled, throwing her off balance and forcing her to stumble back.

She saw the portal and jumped away. "Is that your idea? Locking me away in your cute little meadow? That won't stop me, little halfling."

The ground beneath us shook. We stumbled back. My ankle bent, and I fell. For a moment, I couldn't think through the sudden pain.

Then Erik was there, helping me up. The ground shook again, throwing Melinda off-balance. I grabbed desperately at all the magic I could feel coiled in my stomach, waiting to be used, and I pulled *hard*. I gasped as the magic tore through me, leaving me feeling empty. Wind erupted from me and hit Melinda, throwing her straight through the blue swirls.

My eyes drifted closed and I tried to think through the pain in my ankle, leaning on Erik for balance, when Tilda yelled, "Lia! Close the doorway!"

I opened my eyes and saw Melinda trying to scramble out of the doorway.

Oh no you don't.

I dropped to the ground and fumbled for my notebook, heart in my throat. I couldn't let Melinda escape. I finally found it on the ground as Erik threw his hand out and Melinda was thrown back through the doorway. I picked it up with shaking hands, tears streaming down my face from the pain in my ankle, but I wrote.

The doorway is forever closed.

The blue swirls died away, and the night air became quiet.

We got home through another doorway, me leaning heavily on Erik for support since pain shot through me every time I tried to put weight on my ankle. Tilda looked a little scraped up and shaky, and Erik was very careful of his wrist, but otherwise we were alright. Noah... Noah was a different story.

He looked dazed and bruised, and though the spell Melinda had cast on him seemed to have broken, I couldn't help but worry. What was it she had said? *He will always miss the forest, until he wastes away to nothing.*

But I didn't have too much time to worry about it. When we stumbled through a doorway and appeared in our living room, Mom, who'd checked on us before going to bed only to find both our beds empty, looked a wreck. But when she realised she were all hurt, she took charge, bundling all of us into the car, and called Noah's mom on the way to the hospital. Erik helped me into the car and gave me a quick, chaste kiss on the lips before he stepped away. Mom tried to get him to come to the hospital, saying his wrist needed to be checked, but he refused, and I watched him walk away into the night, unable to do anything about it. My heart broke, knowing he would be going back to that horrible place underground, all alone, but then we were driving off and I couldn't think about him anymore.

At the hospital, nurses took Noah to a room straight away to be looked at, while Mom, Tilda and I were seated in the waiting room of the emergency room. Jenny, one of Noah's moms, came sprinting through the doors soon after we were seated, and was taken to his room before we could talk.

After six in the morning, Tilda and I were finally released. Tilda had a mild concussion, and my ankle was broken and in a cast, but we were alive, and we would be okay. When we got home, Mom bundled us both up on the couch, clearly not wanting to let either of us out of her sight. We told her, briefly, what had happened since we'd gone upstairs to bed so many hours earlier, and Mom scolded us for putting ourselves in danger like that, but underneath it all lurked fear and worry.

"But it's over now?" Mom asked after we'd been quiet for a while.

Tilda and I looked at each other. It felt almost too good to be true, after weeks of fear and worry and the pressure of the world resting on our shoulders. But we'd done it; we'd defeated Melinda and sent her away and we'd all made it.

Finally, I nodded. "Yeah. It's over now."

We really had saved the world.

CHAPTER 28
ICE

"I still can't believe you did the final fight without me!" Clara whisper-screamed at me. A few days after Christmas, almost a month since we fought Melinda, Clara and I were at our regular spot having coffee.

I snort-laughed. "Sorry. I'll make sure to stop to call you next time we have to fight a murderous Scandinavian creature and save the world."

Clara frowned at me. "Shut up!"

I laughed and decided a change of subject was due. "So, how did things go with Alva the other day?" Clara had finally gathered her courage and asked Alva out on a date. Alva had accepted, and they'd decided to go out for dinner and a movie after Christmas.

"They went great!" Clara gushed. "She told me she'd been crushing on me for a long time too but was too shy to ask me out. And that she'd been really questioning her sexuality lately. Can you believe it?"

Given the heart-eyes she'd been giving Clara in Communications for weeks, yes, I could totally believe it. "I told you she felt something for you!"

"Yeah, yeah. Anyway, we had a ton of fun, so we're hanging out again tomorrow!"

I smiled, happy for my best friend. "That's amazing!"

Clara nodded. "I know!" She paused. "Have you heard anything from Erik since the battle of the rauk?"

I blinked at her and then burst out laughing. "The battle of the rauk? That's the best you could come up with?"

Clara grinned. "I like it. And don't try to change the subject. Have you seen Erik since then?"

My mood plummeted. After that quick kiss – which I had mixed feelings about – I hadn't heard a word from him. I tried telling myself he couldn't find me, since my meadow was no more, but he'd seen where we lived. Of course he could find me if he wanted to.

My meadow. My safe space was... gone. Destroyed to create a place for Melinda, on another plane where she couldn't hurt anyone. My only safe place, the only place where I could find comfort, was gone.

My heart squeezed. I'd tried to go back to the meadow once, needing to see for myself, and the destruction... the destruction had broken me down. I had to blink away tears as my stomach knotted at the memory of that breakdown. Seeing my safe space like that, the trees grey husks, the grass and flowers nothing but ashes and dust, even the sky nothing but a dark hole, it had killed part of me. I'd sat there, in the middle of all that destruction, and cried. It still made me ache, remembering what had happened to it – what *I'd* done to my meadow.

"I'm sorry," Clara said, forcing me out of the memory. "I know you cared about him."

I shrugged and pushed the memory away. I imagined all the grief and sorrow and missing Erik in a little box in my mind and I locked it away. It was the only way for me to make it through life. "It's okay. I'm okay."

Maybe one day, it would actually be true.

EPILOGUE

After several hours of chatting, Clara and I finally said good-bye and went our separate ways. I'd promised to be home for a family night, so Clara and I would do movie night another day. Surprisingly, I felt okay about moving movie night. With or without Thursday movie night, I knew we would always make time for each other, because that's what best friends did. They were there for each other, no matter what day of the week it was, and considering Clara stayed by my side through what could have been the end of the world, I felt more secure in our friendship than I ever had before.

Mom picked me up outside the café – she didn't want me to walk too much on my ankle, even though I'd had the cast removed a few days earlier. The car stood only a few steps outside of the café, but the short walk still made the cold seep into my bones. Winter had arrived in full force since the fight with Melinda, and it was colder than I'd ever experienced before. Some nights, while I lay in bed, I couldn't help but remember the nightmare I'd had with the cold and the fire. But I pushed those thoughts away – we'd stopped Melinda and stopped Ragnarök.

Dinner was ready when we got home, and the flat smelled of cheesy, crispy goodness and tomato sauce when I opened the door. Lasagna.

Yum. Kiwi rushed at me and ran circles around me until I picked her up and let her lick my face.

That evening, we caught up on our crime show, played some games, and had a great time. Before bed, we all took a long walk with Kiwi, like we always did these days. I think we were all a bit scared of losing each other after the horrifying fall, and we did as much as we could together these days. Even if it meant me hobbling along on my crutches in the dark and cold evening air.

Tilda and I were talking in my room when I saw a strange shimmering in the air. I blinked, and a woman stood in front of us. Tall and willowy, with hair an almost white blonde reaching her feet. She wore a white flowy robe, and golden circlets tinkled at her wrists. Her feet were bare.

"Hello, Lia. Tilda." Her light voice seemed to float through the air. "I'm Freja, and I need your help."

I frowned, but Tilda beat me to it. "Freja, as in the goddess?"

The goddess smiled softly. "Yes, Freja, goddess of love, war, death, and sejd."

Sejd? Wasn't that the precognitive magic Melinda used?

"What do you need our help with?" I asked. Dread curled in my stomach. We'd already saved the world, stopped Ragnarök... What was wrong now? What could they possibly need our help with?

My heart sped up. *Oh gods, please let everything be okay.* The worry I'd been pushing away for weeks came to the surface, that nagging feeling that it couldn't be that simple. What if we hadn't succeeded in stopping her? What if Melinda was back? Had she taken Noah again?

"You have done such a good job, but unfortunately, the damage was already done. Ragnarök has started."

I opened my mouth, but no sound came out. Ragnarök had started? Everything we'd done had been for nothing?

I waited for the panic, the anxiety, to force the breath out of my lungs, but it didn't happen. I felt strangely... numb. *I have truly lost it this time.*

Tilda wasn't nearly as speechless as me, though. "What do you mean, Ragnarök has started? We stopped Melinda! Lia locked her away." Her words were sharp enough to hurt.

Freja spoke softly, like that might make it any better. "I know. You did everything we could've expected of you, but it was too late." She paused and looked away, guilt flickering in her eyes. "She had already gone too far, and some of us couldn't stand by and watch anymore. When we entered Midgård, it set things in motion that even stopping Melinda cannot undo."

Tilda narrowed her eyes. "You'll have to be a little less vague than that. Maybe if someone had given us actual answers instead of vague non-answers, we would've been able to stop Ragnarök before it started!"

Freja had the good sense to look contrite, at least. "Centuries ago, in an attempt to avoid Ragnarök, the gods pulled away from Midgård—" At Tilda's sharp look, she clarified, "The human realm. We sequestered ourselves in our own realms in the hope that it would stop Ragnarök from happening. We were forbidden to ever enter Midgård again.

"In the event that we were unsuccessful, Oden cast a spell so that if Ragnarök ever approached again, two children with the blood of the Vanir and the Aesir would be born with the power to save the world. Children of both mine and Balder's blood, with the power to create and control reality." Freja fell silent for a long moment. "I never agreed with the decision to leave Midgård, but Oden insisted we had no other choice. But seeing you two fight to save the world – a fight that is not yours to fight, but ours – convinced me and a few others to leave the safety of our own realms and come to help. Unfortunately, our appearance in Midgård did exactly what Oden feared – it set things in motion. Ragnarök started. Soon, Yggdrasil, the tree of life, will fall, and the world as we know it with it."

I finally found my voice as the numbness coating my insides faded, replaced by anger so potent it scared me. "Let me guess, now you want us to fix it for you?"

Freja flinched at my harsh tone, but I was tired of being used by the gods. Freja was right – it was their fight, not ours.

Regret shone on her face as she said, "If Yggdrasil falls, that is the end of the world. I wish I could do it alone, but I do not have the power to save it. You do. You have the power of two gods inside you – the magic of me and Balder. But I will not repeat the mistakes of the past. You will not have to do it alone. You will have the aid of me and my brother, Frej, every step of the way."

I looked at Tilda next to me. Her eyes were wide with fear, even as her mouth set in an angry line. The worry in her eyes, more than the goddess' words, convinced me of what I had to do. I could hate the gods as much as I wanted, but at the end of the day, they weren't the ones who had to live on this planet. *We* were. My family. My friends. And if I had learned anything from the last few weeks, it was that I would do anything for the people I cared about.

I sighed as a sense of calm certainty settled over me. I reached out to grab Tilda's hand and met Freja's gaze. "What do we have to do?"

THE END

Want to know if Lia and Tilda manage to save Yggdrasil in time? Stay tuned for *Fate of Gods*, the thrilling conclusion to Lia's story.

Note from Author

Thank you for reading *Sorcery of Words*! I hope you enjoyed spending a little time in the world of Norse mythology and Scandinavian folklore.

When I started writing Lia's story, I had just started questioning my own sexuality. I was fairly certain I was on the asexual spectrum, and that realisation made me rethink everything about my life. I was also struggling with anxiety and panic attacks, much like Lia is in the story. Because of this, Lia's struggles are very much inspired by my own struggles. My hope with this book is that it might help someone else who is going through a hard time feel seen and validated in their struggles. But I want to note that asexuality is a spectrum, and there are so many different experiences under that umbrella. Lia's story is by no means the only asexual experience; it is one of many. If you want to learn more about the asexual spectrum, *The Asexual Visibility & Education Network* (asexuality.org) helped me a lot when I was questioning. Even if you're just curious about it, it's a great source of information.

In the same spirit, anxiety and panic attacks can take many shapes. There are so many different symptoms, and some people experience some of them, while others experience all of them. Lia's experience is, again, only one of many varied experiences. I've linked a few resources in the *Content Warning* if you want to learn more about anxiety and its symptoms, or find out where you can get help. And if you, like Lia, struggle with mental illness of any kind, don't hesitate to find help.

Finally, I would like to make a note on the setting and the mythology in this story. As you've probably guessed by now, this story takes place on the island where I grew up, Gotland. And I have done my best to stay true to reality. All the little tidbits of facts that I've sprinkled in are real events. The invasion of Denmark did happen, in 1361. The tunnels underneath Visby are real – and I have to thank my sixth grade teacher for taking us to see them, or figuring out Erik's lair would've been a lot more difficult – although they are most likely not quite as livable as they are portrayed in this story.

I have also done my best to stay true to the mythology and folklore which inspired this story. The whole magic system is actually built on something I read somewhere when researching Norse mythology. Stupid me didn't save the exact quote or the source, but it went something along the lines of, words create reality. As someone who's loved reading and writing nearly her whole life, this struck a chord with me and stayed with me, and became the beginning of the creative magic seen in this book.

As for the mythology and the folklore, I was lucky. Norse mythology is very well-documented, which gave me plenty to work with when building this world. But it was also a challenge to stay true to the story I was trying to tell *and* the mythology at the same time. If you are interested in the mythology and folklore that inspired me, I have a few sources that were my go-to. The books *Vaesen* and *Norse Gods*, both by Johan Egerkrans, were by my side through most of the writing process, and my creatures are highly inspired by his illustrations. *Norse Mythology for Smart People* (norse-mythology.org) filled in whatever information I couldn't find there. It's the most extensive Internet source I've found on Norse mythology. Finally, if you want to really dive into the Norse mythology, you cannot overlook the *Poetic Edda*, author unknown, and the *Prose Edda* by Snorri Sturluson. These are the main reason why we know so much about the Norse mythology, and I've done my best to stay true to them.

Acknowledgements

I don't know where to even start this. *Sorcery of Words* was truly a team effort, and I'm overwhelmed by all the amazing people who have helped me on this journey.

Thank you to my unbelievable critique team, Chelsey Fey, bv Sloan, HM Brandon, R. Joy, Heather Ashbury, and Aimee Clinton. You ladies helped me finish the first draft when I'd been stuck for months, and without all your support and help, I still would've been stuck drafting. An extra thank you to bv Sloan for being the first to ever read the mess that was this book, for cheering me on when I lost my way, and for being my constant sounding board. As cliché as this sounds, there truly aren't enough words in the English language to describe how grateful I am for your unwavering support.

Thank you to my beta readers, Anna, Dottie, Maraia, Lindsey, Nora, Keanna, Emily, and Kav. I am so grateful for all the time you dedicated to helping me make this book the best it could be. And an extra thank you to Anna, for listening to my numerous ace freak-outs. When I say *Sorcery of Words* wouldn't exist without you, I mean that literally – the idea would've never been born if you hadn't helped me figure out my identity. You showed me that there were other people who felt the same way I did, and I hope, with this book, I might be able to do that for someone else.

Thank you to my gymnasium Swedish teacher for all your support and excitement. Your constant interest in my writing pushed me to write my first full-length novel. Look, I did it! I published a book!

Thank you to my family for listening to me ramble about books and writing for years on end. An extra thank you to my mom, for believing in my dreams, always, even when I didn't believe in them myself. For supporting my writing when I was nine years old and writing stories about dolphins at school, when I was fourteen and writing fanfiction, and now that I'm twenty-three and sharing my stories with the world. I truly could not have wished for a better mom, and I am so grateful to have you.

Finally, thank you to you, the reader. It means the world to me that you spent this time with my characters, in this little world I built in my head. *Sorcery of Words* started as my little passion project, and is a mix of all the things I love, and I cannot tell you how much it means that you wanted to spend a little time with Lia & Co. So thank you.

ABOUT MOA

Moa Eriksson is a teacher from a small island in Northern Europe, where she lives with her dog. When she's not teaching or writing, you can find her with her nose stuck in a book.

She has dreamed of being an author since early childhood, when her writing journey started with a series of stories about the dolphin Delfi, which soon turned into longer stories full of magic and romance.

Moa's stories are inspired by mythology and folklore, as well as the beautiful nature of her island, which is why nature plays a large role in her stories. Her stories also include plenty of magic and queer characters. Common themes in her works are friendship and found family, with a hint of romance.

Want to stalk Moa's social media?

You can find her on Instagram, Twitter and TikTok by the handle @thereadingfaery. Or check out her website: authormoaeriksson.com.